A VELVET SCREAM

A VELVET SCREAM

A Joanna Piercy mystery

Priscilla Masters

This first world edition published 2011
in Great Britain and in the USA by
SEVERN HOUSE PUBLISHERS LTD of
9–15 High Street, Sutton, Surrey, England, SM1 1DF.

British Library Cataloguing in Publication Data

Masters, Priscilla.
  A velvet scream. -- (A DI Joanna Piercy mystery)
  1. Piercy, Joanna (Fictitious character)--Fiction.
  2. Women detectives--England--Staffordshire--Fiction.
  3. Rape--Investigation--Fiction. 4. Missing persons--
  Investigation--Fiction. 5. Detective and mystery stories.
  I. Title II. Series
  823.9´2-dc22

ISBN-13: 978-0-7278-8109-0 (cased)

All Severn House titles are printed on acid-free paper.

Severn House Publishers support The Forest Stewardship Council [FSC],
the leading international forest certification organisation. All our titles that
are printed on Greenpeace-approved FSC-certified paper carry the FSC logo.

Typeset by Palimpsest Book Production Ltd.,
Falkirk, Stirlingshire, Scotland.
Printed and bound in Great Britain by
MPG Books Ltd., Bodmin, Cornwall.

To Monty – grandson number 2!

ONE

However cold it was outside, it was hot and noisy inside. He had to shout to be heard over the throbbing music. 'Come outside?'

She squinted at him against the strobe lights. He was in silhouette; slim with craggy, angular features, a hooked nose. 'I thought you'd gone off.'

He patted the silver skirt. 'Yeah,' he leered. 'I did for a bit but I always come back, don't I?'

She shrugged.

'So are you comin' outside for a smoke or not?'

The trick was to act nonchalant. She shrugged again. 'Don't mind if I do.'

They wandered away from the noise, past the bouncer who was standing like a sumo wrestler at the door.

He walked ahead of her. She caught up with him, wobbling on her skyscraper heels. 'Got any smokes?'

He held out a pack. 'Take a couple, love.'

She laughed. 'Tryin' to buy me with a couple of fags?'

He laughed too. 'Not likely, love. I don't put your price that high.'

She bunched her fists ready to fight and he laughed again. 'Only jokin', darlin'.'

'Yeah. Right.'

His eyes scanned the car park. 'Let's go somewhere a bit more private.'

'Yeah – and?'

He looked closely at her. 'How old are you?'

'Old enough.'

'Old enough for what?'

'Anyfink.'

'Yeah. Like, or *not old enough for anyfink*?' He was mocking her. 'Come on, love.' He seized her. 'Who are you kiddin'? You ain't even old enough to smoke tobacco.' His face seemed to tighten up. 'Stop playin' around with me or I might get upset.' His fingers were hurting her.

She couldn't say exactly when she became aware of feeling like she was standing in a freezing river, icy water rushing past her. At first her body warmth, her bravado, the alcohol and her surroundings cocooned her, kept her from realizing. She was having a good time, wasn't she?

Wednesday, 1 December. 7.30 a.m.

She was still angry with him, slamming the car door behind her and grumbling all the way as she drove gingerly along the icy road. 'You should have got a taxi in. This is right out of my way. I'll be late for work.'

A gritter trundled past them, orange light flashing. It spattered gravel across the windscreen, so she had something else to grumble about apart from the fact that her screenwash was frozen solid. 'Bloody gritter,' she said. 'Damn thing'll scratch my paintwork flinging stones out like that.' She peered through the windscreen then shot him another venomous glance. 'And all for a "night out with the lads", eh, Steve?'

He sat silently, nursing a sore head and exploring the fur and roughness inside his mouth, hating the smell of his alcohol-laden breath. Hangovers, he thought, putting his hand in front of his mouth. They were horrible. But, hell . . . Behind the hand Steve Shand grinned to himself. He didn't want Claire to see. It had been a 'hello' of a good night. The totty had been there in full force. Ready and willing. The very best all lined up for the taking. He recalled one tiny skirt shimmering in front of him. The girls had been so friendly, so available. So drunk. He grimaced and recalled shimmying down on the dance floor alongside that very same skirt, hands everywhere they shouldn't have been, and almost groaned. Nights out with the boys. He wouldn't give them up for all the Claires in the world.

'Drop me off here,' he said.

She responded sourly. 'Oh. The unpaid chauffeur. Certainly, my lord.'

'Don't be silly,' he said, impatient with her. 'Leave it, Claire.' But she couldn't. Forced on by jealousy and anger, she pursued him into a corner. 'And who were you dancing with last night?'

His answer was a deep, regretful sigh. So she supplied the answer herself. 'Some cheap little tart.'

He looked across at her. Really looked at her and could see that in a few years she would look just like her mother. Her mouth was thin. Hard and bitter. In that very minute he made up his mind. He'd had enough of this. He was going to move back in with his dad. And just to show there were no hard feelings and to give thanks for his lucky escape she could even keep the ruddy ring.

'You might give me a kiss,' she snapped.

He gave her a dutiful peck on the cheek which did nothing to temper her mood.

'You stink of stale booze,' was meant to be her Parthian shot. But as he left the car she relented and called out, 'Bye, then. See you later,' and roared off, giving a little beep of her horn as she turned the corner. And even that irritated him.

Steve Shand drew his keys from his pocket and looked around at the empty car park. It must have snowed more in the night. It had formed a ridiculous three-inch high hat on the top of his car which was starting to melt and drip down the windscreen as the temperatures slowly rose into the day. In his thin work suit he shivered and worried. What would he do if his car wouldn't start? He'd be stranded in this freezing weather. He fingered his mobile. But in her state of mind Claire wouldn't come back for him. He'd have to walk home.

Go back to bed and nurse his thick head.

It was a tempting thought but that would mean trouble at work. His company didn't take kindly to odd days being taken off by their employees. He stepped through the slushy mess. His was the *only* car standing here. *In grand isolation*, he thought. Not like last night, when he had taken up practically the last space. The weather hadn't kept the revellers away. A gust of wind cut through him to remind him. It was freezing. A real arctic blow.

He reached his car and pressed the lock release on his key fob. Nothing happened.

Damn it. The lock was frozen. He bent down and breathed on it, tried the remote again. Nothing. He bent down for a second time, using his breath again to try and open it. This time he was successful. The locks clicked open. He pulled the door.

Then he heard it. A low moan.

He turned around and glanced round the car park, wondering if he had imagined the sound. The place was empty.

Instead of climbing into the car he stood and listened. In the town traffic was starting to build up. Leek was waking to another snowy morning. He bent down, ready to climb into the driver's seat and leave this bleak environment. Then he heard it again: that low moan. It was coming from behind a low wall at the back of the car park where a couple of wheelie bins stood half concealed. Probably a cat or something, Shand reasoned. He was tempted to ignore it. He simply wanted to get into his nice warm car, go to work and recover from his hangover. But Steve Shand was an inquisitive fellow so he went to investigate, sloshing over the melting snow and leaving a trail of damp, grey footprints.

He saw nothing untoward at first. The line of bins, green, blue and brown; a pile of rubbish, spilling out of torn black plastic sacks, everything dripping wet or iced with frost, the only movement a cat jumping off the wall. That was probably what he had heard. Steve Shand smiled to himself. He had been spooked by nothing more than a pussycat. What would his mates say about that? Everyone knew cats made odd noises. He was about to return to his car when something in the pile of rubbish moved.

TWO

Wednesday, 1 December. 7 a.m.

Detective Inspector Joanna Piercy flipped the calendar over to the new month with a feeling of apprehension. She stood and looked at the picture. It was of a sledging scene set in Leek Park. The calendar was called Around the Staffordshire Moorlands and had been Korpanski's Christmas present to her one long year ago. She paused for a moment, staring at the bobble-hatted children, the stick trees against a bright sky, the dark shadows thrown by people across the snow and the caption underneath: 'A sledging scene in Leek Park'. And then the explanation: 'The bandstand in the background, although Victorian in design, was built when the park opened in the 1920's'.

Thirty days to go.

By the end of this month she would be married – and possibly jobless – if the disciplinary hearing went against her. She looked at the days of December and wondered what they would bring. Normally so active and frenetic, she allowed herself a pause for thought. A lot had happened in this last year: her engagement, Korpanski's shooting, a few arrests and some convictions – tough to win as always and easy to lose. She wouldn't have minded a few more felons behind bars and some longer custodial sentences. It might have served her well for tomorrow's hearing.

She took a quick peek at the dates ringed – too many of them.

The thirtieth. A Thursday. Wedding day. Matthew had drawn in a couple of clumsy bells and a love heart pierced with an arrow. She smiled. He was no artist but she could read his message. And in the piercing was – a threat?

She knew that Matthew would want a 'traditional' marriage: a wife and child, while she was firstly a cop. And children or even a child was not part of that plan. It wasn't only that. Matthew had a daughter, Eloise, a teenager who made no secret of the fact that she disliked Joanna and blamed her for the break-up of her parents' marriage. It was because of these reasons that she looked forward to the wedding with mixed feelings.

But before that, in thick black letters was ringed Thursday, 2 December. The hearing which she was dreading. In a previous case she and Detective Sergeant Mike Korpanski had staked out an isolated farmhouse which had ended in a shooting. She had put his life in danger. And the hearing was in the morning. Nothing to look forward to there. And to top it all no doubt at some point Miss Eloise, soon to be her hostile stepdaughter, would be visiting, dropping by casually, as she did these days, sometimes announcing her arrival with a phone call en route, sometimes not even that. Eloise Levin was a local now, at Keele University, studying the very same subject her father had: medicine. Which gave her plenty of excuses to spend long evenings with him, poring over textbooks, asking questions and seeking advice, deliberately discussing topics when she knew Joanna had absolutely no idea what they were talking about. But as she watched the two blonde heads so close – one pale white and straight, the other sandy, rebelliously curly and thick, she realized that Matthew loved it. To him it was partly reliving his happy student days and partly rediscovering the close father/daughter relationship which had been strained by his marital infidelity and subsequent divorce. Joanna made a face. She hated this new détente, disliked and mistrusted Matthew's daughter and resented her taking their cottage for granted as a second home. Only to her selfish and private self would she admit that when Matthew's daughter was around it was *she* who felt like the outsider.

She had almost been deceived into believing that there had been a general thaw in her relations with Eloise right up until the moment when they had got engaged. Matthew had invited his daughter to lunch so he could break the news face-to-face. Eloise had stared sullenly at the black pearl engagement ring and scowled at her father's fiancée, unable to proffer even the most insincere of congratulations. Things had gone downhill ever since with the girl hardly even speaking to her future stepmother. Joanna smiled. Now there was a scary thought. Eloise's step-mother. It would be akin to being stepmother to the child from *The Omen*. And oddly enough, when she caught Eloise Levin glancing at her, she knew that she felt the same, that she had inherited another strapline: The Stepmother from Hell.

Joanna turned away from the calendar. Matthew was coming down the stairs, two at a time in a jerky, jumping movement. He was still wearing his dressing gown, which flapped behind him. Seeing her standing near the calendar, he bent and gave her a big smacking kiss on her lips, tasting of toothpaste and mouth-wash. 'Good morning,' he said jauntily. 'Countdown to the ball and chain, eh?'

She turned around. 'And whose ankle is this ball and chain attached to?'

He peered into her face and tilted her chin up so she could not hide her expression. 'Well, traditionally, Jo,' he said carefully, 'it is the bridegroom who is afflicted. But in this case . . .' He turned away then but not before she had read the expression in his eyes: one of doubt and concern and hurt.

She felt awful. 'Hey,' she said, pouring him some coffee, 'how about you give me a clue as to where we're going on honeymoon?'

'Not a chance.' His good humour was quick to return.

'Not even whether it'll be bikini or fur coat weather?'

He chuckled mischievously. 'You won't get it out of me,' he said. 'I'm a pathologist, remember?' He grinned. 'I'm used to keeping the secrets of the dead.'

'And I'm a detective,' she responded, 'used to prising information out of the toughest of characters. And I am going to winkle it out of you by interpreting clues.'

Matthew grinned. 'Want a bet?'

She gave him a chaste kiss on the cheek. 'Yes, I do, Doctor Levin. I bet you one whole bottle of champagne on our wedding night that I guess where the honeymoon is.'

His eyes took on a luminous look. Catlike and cunning. 'What sort of champagne?'

'Krug.'

'Then you're on.' He was quiet for a moment, then added: 'Or we could swap secrets,' he suggested. 'You could tell me what your wedding dress is like and then I'll tell you what to pack on the honeymoon. And buy the champagne.'

Joanna made a face at him. 'That is one secret you will not winkle out of me, except to say that I shan't be dressed as an angel without wings. In other words, all I'm telling you is that it isn't white.'

'Well, there's a surprise,' Matthew teased. 'Thank you for that, Miss Piercy, soon to be Mrs Levin. And now, I suppose, I'd better have my shower.'

Wednesday, 1 December. 7.45 a.m.

His hand was shaking as he pulled his mobile phone from his pocket and pressed out the three numbers.

'Police,' he managed, then: 'No, I mean ambulance. Please. Hurry. Please. I think.' He glanced across at the girl. She was still moaning but not conscious. Hardly moving except for shallow breaths. He didn't dare move her himself or do anything except put his coat over her. He felt helpless. He'd touched her briefly and she had felt ice cold. Practically dead already, part of the snow scene. 'Hurry up,' he shouted into the phone before hunkering down beside her, still speaking into the mobile. 'She's barely alive. She's freezing to death while you ask your questions. It's no use you asking me who she is. I don't *know* who she is. I don't know what to do with her. She's really cold. Yes, I have put my coat over her. I don't *know* whether she's broken anything. No, she's not bleeding.' Shand got suddenly angry. 'I'm not a bloody doctor, you know. I'm just a guy picking up my car.' *Hung-over.*

The thought was sudden and uncomfortable. He'd summoned the police, hadn't he? He'd been about to climb into his car and drive. What if he was still over the limit and they breathalysed him? He'd had a shedful last night. Bugger. His eyes drifted towards the furthest wheelie bin. Draped across it was a tiny silver skirt, shimmering in the anaemic winter sunshine, dripping as the snow melted.

Oh, hell, was his first thought. Then: *double bugger*. And he'd be late for work. He felt like kicking the girl, not saving her life.

Bloody women: nothing but trouble. He was bound to be questioned over this and while he'd just decided to dump Claire, as he sobered up he realized he wasn't quite so sure about a life of endless mates' nights out and troublesome women wearing hardly anything but tiny, sexy, shiny skirts. Suddenly, more than anything, he simply wanted to be safe.

Joanna was looking out of the window at the snow when Matthew came tripping back down the stairs, dressed now in a pair of khaki coloured jeans and a navy sweatshirt. As he wore 'scrubs' practically all day he only wore a suit if he was either in court, at a medical meeting (of which there were plenty), or teaching students. He was combing his still-damp blond hair with his fingers. He followed her gaze out of the window, on to the snow scene.

'You're not thinking of cycling to work through that, Jo, are you?'

Resenting his proprietary tone, she turned away. 'No,' she said. 'Even I'm defeated by this weather. Not only is it slippery on a bike but there's always the chance that some mad car driver will slide right into you.'

'Never mind,' he said, pouring himself a huge bowl of muesli and sitting down at the breakfast table. 'In four weeks time we'll be on our way to Barbados . . .' He waited, grinning and aiming a sideways look in her direction, 'or Russia or Canada or South Africa or Australia or even somewhere else.' He gave her another sneaky look. 'We might be skiing or scuba diving or sitting on a train across the Rockies or photographing the Taj Mahal. On the other hand we could also be climbing Machu Pichu or cycling across the Ho Chi Minh Highway.' He grinned at her, chewing his breakfast cereal slowly. 'Isn't it fun thinking of all the things we *might* be doing?'

'You,' she said, dropping into a chair opposite and cupping her chin in her palm, 'are being very irritating and I won't know what clothes to take.'

He gave a noisy yawn and a look of mock reproval. 'Of course, the honeymoon is conditional on my approving this wedding dress you're being so secretive about.'

Joanna had a moment of terrible doubt. Perhaps all brides do. What would he think of it? Matthew could be, at times, quite conventional. 'Matt,' she said tentatively. 'It's not . . .' She paused, searching for the appropriate word, 'the usual dress.'

He stood up then, came behind her, put his arms around her shoulders. 'As long as it's not black.'

'Umm.'

'Jo,' he said, his green eyes clouding. 'You wouldn't do that to me, surely?'

'Umm.'

'Well,' he said. 'I never thought you'd turn up to the altar in the usual white meringue. But black! My parents will never forgive you.'

'They'll never forgive me whatever I wear, will they?' She tilted upwards, putting her face close to his. He kissed her mouth. 'Mmm,' he said. 'Orange juice and coffee.'

It was she who broke it off. 'Time I went to work, Matt.'

'Mmm.'

'And I didn't say it *was* black,' she hesitated, 'or that it wasn't.'

She put a coat on over her skinny black trousers, red sweater and skiing jacket and gave a vengeful look at the inches of snow. Yes, it was definitely the car today, though she could have done with working off some of her anxieties with a stiff bike ride. She slammed the door behind her. Matthew wouldn't need to leave for another half an hour.

The one advantage of using the car was that she arrived at work at 8.15 a.m. and was already at her desk by the time Korpanski rolled in, which made her feel smug.

'Morning, Mike.'

'Hi, Jo.' He hovered. 'Coffee?'

The phone on her desk interrupted her answer, making her jump with apprehension.

'Piercy?'

It was Colclough. Or to give him his full title, Superintendent Arthur Colclough. He of bulldog jowls and normally paternalistic attitude towards her. Not today. He sounded like a fierce bulldog. In spite of herself, she smiled. A fierce *Staffordshire* bulldog.

'Yes, sir.'

'You're ready for tomorrow's hearing, I hope?'

'Yes, sir.'

Superintendent Arthur Colclough gave a long, puffy sigh. 'I never thought I'd see this day, Piercy,' he said. 'I'm disappointed in you. I've always thought I could rely on you, at least, to toe the line.'

'Yes, sir.' She deflected Korpanski's sympathetic gaze.

'It reflects on us as a force, you know.'

'Yes, sir.' There was no other response she could make.

'And so near to my retirement,' he finished mournfully.

Joanna rolled her eyes at Mike. What this had to do with her dressing-down was unclear but she kept silent. He'd been threatening retirement for years.

It was one of those things, Joanna had believed, which would never happen, although she knew, inevitably, that one day it would. She felt a bit sad. She had felt affection for Colclough. He had always stuck up for her. She had been his protégée. Thinking he was being a modernist, he had wanted a woman officer in a senior position in his station. And she'd fitted the bill. But right now his involvement was costing him dear and he wanted to let her know this. So he was lecturing her like a father. Well, not like *her* father. Christopher Piercy, or Kit, as he had liked to be known, had never lectured anyone in his life. That would have needed some measure of maturity – something her dad had never quite acquired. Sometimes, when she thought about him, which wasn't often, she decided that it would have been a toss-up to discover who would grow up first: Peter Pan or 'Kit' Piercy. She wouldn't have bet on either.

'Nine o'clock, then. Sharp.'

'Yes, sir.'

As she put the phone down she met Korpanski's eyes across the room. She read his gaze of sympathy but something more too. She glanced at his shoulder, still padded with a dressing. The injury was taking its time to heal. He still had to go for physiotherapy three times a week – in police time. Frances, his wife, would never forgive Detective Inspector Piercy for risking her husband's life. Joanna wasn't sure that she could forgive herself, either.

Korpanski went to fetch the coffee and put it down on her desk. 'December,' he commented. 'It's come round quick.'

'Yes.'

He tried a cheery tone. 'Not long now till the great day.'

She peered hard into her screen.

'Jo,' he said tentatively, 'are you sure you're doing the right thing? I mean, you're a copper. Levin's going to want some sort of—'

She spun around in her chair to challenge him. 'Oh, you know what he wants, do you?'

Korpanski shrugged. 'At a guess: same as any man. A wife at home, kids.' He ignored the fury rising in her eyes. 'Well, you know what this job can be like.' He looked awkward. Korpanski was not good at expressing himself. 'The hours are crap,' he continued. 'It's tough enough for a man, let alone a woman. Besides . . .' He took a long, thoughtful swig of his coffee. 'You've answered my question, Jo. You wouldn't be so prickly if you knew you were doing the right thing.'

'Well, thanks for that bit of philosophy,' she snapped and turned back to her screen, glaring into it, so angry she could not read a single word. They worked in uneasy silence for a few minutes. When the phone rang again it was Korpanski who took the call, listening carefully, his face a mask. Joanna stopped staring into her computer screen and watched him instead, knowing something was happening by the stiffening of his shoulders, the beefing up of the muscles in his thick neck and the raising of his tone. Finally he put the phone down and turned to her. 'We've got a suspected rape, Jo,' he said.

'A rape? Where?'

'Outside the new nightclub, Patches. The girl was left for dead. Nearly died of hypothermia. She's been out there all night. It's a miracle she's survived. She was hardly wearing anything. Passed out, I expect.' Typically, Korpanski had already started to put his own interpretation on events. 'Drunk. Perhaps drugs. Uniformed guys were called out there . . .' he glanced at his watch, 'nearly an hour ago. She's in Stoke hospital now, warming up.'

'Is she conscious?'

'Barely.'

'Do you have a description of her?'

'Five foot four, very slim, long, straight brown hair, brown eyes, wearing one high-heeled silver shoe and a black boob tube.' He looked up. 'And little else. A short . . . uniformed guys say *very* short, silver skirt turned up nearby together with the second shoe.'

'We need to get down to the hospital as soon as possible with one of the WPCs to get a statement. Who's done rape training?'

'I think Dawn has.'

'Right. Bring WPC Critchlow along. We'll have to get swabs and stuff.'

She looked into Korpanski's fathomless eyes. 'I take it this isn't one of those I said yes, I said no?'

'We won't know till we get there, Jo, but it doesn't sound like it considering she was left out there to die. Pretty heartless.'

She thought for a moment, drumming her fingers on the desk. 'I think we'd better go to the scene of the crime first and make sure that's being dealt with properly. Then we'll go to the hospital and see if we can get some sort of statement and some samples.'

Mike was a man who liked action. He was already standing up.

Joanna unhooked her jacket from the hook on the back of the door. 'What do we know about our victim?'

'Kayleigh Harrison. Fourteen years old. Lives with her mum,' Mike turned to look at her, 'who hasn't yet reported her daughter missing. Fairly obviously, judging by her age and the fact that she was probably inside an over-eighteens' nightclub until the early hours, I would guess she's a bit of a tearaway. She should have been tucked up with her schoolbag by her bed.'

Joanna smiled. Even if she hadn't known it, by Korpanski's censorious tone she would have guessed that he had a teenage daughter of his own to protect. They were already out of the door and heading towards a squad car now. 'Have they spoken to her mum?'

'They haven't been able to get an answer at the house.'

It was now nine o'clock. 'Maybe she's at work?'

'Not according to the neighbour. More likely to be blotto,' he said, 'according to the uniformed guy who called round.' He inched the car across the slippery car park.

'Blotto,' she commented. 'This early?'

'There's more. The guy who found her this morning had left his car in the car park last night because he'd had a "good night out" last night. Unfortunately for him the effects of the "good night" were still in his bloodstream so the uniformed guys have advised him not to drive. He's cursing, saying it'll cost him his job if he doesn't get to see a client today.'

'I would have thought he's got reason enough to miss a call today.'

Korpanski said nothing but kept his eyes on the road.

'So this "guy" was also in Patches last night?'

'Seems so.'

'Fairly drunk and with a gang of "mates"?'

'That's right.'

They'd arrived. Though Patches nightclub was on the opposite side of the town to the station they were there within minutes. Leek is not a large town.

Even as they climbed out of the car, Joanna realized that no one could be in any doubt that *something* had happened here last night. The car park was cordoned off, already a scene of activity, with a few curious onlookers watching and exchanging – what? Misinformation, probably. It was generally the case.

Sergeant Barraclough, 'Barra' to all, was directing the fingertip search of the car park, which was damp and grey with slush, the scene furred by fog that clung around the area. Joanna didn't envy them. A fingertip search is an unpleasant job: on your knees, even with 'waterproof' trousers which never quite were. The scene bore the indistinct uniform greyness of a Lowry, peopled by stick men and women whose focus was on the ground, all dressed in identical suits, hats and overshoes, each one anonymous.

Do Not Cross tape had been strung around the entire area and the team, in their now sodden white suits, were moving forward in a slow, swaying movement. Joanna watched for a moment as they moved through the scene, the main sound a sort of sucking wetness with the odd shouted instruction. She glanced across at the nightclub. As do most clubs in the day, Patches looked decidedly seedy. It was a large, square building which had been a silk weaving mill two hundred years ago, but that had long since closed. It had then, briefly, been an antiques centre, but that had closed too and it had recently been converted into a nightclub with a coat of post office red gloss paint and blue window frames. There wasn't much choice of venue for a night out in Leek. Apart from the pubs and The Winking Man, which was way out high on the Buxton Road, there was only here, so the local youngsters tended to congregate at Patches. With the fresh snowfall last night the A53 Buxton road would have been impassable, so unless any revellers could be bothered to venture into Hanley they were stuck with Patches.

The car park was empty apart from the one splash of colour, a red Audi TT, with the number plate SEC5 21. The five had been curved to make the clumsy words, SECS 21. Joanna smiled. The plates were, strictly speaking, illegal, though they still struck her as funny. Though, in the circumstances . . .

Barra came forward to speak to them. He jerked his head in the direction of the car.

'Belongs to Steve Shand,' he said. 'He left it here last night because he'd had a drink too many – or six. When he came for it,' he said, following their eyes, 'he found young Kayleigh. Lucky he did and even more lucky he noticed her. She was partly hidden behind the wall and barely conscious. But he was here a while, so he said, because his locks were frozen. He was blowing on them when he heard a noise. He said it sounded like somebody moaning or groaning. He thought it was a cat or something, then took a look and found her. Otherwise she could have been dead.'

'What time was it?' Joanna asked.

'Seven thirty. He was going to work.' Barra gave a rueful smile. 'Needless to say, we've detained him. He wasn't fit to drive anyway.' His eyes flickered back towards the vehicle. 'We've kept the car. Just in case.'

Joanna nodded and Barra continued. 'We'll do a quick check of it and if it's all right with you he can have it back this evening.'

'Yeah. Fine. What does he look like?'

'Thick set. Muscular. Looks like he "works out". Early thirties.'

'Have we got any sort of statement from Kayleigh about her attacker?'

'Not much of one so far. She says he was tall, skinny, London accent.'

'Not a local lad then?'

'It would seem not. No one she knew anyway.'

'OK. Well, it's not much but it's something to go on.'

Barra nodded.

'The accent of our Audi owner?'

'About as local as oatcakes.'

'Sort of lets him off the hook then, along with Kayleigh's description.'

'Sort of.' She could tell that Sergeant Barraclough was not quite convinced.

'What job does this guy do?'

'He's a rep for a pharmaceutical company. Visits doctors in their surgeries and such like.'

Joanna looked around. 'Have you found much here?'

'Bits and pieces. Not a lot. The sort of stuff you'd expect. Plenty of condoms. A couple of fag ends and lager cans but it's so wet and cold.' He paused. 'The snow really hasn't helped.'

'No. Right. And how is the girl?'

'Physically, she's recovering.'

'I'd better go and see her.' Joanna said. 'Just show me exactly where she was found, Barra.'

'Over here.' He led her between lines of tape, to the far corner of the car park where a low wall stood, probably a relic of some long destroyed outbuilding. Now it served as a store for bins – and was well hidden from the rest of the area. 'Quite clever, really,' Barra observed. 'She'd have been out of sight. And considering the music would have been blaring, out of hearing as well. They just kept the old bins and stuff here. Bits of rubbish. Shand, the guy who found her, said she was covered in rubbish; looked just like an old pile of nothing until she moved. Lucky she did or this would have been a murder investigation.'

Joanna looked around her. 'Do you think our perpetrator recced the place first and chose this spot deliberately, or just hit lucky?'

She knew exactly what she was asking. In spite of the cockney accent, was this a local man with local knowledge?

Korpanski, too, was looking around – along the ground, then upwards. 'Hit lucky or unlucky?' he asked. 'If he'd taken a look around first surely he'd have seen that?' He indicated a CCTV camera set high on the corner of the nightclub, pointing down towards the car park.

'I think he must have recced the place first,' Barra said. 'It's just a little too lucky and well hidden here. But the camera's set quite high up. I wouldn't be surprised if the angle's all wrong. Maybe we'll find he's done the old "hoody" trick and isn't that recognizable from up there. It's a bit too high. If I'd been advising the owners of the club I'd have said to bring it down a foot or two and get an angle which would at least give us a sporting chance of a face and identification. From up there we'll just get the tops of heads and boots.'

'I wonder,' Joanna mused, 'if he is a stranger? He could still be a local man with a London accent. Hopefully we'll find him soon with or without the CCTV. Anyway, we'll take a look at all that later.' She peered down at the spot where Kayleigh had been found. It was a depressing little area, even without the memory of the sordid scene that must have been played out here last night. Melting snow, grey and cold, plenty of slush, dented lager cans, cigarette butts, polystyrene burger boxes, the general detritus of scruffy humans who can't be bothered to bin their rubbish even though the bins stood right here, mere inches away. In spite of the open air there was a stink around the place too, of something unpleasantly rotting mixed with stale urine. The men spilling out of the club must have used this place as a pissing wall.

Joanna turned away.

'We've retrieved her knickers,' Barra said, 'from over the wall where he must have chucked them along with the other shoe, but we haven't found a coat.'

'She probably didn't wear one.' Joanna had seen the girls shivering as they queued up to enter the clubs both here and in Hanley. She had stopped once and asked them why they suffered the cold. The girls had been quite happy to tell her: because it cost five quid to leave it in the cloakroom, queuing up to dump it in the cloakroom lost them valuable dancing time and the coat would probably be nicked if they left it while they had a dance. 'Right.' She didn't need to tell Barra to bag the knickers up together with anything else they found and send them to forensics. It wasn't necessary because Barra must have combed a thousand crime scenes before. The last thing he needed was Inspector Piercy breathing down his neck. 'I'd like to take a quick look around the nightclub. Is the owner here?'

'Yes. I saw him twenty minutes ago.'

'How much does he know about what happened last night?'

'I just said an alleged serious sexual attack on a minor. Naturally he insists as it happened in the car park it's nothing to do with the club and he can't help us. It's for over-eighteens. Strictly.'

'And Kayleigh's fourteen.'

'Poor kid,' Barra said sympathetically. 'She's bound to be a wreck after this. She was probably heading that way before the assault. Now – well.'

They crossed the car park and approached the building, Mike striding at her side.

'We're going to get this guy,' she said as they reached the door. 'I just know it.'

He grunted. 'Is that before or after your honeymoon?'

She almost, *almost*, responded: what honeymoon? Because now the case was all-absorbing and the wedding, even the disciplinary hearing tomorrow morning, was forgotten, but she stopped herself just in time, horrified by the answer that had arrived so automatically. She met Mike's eyes with an expression of rising panic. She knew that he had spoken the truth this morning: that the job would always absorb her to the exclusion of all else, even Matthew. Worse still, Matthew knew it too. Bloody Sergeant Clever Korpanski had even been uncomfortably near the truth about Matthew wanting a trophy wife and two point four kids. She strode towards the entrance, quickening her pace. Korpanski opened his mouth to say something but she was leaving him behind. At a guess, knowing Mike, it would have been something cheerful and funny, but when he caught her mood he clamped his lips tight shut before a single word escaped. Instead, he gave her a ghost of a smile followed by an awkward, almost apologetic twist of his mouth.

Barra had already put the boards up outside the nightclub, inviting people to speak to the police following a 'Serious Incident'. Date and time were there together with a hotline telephone number. Hopefully someone would recognize the man from the description that Kayleigh Harrison had given. Maybe the investigation would hit lucky and someone would even identify him. If he *was* a local man with a southern accent he would stick out a mile in this moorlands town which had not only an accent but also a vocabulary and grammar all of its own. People would know him. If, on the other hand, he was from outside the area, what was he doing in Leek at this time of year, so outside the holiday season and with roads which were frequently closed to traffic because of the weather?

It was different in the summer with an influx of seasonal holidaymakers who rented cottages in the Peak District, visited Alton Towers and the factory shops in the Potteries. But few visitors came to Leek in December except the extreme climbing fraternity, who found the challenge of The Roaches in snow and ice exciting and bought both their equipment and provisions in the town. But they were easy to spot. Healthy, hearty, noisy, muscular, tanned men and women wearing North Face, Berghaus and Gore Tex: people in big boots, thick socks and healthy strides. They wouldn't be outside a nightclub raping a fourteen-year-old.

The manager of Patches was an American called Chawncy Westheisen. He was a bluff fellow, burly and over six foot high, with an impressive paunch. He greeted Joanna and Mike very cautiously. 'I'm horrified to hear what happened,' he said. 'One of the reasons I came to Staffordshire from the Big Apple was to escape the violence. I had a club over there and we had a shootin' one night. Two of my bouncers were badly injured. One never worked again. It upset me greatly,' he said, leading them into his first-floor office. 'Troubled me so much I came over to the UK to look for some sort of small townsville where I could open another club. I brought the name with me from New York. It's been quite successful here as a drinking place – a couple of bars, a dance floor and quiet zones too. I learned that,' he said, with a frank sweep of his blue eyes, 'from my days in New York. You know what it's like, Inspector. Places become fashionable and they make money and then so . . .' He left the sentence hanging in the air; neither of the two police officers could quite have finished it.

Joanna's mind was already asking questions. What then, she wondered? Had the shooting in the New York Patches been connected with a protection racket? Bribery? Drugs? What? Joanna looked at Mike and shrugged. She didn't know. Neither did she have any idea whether it had any bearing on the assault on Kayleigh Harrison.

'Quite, Mr Westheisen,' she said briskly. 'At least it's a place where the youngsters can come without getting into trouble or heading into the city.' Kindly she didn't mention the couple of drugs raids they'd had at Patches in the last six months or the death of a young woman who had 'chilled out' on Dexedrine. They had tracked down the suppliers but catching a drugs supplier could be likened to cutting off the head of the Hydra. Two more appeared in its place. Then four. Then eight. "And then so".

Westheisen had escaped without a conviction. The truth was that the local force found it easier to keep an eye on one nightclub than all the street corners, gyms or pubs – of which there were many – where transactions could be exchanged. But now Westheisen had a rape case to contend with, and that would be more tricky. All three of them knew that clubs had been closed down for less. This could easily be the end of his club. What responsible parent would want a daughter to come here now? And females are essential to attract the males. The club would gain a bad reputation – and slide slowly down the sinkhole. Maybe that was Westheisen's "and then so". Even though, after an event a club was probably at its safest – with everyone, including the police, on high alert.

OK. It was shutting the stable door but this is a fact of life. It's what we all do.

Joanna stole a swift glance at Chawncy Westheisen. He was a wise and canny New Yorker. He would have worked all this out for himself by now. 'Did you bring your family over here, Mr Westheisen?'

'My partner,' he corrected her. 'We worked together in New York. His name's Marvin Solfa.'

'And was Marvin here last night?'

'No. It's often kind of quiet here on a Tuesday. Usually just one of us comes. Last night I drew the short straw.' He seemed to think he needed to add something. 'Marvin would have come in if I'd have asked him to, if it had gotten busy.'

'Right. Did you see a young girl wearing a very short silver skirt last night? She had long, straight brown hair, silver shoes and a black boob tube?'

Chawncy was instantly wary. 'How young?'

'She's actually fourteen.'

'Certainly not,' he said. 'At fourteen she would have been way too young for Patches.'

'Girls can look years older than they are,' Joanna commented.

'I've owned a club for a long time,' Westheisen said. 'I know the score. I'd lose my license both here and in the States if I violate a law. She wouldn't have got past me.'

'Well, it looks as though she got past whoever was on the door last night,' Joanna said waspishly. 'She wasn't wearing her school uniform, you know.'

'I'd have asked for ID.'

'Who was on the door last night?'

'A guy called Andrew Crispin. And he'll lose his job if he let in a fourteen-year-old.' He thought for a moment. 'You don't know that she was actually in the club, do you?' It was a very optimistic attempt at clearing Patches of any involvement.

Nice try, Joanna thought. Aloud, she said, 'Dressed like that she wasn't out of doors all night.'

'Was she wearing a coat?'

Joanna shook her head. 'Not that we've found. I'll need to talk to Marvin too at some point,' she said.

'Why? He wasn't even here last night.'

'We just do,' Korpanski said and, looking at the meaty sergeant, well over six foot tall, Chawncy Westheisen didn't demur. He satisfied himself with a mutinous look Joanna completely ignored.

'Was it busy here last night?'

'Yeah. More than usual. I guess it's because it's December. Christmas and all that. The kids – they want their seasonal romance.'

'Right. I'll need the name of everyone who worked here last night: the bouncer, the person on the door, bar attendants.'

Westheisen frowned. 'I'll need to take a look at the rota to see who was behind the bar.' He chewed his lip. 'We do run a membership system here,' he said. 'It's possible she pinched another girl's card and got in on that and Andrew simply glanced at it without checking properly.'

Joanna was anxious not to deflect the course of this investigation. Right now her priority was not to fall foul of Westheisen but keep him sweet and cooperative and dangling on the hook of losing his license. This should keep his memory alert so it retained any evidence. He might have useful information and she might need to go through his membership list. But to find the person who assaulted Kayleigh Harrison there were certain questions she must ask sooner or later.

'Do you check ID when people become members?'

Westheisen nodded. 'More than our license is worth if we get it wrong,' he said, agitated now. 'We have an obligation to check ID.'

'Indeed you do. Do you mind if we take a look around?'

'Not at all. I'll be delighted to show you.'

He led them through the main dance hall with its long bar to the 'quiet' room and upstairs through the offices. Joanna noticed four CCTV cameras strategically placed. Patches was as good as it got for a small-town club in rural Staffordshire. 'In summer we get the kids coming out from Stoke and round about too,'

Chawncy said proudly, over his shoulder. 'Even Manchester once or twice.'

'London?'

'Hey.' Westheisen laughed. 'We're getting a reputation but not that far afield.'

When they'd finished the tour Joanna asked for both the internal and external CCTV videotapes from the night before. Westheisen didn't argue but made a showy gesture of handing them over. Joanna bagged them up. Some of the junior officers would love to sit and watch the skimpily clad girls strut their stuff.

They returned to the station and dropped them on Timmis' and McBrine's desks. It would make a change from their normal duties: moorland patrol, finding sheep that had strayed, rescuing over ambitious climbers, finding lost children, protecting the sparrow hawks, making sure campers' fires didn't spark off a major alert and even a spot of cattle-rustling. 'Take a look at these,' she said, 'and see if you can pick Kayleigh Harrison out. She's the one in a tiny silver skirt and black boob tube. See who she's with, will you?'

The two officers looked at each other. 'My dream job,' Saul McBrine said with a grin. 'Just don't let my girlfriend know I've spent hours ogling girls in silver miniskirts and boob tubes. She'll kill me.'

'You'll survive,' Korpanski said, joining in the laughter with the two officers.

'Come on, Mike,' Joanna said. 'Let's get a couple of sandwiches from the cake shop and take a quick look at the tape from the outside camera trained on the car park. Then we must go down to the hospital and speak to our girl.'

THREE

*S*he didn't even look fourteen, was Joanna's first thought. More like twelve. Lying with a white, terrified face; big eyes peering over the sheet. Her face was thin, drawn.

Whatever she had looked like last night, in her silver skirt, tall heels, boob tube, et cetera, she was just a child, a frightened little girl. WPC Dawn Critchlow was sitting at the side of her bed, watching her but not speaking. She gave a terse nod as Joanna and Mike entered. Kayleigh opened her eyes even wider. 'Hello, Kayleigh,' Joanna said softly. She sat down in the armchair and faced the child.

'I'm Detective Inspector Joanna Piercy,' she said, 'from the Leek Police. I want you to tell me what happened last night. As much as you remember.'

Tears ran down Kayleigh's face. She put her hands up to hide them but it did nothing. The girl scooped in a couple of deep, noisy breaths.

'Please,' Joanna said, 'tell me what happened.'

The hands moved a centimetre down the face so the eyes met hers. But Kayleigh pressed her lips together – if anything more firmly.

'If you were assaulted,' Joanna said, 'what happened to you could happen to another girl – maybe even worse. You were left to freeze. You could have died, Kayleigh.'

Slowly the girl slid her hands back to her side. Her eyes looked into Joanna's with a trusting look that was painful. But Joanna did not shy away.

'Would you like your mother or a social worker with you?'

It provoked a quick response. 'No fear.'

Joanna gave Mike a quick glance before continuing. 'Right. So. Tell me what happened, in your own words. Did you meet someone inside the club?'

Kayleigh shook her head and Joanna twigged. 'He got you in, didn't he?'

Kayleigh bit her lip and nodded. 'He put 'is arm round me and sort of hid me from the bouncer. Inside he bought me a drink.'

'What did he look like?'

She looked panicked by the question, then blurted out: 'He were tall and skinny.'

'What was his hair like?'

'Sort of spiky. It felt a bit sticky.' She frowned. 'I think it had gel on.'

'What colour was it?'

'Brownish, I think.' She frowned in concentration.

'What was he wearing?'

'A sort of leather bomber jacket and jeans. They allow them on weeknights,' she defended.

'How old?'

'About thirty or so. It's hard to tell, really.'

'Was he local – someone you knew?'

Kayleigh shook her head. 'He had a London accent,' she said. 'And the way he talked, the things he said.' She smiled and changed her voice. '"Oh dear, oh dear. Look what you've made me do – spill me drink".' She met Joanna's eyes. 'That's how he talked, Inspector.'

'Do you remember anything else about him? Anything that might help us find him?'

'He had big teeth,' she said. 'Big and yellow. Like a wolf's, they were.'

Joanna looked at her closely. Kayleigh had very pale skin, devoid now of make-up, brown eyes, long, straight hair brushed away from her face. Dressed in a hospital nightdress she looked far too young to be having this conversation.

'Can I have a word?' She spoke to Dawn Critchlow and they went outside the door. 'You have all the swabs and samples?'

Dawn nodded. 'Poor kid,' she said, eyes drifting towards the porthole in the door. 'It was pretty ghastly. I thought she'd have wanted her mum there at least – but no.'

Joanna then went to speak to the doctor in charge of Kayleigh's case, who turned out to be an elegant Indian lady in a dark red sari by the name of Dr Rani Bopari.

'She is lucky to be alive,' the doctor said. 'Her temperature on admission was twenty-nine degrees. Below twenty-five and she would probably have died. We would not have been able to save her.'

'Does she have any other injuries?'

'Internal bruising, a labial tear, some bleeding too.'

'So, rape?'

She gave a wise smile. 'You cannot draw me on that, Inspector. Rough sex but I don't know whether it was rape or consensual.'

'Was she a virgin before this?'

'I cannot say.'

'Was she drugged?'

'I believe your police surgeon has taken some samples for toxicology,' Dr Bopari said. 'You need to wait for those results. I could not say for sure with exposure to such cold and the alcohol.'

Joanna's ears pricked up. 'How much alcohol?'

'The equivalent of a bottle and a half of wine,' Dr Bopari said without smiling. 'She still had a high level of alcohol in her blood this morning. We've had to work it out backwards using a graph. It's not completely reliable – you know that we all metabolize alcohol differently – but it's as close as we can get. She's fourteen years old. My guess is that last night she was pretty drunk. And again,' she said, the smile returning, 'you will need to wait for the results of the blood tests. The swabs and things will take a bit longer.'

'Swabs and things?'

'There was no semen,' Dr Bopari said, frowning now, 'he probably used a condom, but we might still be able to get DNA and we must obviously test for STDs.

These are what we are looking for,' she enlarged. 'Gonorrhoea, Chlamydia, Trichomonas, Herpes. HIV.'

Joanna flinched. It was a grim picture, this bald truth about the reality of rape. 'I see. Well, thank you.' Joanna handed the doctor a card with her telephone number on it. 'If you have any more information that will help us, please don't hesitate to pick up the phone.'

'I won't,' the doctor said.

Joanna returned to the room. This was the difficult bit. 'Kayleigh,' she said. 'In your own words I want you to tell me exactly what happened to you last night. Everything.'

The girl blinked, wiped her hair away from her face and looked at Joanna. 'You know what happened,' she said.

'No, we don't, Kayleigh.'

The girl stared up at the ceiling and made no response until Joanna prompted her. 'When did you first notice him?'

'Outside. It were really cold and I were shiverin'.'

Joanna wasn't even going to ask about a coat. She let the girl continue, halting here and there. 'He was sort of lookin' at all the girls in the queue and that's when I noticed him. He seemed to pick me out.' A note of pride had entered her voice. 'He started speakin' to me, friendly, like, and he said he'd see me inside.'

'Right. Good. You're doing well so far.'

Kayleigh paused.

'Did he tell you his name?'

She shook her head.

'Did he ask your name?'

'Yeah.'

'And you told him?'

She nodded. 'He said it were a nice name.'

'Was he with anyone?'

'Not as I saw. He were on his own.'

'So you went inside with him. What about the bouncer? Didn't he realize you were underage?'

Kayleigh gave a mischievous giggle as she shook her head. Again there was this air of pride. 'He puts his arm round me and starts snoggin'.' She couldn't resist a smile. 'The guy on the door just starts laughin' and lets us through.'

'Did he appear to know anyone inside the club?'

She shook her head.

'Did you stay together?'

'No. He was sort of playin' around. I didn't mind. I was inside. It was warm. I had a drink or two inside of me. That was all I cared about.'

'Was he with any other girls?'

'He had a couple of dances but after a while he came back to me.'

'And then?'

'We went outside for a smoke a couple of times.'

'He was a smoker?'

'I don't think he was, really,' she said perceptively, her eyes screwed up now. 'He didn't inhale, just blew it around, tryin' to look clever. And his clothes. They didn't smell of smoke, neither.'

Joanna stored all the facts away. 'Go on,' she prompted.

'It got to about two and I knew the club'd be closin'. Most people had already gone with it bein' a week night and snowin'. I asked him if he'd give me a lift home.'

Joanna felt her hopes rise. 'He had a car?'

The girl shrugged. 'I don't know.' She thought, frowning. 'I didn't see one.'

'OK.'

'We went outside. It was freezin'. Real brass monkey weather.' She gave a vague smile. 'I wonder why they say that, about a brass monkey.'

'It's something to do with cannonballs.' Korpanski spoke from the doorway, giving Joanna a bland but triumphant smile.

'Oh.' Kayleigh looked vague and as though she didn't care anyway.

'Did anyone see you go outside?'

Kayleigh shrugged. 'I don't know.'

'Then?' Joanna prompted.

'I thought we'd go back to Coffin Corner.'

'Sorry?'

'Coffin Corner. It's the name they've pinned up on the sort of stand thing where the smokers go since the smoking ban.'

'Ah.'

'But we didn't.' Something in the girl's voice changed. It became, if anything, more certain; her words were spoken quickly, as though she wanted to get the story over with. 'He pulled me over to where the bins was. I thought he'd just want a snog or something but he puts 'is 'and over me mouth and pulls me skirt down. I was frightened. I kept sayin' leave it and I want to go 'ome. I felt really ill. Dizzy and very sick. I said I thought I was goin' to puke. I really thought I would. Then he was on top of me and . . .'

She put her hands over her face, ashamed.

Joanna gave her a couple of minutes, then said, 'And it was this man who assaulted you?' She baulked at the word rape. It sounded so graphic, so cruel, so descriptive.

'Yeah. No doubt about it. It was the man who'd been so nice to me all evening. And then –' she covered her face with her hands again and spoke through her fingers – 'it was snowin'. Great big fluffy flakes driftin' down. I used to like the snow, Inspector.' The words had more than a touch of pathos.

Joanna reached out and touched the girl's hand. 'You've done very well, Kayleigh. But I need to know what happened then?'

'I don't know,' the girl said. 'I felt him inside me. Pushin'. I was so cold and wet. I was freezin'. I could feel the snowflakes landin' on my face, and then I don't remember anything more. It's as though a piece of black cloth just dropped in front of my eyes. I must have passed out. I don't remember anything more until . . .' She squeezed her eyes tight shut. 'I heard a voice. It was getting light. Then I heard the ambulance screamin' and I knew it was for me,' she said, the shock making her face pinched. 'That's it. That's all I remember, Inspector.'

Joanna touched the girl's shoulder. 'You've done really well, Kayleigh,' she said. 'You've been very brave.' She smiled. 'Well done. If you remember anything more I want you to tell WPC Critchlow. She'll stay with you for now and we'll go and talk to your mum.'

Kayleigh turned her face to the pillow. 'Good luck,' she muttered, now sounding more like a stroppy teenager.

'Is there anything you want her to bring from home?'

'Mobile phone charger, my iPod and some money.'

'Right.'

As Joanna and Mike left the hospital she turned to him. 'Now,' she said, 'time to visit the mother. What's her name again?'

'Christine – umm, Bretby. She married a guy called Neil Bretby after divorcing Kayleigh's dad.'

Kayleigh and her mother lived in a terraced house whose front door opened right on to the pavement. It was on the southern edge of the town, up a quiet side street with cars parked on both sides, leaving one narrow lane for through traffic. There were plenty of these terraces in Leek, built in the nineteenth century for the mill workers, well before the age of the car. A police vehicle already stood outside number seventeen, telling anyone who saw it that a drama was being played somewhere along this quiet and very average street. As Joanna and Mike pulled up a large woman crossed the street towards them, heavy thighs bumping together in unflattering black leggings.

'What's goin' on 'ere,' she asked and without giving them a chance to answer ploughed on. 'It's that bloody Kayleigh again, isn't it? She's up to something.' Her lardy face displayed piggy eyes and yellowed teeth.

'And you are?' Joanna queried politely.

'Pauline Morrison. I live next door and I've had enough of that kid. She's nothing but trouble.'

'I'm afraid that Kayleigh has had a sort of accident,' Joanna said calmly. 'I think she and her mother are going to need all the neighbourly support they can get. I'm sure they can count on you, Ms Morrison?'

Pauline's mouth dropped open. This was not what she had expected. She stood with her hands on her wide hips and searched for something to say, finally mumbling. ''Course.' She turned on her heel and opened the front door to what was, presumably, her own house. Joanna gave Mike a tiny smile. 'Round one to me?'

His eyes rested on her warmly. 'It's something I've never quite got used to,' he mused.

She raised her eyebrows questioningly.

'The way you use politeness as a weapon.'

She giggled, then stopped when they spied Pauline watching them through the window, mobile phone pressed to her ear, talking animatedly, waving her free hand in the air.

The jungle drums were beating.

Joanna knocked on number seventeen and the door was opened by WPC Bridget Anderton: a small, plump officer who loved dogs and children and, unusually for a policewoman, rarely saw any harm in anyone. She had a difficult home life: three children and a husband who was on long-term sick leave with depression. She gave Joanna a wide smile, showing beautiful teeth. 'Afternoon, Joanna, Mike,' she said. 'I suppose you've come to speak to Kayleigh's mum.' She stood back against the door, allowing them to enter.

Christine Bretby was sitting on the sofa, staring ahead of her; a slim woman who looked older than her years. According to their records she was thirty-four but she could have passed for late forties. She looked across wearily as Joanna and Mike filed into the small, square room. It was a little plain and character-less, with beige emulsioned walls. There was little in it apart from a large, flat-screen television, standing in the corner on a smoked-glass unit and a huge framed print of Klimt's *The Kiss* over the faux log gas fire. Joanna couldn't help but focus on the gaudy print.

Christine followed her gaze and gave it a sentimental look. 'He gave me that,' she said. 'Neil. Lovely, isn't it?'

'Very nice,' Joanna responded without meaning it. To her it was one of those paintings whose original meaning and significance had been lost because it had become a cliché. A birthday card, a poster, a cheap print seen everywhere. On mugs, plates, wrapping paper and in shop windows.

She sat down on the other end of the sofa. 'Christine,' she began, 'do you know what happened to your daughter last night?'

Christine stared back at her, her eyes angry and her lips tight. 'Let's get one thing straight, Inspector,' she said, 'my daughter is a cunning little liar. Ask anyone who knows her what she's like. She's bad news. Don't you fall for her stories.'

'Kayleigh claimed she was raped last night.'

Christine's finger pointed at her. Straight and uncompromising. 'I'm telling you, don't get fooled by her. You don't know her like I do.'

'Mrs Bretby,' Joanna said, beginning to lose her patience. 'Whatever the truth your daughter nearly died last night from hypothermia following an assault. I could be picking you up right now to take you to the mortuary instead of to the hospital. Whatever happened last night . . .'

'She'll have been askin' for it.' Christine's voice was harsh, ragged, unsympathetic. 'What was she wearin, Inspector? Where was she? I'll tell you. She was in a tarty little skirt, showing all her bits, in a club what's meant for over-eighteens.' Christine's eyes opened wide and she hunched her shoulders up. 'She's fourteen years old. What does she expect? Answer me that. You know what men are like: think women are lined up just for them. Girls like Kayleigh, well, they're just askin' for it. And if he left her there, half-dressed in the snow, it was no more or less than she deserved.'

For a moment Joanna was too stunned to respond. She glanced at Mike for help, but he was wearing his famously wooden expression. No help there, then. She tried again. 'Mrs Bretby,' she appealed. 'Whatever the truth about last night your daughter has had a truly dreadful experience which has very nearly cost her her life. Please—'

Christine Bretby shifted on her seat to inch a little closer to

Joanna. She put her face near enough for Joanna to smell tobacco and wine on her breath; see the bloodshot whites of her eyes and the pores glistening on her skin, which was coarse and aging quickly. 'How well do you know my daughter, Inspector?' she demanded. Then, triumphantly: 'Answer, you don't. Right, then. Let me tell you.' There was more finger pointing. 'Her dad was a nasty, violent blighter not above raisin' his fists to anyone when he'd a few too many. I was stupid enough to marry him when I was seventeen years old and knew it had been a big mistake before I was eighteen. Got the story so far?'

'Go on,' Joanna said quietly, suppressing the hostile tone in her voice.

'I divorced him after five years. I'd finally had enough. So there I was, twenty-two years old, on my own, with a kid of two. I can't earn a lot of money. I never trained to do anything. And let me tell you this. Don't think it's a great big exciting bed of roses being single out there, particularly in a small town like Leek where everyone knows everyone else. There's not loads of fellas queuing up to be the perfect dad to someone else's 'orrible little kid, wantin' to shower you with champagne and roses, take you on cruises and stuff. It's bleedin' hard out there and even at twenty-two there's plenty of younger competition. Girls may like older men but men sure as hell don't like older women – except for a quick screw,' she finished bitterly. 'And then, when I was thirty I finally hit lucky. I met Neil Bretby. He was a lovely guy: divorced, quiet, a plumber who worked hard and was decent. Everything.' Her gaze couldn't help but drift up towards the Klimt and she gave a great sigh. 'Of course, little Kayleigh had had me all to herself up until then, but . . .' *Wham!* She slapped her hand on the seat between them. 'All of a sudden this little ten-year-old has to share her mum and she don't like it. 'Specially when we get married a couple of years later and he moves in.' Her glance drifted upwards again. 'He was so romantic, so lovely, so handsome and just a really great bloke. When he asked me to marry him it was the best day of my life. And the same was true of my wedding day. It was how things should be, apart from Miss Sulky Pants who didn't like her bridesmaid's dress.' Her voice, which had turned harsh, softened again. 'It was nothing

short of true love. I had everything I never had with Peter, my
first husband, Kayleigh's dad. It was as though I'd married a real
grown-up man. I was happy. But little Miss Sulky Pants didn't
like it. She was jealous so she made up a story about Neil.' Her
eyes clouded. Now she looked more sad than angry. 'And however
much I didn't believe it the mud was stickin'. When I was on
my own I'd find myself startin' to wonder. What if? What if?
What if it was true that he married me just to get at my own
daughter?' She finished on a breathless, wondering note. 'In the
end I 'ad to let 'im go. It was no good any more. The magic had
gone. It was all spoilt.' She eyed the pack of cigarettes on top
of the television. 'So now I'm back on my own. Stuck with 'er.
And I can tell you now, it's even harder this time around. I won't
strike lucky again.'

Joanna was silent for a minute. She owed the woman this
tribute, at least. But . . . 'Christine,' Joanna said. 'Whatever's
gone on before, Kayleigh has had a truly dreadful time. A girl
needs a mother at a time like this.'

Christine's face twisted then into an ugly sneer. She had given
up searching for sympathy for her side of the story. The gloves
were off, the fists raised. 'Does she indeed? Does she really?'
She gave into the craving, crossed quickly to the TV and lit one
of the cigarettes, dragging on it so deeply her lips practically
disappeared. Then she lifted her index finger in a last didactic
gesture. 'Let me tell you what I think happened, Inspector: my
version of the events of last night. She sneaks into the club with
some guy probably old enough to be her father. Drinks until she's
blotto. The guy sees she's three sheets to the wind, drags her
outside, maybe slipping her a Mickey Finn or somethin'. He
shags her and dumps her.' Her eyes blazed. 'Got it? Who's the
criminal here?'

Behind her Joanna could hear Korpanski shifting his weight
on his feet. It sounded like a heavy, rhythmic thud. She knew he
hated the 'Take them, fuck them, leave them' epithet applied to
men sometimes. And he had strong feelings about motherhood,
too, which he had expressed before. She gave him a quick, warning
glance. Korpanski's neck had turned red. A sure sign he was about
to blow. She shook her head at him, warningly. He met her eyes
with a steady gaze and a tightening of his neck muscles. Slowly

his neck resumed its normal colour and his breathing slowed. She heaved a quiet sigh of relief. The danger was over.

Christine seemed not to notice any of this and continued with her story with barely a pause. 'She passes out and then, when she comes round, she makes up this cock and bull story to explain what's been going on. Take my word for it, Inspector: that is what happened.' She lay back on the sofa exhausted. 'Need a police investigation for that, Inspector?' she mocked.

Joanna glanced again at Mike, who was scowling, then at Bridget, who was watching the drama with her lips slightly parted, sitting very still. Joanna couldn't begin to work out what her response to all this was. Bridget's life had made her adept at the art of concealing her emotions.

'Would you like WPC Anderton to drive you to the hospital to see your daughter?'

Christine puffed on her cigarette. ''Spose I'd better,' she said reluctantly, stubbing the cigarette out in a small brass ashtray and standing up. 'It'll look bad if I don't.'

'Kayleigh asked if you would bring her mobile phone charger, her iPod and some money.'

Even this seemed to upset Christine. 'Oh, she did, did she? Anything else Lady Muck wants?'

'I don't think so.' Joanna could have added so many words, so many sentiments, but wisely she kept her mouth shut and left with her sergeant.

As she reached the door, she turned. 'By the way,' she said. 'Kayleigh's father. Where is he now?'

'Scarpered off back to London,' Christine said. 'I haven't seen him in years.'

'Was he a Londoner?'

'Oh, yeah. When we split up he went straight back. Once a Londoner, always a Londoner.' She gave a cynical smile. 'Bit like Leek, I s'pose. You never quite leave the moorlands behind.' She qualified the statement. 'Not completely anyway.'

'He had a London accent?'

'What on earth has that got to do with this?'

'Kayleigh said that her attacker had a London accent.'

Christine almost laughed. 'There's probably millions of people with a London accent.'

'Not in Leek.'

'Yeah, well. Born and bred there, he was. I'd gone down there to work. You know . . .' Again Christine Bretby smiled. 'You know, it's the kind of the thing you do when you're in your teens and I was a bit of a tearaway. Bit like Kayleigh, really. Leek wasn't big enough for me so I worked in a hotel in Leicester Square. That's when I met 'im. He was a right charmer. We got married. He came back up 'ere with me but I don't think he could cope with rural life. He missed the "Old Smoke".'

'Has he ever come back to Leek?'

Christine shook her head. 'Not as far as I know. He wasn't ever over keen on the place. Never really settled here. Couldn't wait to get back to London.'

'Has he got any friends still here?'

Christine looked guarded. 'One or two.'

'Can we have their names, please?'

'As far as I remember he knew a guy called Johnny Ollerenshaw. I didn't really know him. And there was someone else.' She screwed up her face. 'A farmer from out Rudyard way – Terence Gradbach, I think his name was. Those were the only two he was really friendly with. He didn't make friends easy. He was a bit of a loner. But they used to go fishing together on the canal. I don't think there's anyone else he would have kept up with – if he's even kept up with them.' She looked up. 'But Peter can't have had anything to do with this. We're history. He's not wanted any contact with Kayleigh since he's gone. You're barkin' up the wrong tree there, Inspector Piercy.'

'Was he a smoker?'

Again Christine looked bemused by the question. 'What the heck are you asking these questions for about her dad? What's this got to do with whatever happened to Kayleigh last night?'

Joanna hid behind, 'Just answer the question, please.'

'He was a social smoker,' she said grumpily. 'Not heavy.' She gave a sour smile. 'Not like me.' She glanced at the only ornaments in the room: the packet of cigarettes and plastic Bic lighter on top of the television. 'Addicted.'

'OK. Right. Thanks for that.' Joanna smiled. 'And his teeth?'

Now Christine looked at her as though she'd left her senses. 'His teeth?' she chortled. 'Same as everyone else's.'

Joanna persevered. 'There was nothing –' she paused – 'notable about them?'

'No.' The answer came flatly.

'Do you have a photograph of him?'

The question provoked both anger and humour. 'Not bloody likely. I hardly had any affection for him after I'd gone. I wasn't going to keep mementoes.'

'OK. One last thing, Christine. Do you have a recent photograph of Kayleigh?'

For a moment Christine sat still, as though thinking. Then she stood up and left the room, returning with a glossy picture. Joanna studied it. She would have found it hard to believe that the pale child in the hospital bed and this giggling, heavily made-up girl in a very skimpy dress were one and the same. The power of make-up and clothes, she reflected. They transform.

'Thank you,' she said.

Most mothers in this situation produce a school photograph – something to underline the fact that their child is clean and pure, even when facts point resolutely in the opposite direction.

Not Kayleigh's mother. She wanted to portray her daughter as glamorous, tarty, older than her years: inviting sexual advances. If anything she appeared to want to blacken her daughter's reputation, not enhance it.

Interesting.

FOUR

As Barra had predicted the images from the CCTV outside Patches nightclub showed little. Most people were muffled up against the weather and stood with their heads bowed and their shoulders hunched. It was disappointing. Everyone was anonymous. There were plenty of couples walking together: clusters of girls and clusters of youths laughing, talking, smoking, drinking. All appeared perfectly normal. They ran through the tapes and then, a little before 2 a.m., they spotted Kayleigh by her silver skirt which shimmered and glistened in the lights. She was drunk. Very drunk, and staggering against a man who looked tall and thin and had a loose-limbed, gangly gait.

Joanna zoomed in but the picture was too grainy. They could get it enhanced but this was risky. Filling in too much detail could mislead people if they got the details wrong. Kayleigh had been accurate, though, in her description. The man was a good few inches taller than her even though she was wearing skyscraper heels that she was having great difficulty balancing on, sliding around in the snow and occasionally clinging on to the man's arm. They needed to measure Kayleigh's height plus the shoes she had been wearing to work out her attacker's height. But at a guess he was six foot one, six foot two. He was indeed wearing a dark leather bomber jacket. It could have been black or brown. Tight trousers displayed his skinny legs. His feet looked unusually small. Maybe a size six – round about the same size as Kayleigh's. He had light coloured hair. Not blond. It wasn't that light. It could have been grey or light brown and again, Kayleigh's description had been accurate. His hair was short and spiky, around half an inch all over, sticking up, but his face was bent down. They could not make out his features except for a thin mouth. He looked faintly disapproving. Kayleigh and her alleged rapist looked like any other couple, staggering drunkenly together, the man in much better control than the girl. No one would guess that the girl was a minor of fourteen years old or that the man was about to rape her then abandon her in sub-zero conditions, without caring whether she lived or died. Joanna watched the video again at normal speed then slowed it down and had to acknowledge that under the circumstances it did not look suspicious. That was the beauty of it. They were just another couple. No one would have given them a second look. But it was to be hoped that someone had. That someone had picked up on details which Kayleigh had missed.

'Is he still around Leek?' Joanna murmured, fiddling with the zoom-in button and trying to decipher the man's features, which stayed stubbornly in the shadows, almost as though he knew the camera was following him. 'Or has he gone somewhere else to try his luck? Maybe even gone home to a wife and kids?' She looked up at Korpanski. 'And what if Kayleigh is lying? What if it was consensual sex?'

Korpanski's chin was square and firm. 'We could still get him on having sex with a minor.'

Joanna raised her eyebrows.

'Attempted murder,' was Korpanski's next suggestion.

'We'd never get the CPS to run with that. He'd get away scot-free. It wouldn't stick, Mike. Even I can dream up the defence. His lawyer would simply say that he assumed the girl would take herself home. That he couldn't have known that she was so drunk she would pass out and lie there all night.' She fell silent. 'This case is worrying me, Mike,' she said.

He looked up. 'Any particular reason?'

'I don't know,' she confessed. 'Only that I feel a bit sick.' She met his eyes. 'Rape is bad enough,' she said. 'But can a man think so little of a woman that he just abandons her?'

'Some men,' Korpanski replied gruffly. 'Only some men.' He looked glum for a moment. Then he brightened up. 'Let's go public, Jo,' he said. 'We've got plenty to go on, and a good description. Let's flush him out of the woodwork and see what happens.'

She smiled at him. 'That, Korpanski,' she said, 'is a very good idea. We'd better prepare our statement. But,' she continued, 'we'll keep it very simple. A description and just say we are anxious to talk to this man.'

They dispatched PC Phil Scott to ascertain how tall Kayleigh was, how high the heels had been on her shoes and what size footwear she wore. Kayleigh was bound to appreciate the company of the tall, blond policeman.

At half past five Steve Shand called in ready to give his statement. He looked very nervous and still a little pale and hung-over.

Joanna tried to put him at his ease by thanking him for calling in so promptly but it didn't help. He still looked very nervous.

'Take us through last night first,' she suggested. 'Who were you out with?'

He answered quickly. 'Four of my mates. It were a night out with the lads.' He spoke defensively in a thick Staffordshire accent and Joanna guessed that Shand's girlfriend hadn't been too happy about his 'night out with the lads'.

'Their names?'

Shand looked uncomfortable. 'Gary Pointer, Andrew Downey, Clint Jones and Shaun Hennessey,' he said, adding: 'they've all been my mates since school. We go out fairly regularly.'

'So they are all from around here?' Joanna asked casually.

'Yeah. Leek born and bred.' Joanna gave Korpanski a quick glance but his face was sphinx still. He was giving nothing away. And she might have imagined the look of disappointment in his dark eyes. There was nothing Korpanski liked better than a quick 'finger on the collar'. She would lay a bet his own fingers were itching right now.

'Perhaps you'll ask your friends to contact us,' Joanna suggested. 'Now, if you could run through the events of the evening?'

'It was Shaun's birthday. The big three-o.' Shand grinned. 'So we thought we'd hit the town. We went to The Quiet Woman first then wandered up to Patches around ten thirty or thereabouts.'

'Was Patches crowded when you got there?'

'No. The snow had kept people away, I reckon. It was pretty quiet. It's usually crammed.'

'Did you notice the doorman?'

'Andy? Yeah.' All of a sudden Shand looked concerned. 'Why?'

'Just curious. Did he check your ID?'

'No. He knows us. He didn't bother. Just gave us the usual warning to behave ourselves. As if,' Shand grunted.

'And then?'

Shand flushed. 'Drinks, a few dances, a bit of a—' He stopped dead.

Joanna and Mike exchanged glances.

Shand looked from one to the other; a rabbit caught in car headlights.

Korpanski reassured him. 'Look, anything you say in here will remain secret – unless it has a direct bearing on the case.'

He could tell that Steve Shand wasn't quite convinced. He eyed them warily.

'I might have . . .' His voice petered away. 'Look,' he said. 'I had a lot to drink. My memory isn't exactly sure what happened. I probably went outside with a girl. Bloody Claire,' he said, 'my girlfriend. She'd kill me if she knew.'

'Who was the girl?' Joanna's voice was deceptively soft and quiet.

'I don't know,' Shand confessed.

'Was it Kayleigh – the girl you found yesterday morning?'

'Oh, no,' Shand said. 'It weren't her.'

'Sure, are you?'

'Absolutely.'

'We could do with knowing who it was.'

'Look,' Shand said, gathering confidence now, 'I haven't even said that I did go off with anyone. I just said I *might* have done.' He scooped in a deep breath.

'What time did you call the taxi?'

'Late,' Shand admitted. 'The club closes around two. I guess it was around about then.'

Something else to check.

'The name of the taxi firm?'

Shand looked wary. He didn't like all this checking. 'Sid's Taxis,' he said grumpily. 'I always use them.'

Joanna waited.

'He took me straight home.'

Joanna smiled. Now it was time to dig a little deeper. She produced the photograph of Kayleigh that Christine had given them. 'Did you notice this girl *inside* Patches?'

Shand hardly looked at the picture. 'No,' he said quickly. 'I didn't.'

Joanna kept silent for a minute, waiting for Shand to speak again when he had put two and two together. 'Is that the girl that . . .?'

'It's the girl whose life you probably saved,' Joanna said.

Shand looked horrified. 'But she looks so . . .'

'Young? She's fourteen.'

He shook his head. 'No. I meant lively. Alive. You can't imagine her freezing to death and, well – ' His blue eyes looked confused as he stared at Joanna. He ran his fingers through the short, spiky brown hair, a movement that emphasized a receding hair line. 'Dying,' he finished.

'She was wearing a silver miniskirt,' Korpanski put in gruffly. 'That might help to jog your memory.'

'Oh, f—!' Shand looked shocked. Until this moment he had not connected the half-dead girl with the sexy thing who had been gyrating around him.

'*Now* do you remember her?'

Like many weak men, Shand hid behind a lie. 'No,' he said firmly.

But Korpanski was not going to let him off the hook so easily. 'Sure?'

Shand looked at the burly sergeant and visibly shrank. 'No,' he said. 'I didn't see her last night.'

Korpanski gave him a straight, innocent stare. 'And yet you say that the club was quiet.'

'It weren't that quiet,' Shand said. 'There was a few people – later on.'

'Right.'

Joanna then produced the best print they had obtained from the CCTV pictures of their suspect. 'What about him?'

Shand gave this a little more attention. 'No,' he said. 'I don't remember him.' He looked up. 'Sorry,' he said.

'OK. He had had a cockney accent. Did you notice anyone with a cockney accent – at the bar, maybe in the gents?'

Shand shook his head. 'No,' he said. 'Sorry.'

'That's OK. So you went home in one of Sid's taxis, and presumably went to bed.'

Shand risked a moment of levity. 'Sneaked into the spare bed, more like,' he said. 'I didn't want to wake Claire.' Man-to-man, Korpanski and Shand exchanged a glance of shared male sympathy and Joanna felt both excluded and resentful. What was it about men that felt they had to play the part of Don Juan?

She hauled the pair of them back to the present and away from amorous dreams that they were irresistible to legions of women.

'And this morning?' she proceeded briskly.

That wiped the smile off Shand's face. 'I got Claire to drop me off at the car park,' he said. 'But I couldn't get into my car. The locks were frozen. I breathed on them and tried again. Then I heard a noise. I saw a cat and thought it must be that. But I heard it again and so I thought I'd better check it out. I went towards the bins. There was piles of rubbish.' He swallowed. 'Just lying there. And then it moved. I was so shocked. I saw it was a girl. I rang nine-nine-nine.'

'OK,' Joanna said. 'As I said, you almost certainly saved her life. Thank you very much. Now I wonder if you'd mind giving us your fingerprints.'

The broad, open grin that had melted away was replaced by a look of wary anger. 'What is this?' he demanded. 'The third degree or something? I'm not under suspicion, am I? I'm the good guy here, surely?' He looked from Joanna to Korpanski. 'I'm the one who found her. If it wasn't for me she'd be dead, wouldn't she? You've said that. Hey,' he continued, 'I'm the knight in shining armour here.'

Neither Mike nor Joanna could deny this. Shand persisted. 'I'm the cavalry, mate.' He was appealing to Korpanski – as another man, Joanna observed. 'I'm the one who called the ambulance and gave her my coat.' He looked from one to the other. 'Why are you asking me all these questions anyway? You must know I had nothing to do with the assault on a fourteen-year-old girl.'

As Shand had elected the male option Joanna let Mike explain. 'Purely routine, sir,' he said calmly.

The politeness didn't mollify Shand. He still looked cheated, as though he'd had a winning lottery ticket and then found someone had pinched it from his pocket.

'Why do you want *my* prints?'

'To exclude them from anything touched at the scene of the crime,' Joanna said.

'I don't think I did touch anything.'

'You almost certainly did,' Joanna insisted. 'You'd be surprised. And it could save us a lot of time, trouble and money.' She gave him one of her wide smiles.

Shand responded and caved in. 'All right,' he said. 'Fine by me. So long as you destroy them after.'

'As soon as this incident is solved, Mr Shand.'

He looked mollified at that. Joanna would have been happy to let him go, but Shand seemed to want to drive home his point.

He drew in a deep breath. 'I was just out with a few mates. All right? Having an innocent night out with the lads. It doesn't make me a rapist.'

'A rapist,' Joanna queried sharply. 'Where do you get that from?'

'Well, it's obvious there was a sexual attack, isn't it?' He was on the defensive. 'She was hardly wearing anything when I found her. I've got a brain cell, you know. There's your interest. And the local radio station said a "serious sexual assault". It doesn't take a lot of filling in.'

He squeezed his eyes tight shut. If only he could blot out that girl dancing provocatively in that shimmering skirt, right in front of his eyelids. Flirting.

Joanna was watching him carefully. Beads of sweat were breaking out like dew on his forehead. As though he needed to pretend they weren't there he didn't wipe them away.

She continued. 'The description Kayleigh has been able to give us is of a tall, thin man with spiky hair, in his thirties or early forties, with a strong cockney accent. Do any of your "mates" fit that description?'

Shand shook his head decisively. He was on safer ground now. 'No,' he said. 'My mates are all from round here. Not a cockney amongst them. Staffordshire born and bred. Like – I – said,' he finished deliberately.

'Right,' Joanna said and tried another tack. 'Apart from the accent, do they fit the physical description?'

Shand thought for a moment. 'I suppose Gary looks a bit like that,' he said reluctantly.

Mike's pen was poised over his notebook and Shand reluctantly gave him his friend's name and address.

'And what was Gary wearing last night?'

Shand blew out through his lips. 'I can't remember,' he said. 'Jeans, I suppose.'

'A coat?'

Shand shrugged. 'Haven't a clue, mate,' he said, again addressing Korpanski. He grinned. 'I don't really notice what my mates are wearing. More –' He stopped at that.

Korpanski took the questioning further, still in the same jokey, matey tone. 'Did Claire mind you clubbing with a few of the "boys"?'

Shand looked angry. 'Whatever's that got to do with this? Whether my girlfriend minded me having a bit of fun with my mates is nothing to do with this. How could it be? You're just prying.' He frowned at them both in turn and picked on Joanna as the softer target. 'You're tryin' it on. Get a kick out of this, do you?'

'Answer the sergeant's question,' Joanna said flatly.

'She doesn't like it much,' Shand admitted. 'Especially there. It's known as a bit of a knocking shop.'

'Is that why she dropped you off this morning and didn't wait to see whether you could get into your car?'

Shand heaved a big sigh. 'Sort of.'

Joanna shot Mike a quick glance. 'Do us a favour,' she said, chummily addressing Shand. 'Ask your mates if they'll pop in and make a statement, will you? Sooner rather than later.' Without waiting for him to respond, she added: 'Thanks. You're free to go now – after you've given us your prints.'

Timmis and McBrine had got themselves a few bags of crisps and some Diet Coke and were enjoying themselves watching the CCTV shots from earlier in the evening, which had captured activities on the dance floor and around the bar. The girls were all flinging themselves around in the tiniest of clothes, some of them see-through. They got the odd flash of knicker and some very good views of cleavage and bosom. There were plenty of bumps and spills as the dancers were overambitious in their moves. There was the odd spat between women over the men and a couple of hefty chinning-ups as beer was spilt accidentally or deliberately over the odd guy. But all in all there was a reasonably amicable atmosphere in the club.

McBrine leaned forward. 'There she is,' he said. 'That's our Kayleigh.' The silver skirt made her easy to pick out. She seemed to be dancing alone rather than with a female friend or with a bloke. They watched her for a while. 'Good dancer,' PC Timmis observed.

'She's fourteen,' McBrine growled.

'I know,' Josh Timmis replied, 'but it's really hard to remember that when you see her move.'

'Behave,' his pal said good-naturedly. 'We've a job to do.'

'Yeah.' Timmis popped open another bag of crisps then leaned forward. 'Hey. Look at that.' Just as the man grabbed hold of

Kayleigh she disappeared from view behind a gang of mixed revellers.

They rewound that bit but all they could see was a man in a white shirt putting his hand over her bottom. He pulled her towards him and then they lost her. There had been three sets of tapes; one from each of the cameras. They snapped the ring pulls of a second can of coke, split opened more cheese and onion crisps and settled back again.

Joanna met up with a few uniformed officers and quickly outlined the case and the direction of her enquiries.

'See if you can find out anything more about Kayleigh's father,' she said to Detective Constable Danny Hesketh-Brown: a keen, fresh-faced officer from the Potteries who had been ragged mercilessly on account of his double-barrelled name but now was accepted as 'one of the lads'. 'One of his fishing buddies might be able to help you. I don't really think we have much to worry about there but it's as well to check.'

Hesketh-Brown nodded.

'Also, it might be an idea to track down Neil Bretby and interview him. It might give us some insight into Kayleigh. This is still being treated as an alleged rape case,' she said to the assembled officers. 'Looking at the CCTV footage we'll be lucky to make a positive ID from it.' Groans from the force. 'It's too grainy and indistinct. We'll see if we can get any trace evidence from her clothes. When Kayleigh is a little better we'll do an identikit picture but she tells us he has a London accent. She was fairly obviously drunk as a skunk so we'll have a word with the owners of Patches about underage drinking and they'll have to be more careful in future about letting in under-eighteens, but for now let's concentrate on the case in hand.' She paused. 'The fallout will come later – how come a fourteen-year-old is in a club for over-eighteens, drinking?'

'And getting raped,' came a voice from the back.

'Quite,' she commented dryly.

'Timmis and McBrine – anything meaningful from the CCTV footage from inside the club?'

McBrine grinned. 'Plenty of eye candy.'

'*Meaningful*,' she repeated.

'We've had a couple of sightings; her dancin' with someone but not yet, ma'am.' They were unabashed. 'We've got another couple of tapes to go.'

'Good.' Joanna ignored the ripple which went round the room.

'Lucky buggers.'

'Some people get all the luck.'

This male banter was something you had to get used to working in the police force. To the general public it may portray itself as politically correct but underneath it was as sexist as ever.

But the women were fighting back.

'Decent *men* there too?' Hannah Beardmore asked innocently.

Joanna smiled. 'Well, we'll be interviewing anyone who feels they have something to contribute and I'll put something out in the press. Dawn, how did the meeting between Kayleigh and her mother go?'

'Frosty, to say the least. No love lost between those two. They really hate each other.'

'Any idea why the feelings run so deep?'

Dawn shook her head. 'Apart from the obvious: Kayleigh having robbed her mother of married bliss.' She met Joanna's eyes squarely. 'I'd say that's enough, Joanna.'

'OK. I'm treating the London accent as an important lead.' She deployed a few officers to check in the shops, pubs and hotels. 'If our perp is from out of the area he must have stayed somewhere. If we come up with nothing from Leek we can widen the area to cover Stoke, Stone and Macclesfield. I'll also be doing a broadcast on local radio and we'll see if that bears fruit. Anything else?'

There wasn't and the officers dispersed.

FIVE

Thursday, 2 December. 8 a.m.

She dressed carefully and nervously in a grey skirt suit, cream silk blouse and black court shoes, feeling as though she was dressing for a funeral – her own. She brushed her hair, applied the lightest of make-up, feeling sick with dread as she peered at herself in the mirror and saw how pale and apprehensive she looked. Matthew came behind her, grinned at her into the mirror and put his arms around her. 'Good luck,' he said, kissing the back of her neck. She turned around to face him, Korpanski's words about Matthew wanting a 'wife at home plus kids' biting into her. 'You'd probably be pleased if I lost my job, wouldn't you, Matt?'

He shook his head. 'No, I wouldn't because it wouldn't be you, Jo.' He tilted her chin up, kissed her on the lips then searched her face. 'I can't imagine you at home all the time, going out to lunch? No thanks. It wouldn't be you.' Oddly enough this was one of the few times he chose to mention his ex-wife. 'That's what Jane was like: happy to chitter-chatter with her socialite friends, days out to London, shopping, partying, going to the theatre, that sort of stuff.' His green eyes clouded. 'I was just a provider. She was never interested in my work or my opinion or anything. She had her own friends and didn't like my medic friends.' He frowned. 'She found them boring. We had nothing in common, Jo.' He gave a short laugh. 'Can you believe it? I was married but I was lonely. Really lonely.' He dropped his arm around her shoulders and she was aware that however strange the timing this was one of the most honest, deep and heart-searching confessions he had ever made to her. He continued. 'When I met you I felt we connected.' He smiled, kissed her again and his face lightened. 'Now that's enough of this maudlin, self-pitying talk. Let's just leave it at this: I can't imagine you being anything other than what you are, Joanna Piercy, soon to be Mrs Levin. I love you the way you are, I promise. And don't forget, we're going out for dinner tomorrow night whatever happens.'

'Oh?'

'And don't forget something else.'

'What?'

He brushed her lips with his own and she felt the heat in them. 'That I love you,' he said simply. Then he drew back. 'Anyway, Colclough won't let anything happen to his favourite cop. He'll protect you.'

She shook her head. 'Not now I've let him down, Matt. He takes it personally.' She smiled sadly. 'I'm his fallen angel.'

'You'll soon fly back into his good books,' he said. 'Ring me when you can.'

Her stomach was too churned up for breakfast so she poured herself a lemon, honey and ginger smoothie then left, shouting up the stairs to Matthew, who was now under the shower.

The drive in from Waterfall to Leek was achingly familiar. Every twist and turn in the road, every incline, every downhill. She might be driving her car today but she'd ridden this way so many times on her bike that she could almost feel the pull on her legs as she finally arrived at the station and turned into her parking slot.

She got a few looks of sympathy as she walked into the station but some officers looked at her with a sort of righteous indignation. DS Mike Korpanski was a popular member of the Leek police force and his injury had upset them all. The finger had been well and truly pointed at his superior, Detective Inspector Joanna Piercy, who had risked his life with her cavalier decision.

She sat outside Colclough's door, her stomach in knots, feeling like a fourteen-year-old waiting outside the headmistress's office to be expelled for smoking or a patient waiting to go under the knife, or a criminal awaiting the hangman's noose or the judge's verdict or . . . Her imagination finally ran out of ideas.

The door opened and she was ushered in.

Police complaints were a serious business. Justice and fairness had to be done. More importantly it had to be *seen to be done*. Besides Colclough there were three other senior officers, two men and one woman, all in uniform and all of whom stared at her, straight-lipped. The thinnest of them introduced himself. 'I am the Chief Constable of Staffordshire, Jonathan Taylor,' he said. 'These are Detective Chief Inspectors Stuart Wrekin and Teresa Finney. Chief Superintendent Arthur Colclough you already know, I believe.'

Joanna couldn't even look at Colclough. She couldn't face the look of disappointment she would have seen there. Instead she focused on the chief constable, who met her eyes fearlessly.

'First of all, Inspector Piercy, you accept that a senior officer is responsible for the safety of his or her junior officers?'

'Yes, sir.'

'Do you also accept that you took an unacceptable risk in staking out the farm without backup?'

'As it turned out, sir.'

Taylor's eyebrows lifted at this weak attempt at self-defence. To him it would be interpreted as impertinence.

'There are rules designed to protect our officers from harm. Particularly where firearms are concerned.'

'I didn't know there was a firearm involved, sir.'

'As I understand it the murder you were investigating was committed with a shotgun.'

'Yes, sir.'

'So you might have guessed that a gun *would* be involved.'

It's so easy to be wise after the event. 'Yes, sir.'

'Yet you decided to stake the place out, taking with you one sergeant and letting no one know of your intention.'

Put like that it sounded black. She caught the four officers exchanging glances and sat stone still, waiting for the axe to fall.

'Detective Sergeant Korpanski could have died in this rash attempt.'

Joanna lowered her eyes, remembering the blast of the gun and Mike's instinctive dive in front of her. This was what Fran Korpanski would never forgive, rather than the risk to her husband's life. Joanna could still feel his swift movement, the jerk when he was hit, then the weight of his body and the warm, stickiness of his blood. She closed her eyes and simply nodded, still crushed by her memories.

Taylor continued. 'You and DS Korpanski have a close and loyal working relationship, it has been noted.'

Again she simply nodded.

Stuart Wrekin spoke. 'There are reasons for the rigid rules we have to abide by, Inspector Piercy. Do you accept that?'

'I do, sir.'

'You regret your actions?' Teresa Finney this time.

Joanna met her eyes. 'I do, ma'am,' she said. 'Bitterly.'

All four pairs of eyes turned on her and judged her.

There was silence in the room. Then the chief constable leaned back in his chair and steepled his fingers. 'Leave us for a moment,

Piercy,' he growled and Joanna knew they were about to decide her future. She wanted to beg that they keep her on. Demote her if necessary but not cut off the lifeblood which was her work.

Please?

She sat outside.

Five minutes passed.

Then the door was opened and Colclough motioned her to enter. She tried to read his expression but he avoided looking at her. It didn't look good.

She followed him back into the room where he took his seat behind the long table on the end of the line.

The chief constable cleared his throat and spent a minute or two studying her.

'Piercy,' he said softly. 'You've been lucky this time.'

'Sir?'

He drew in a deep breath. 'You have a very good work record. Many of your colleagues have spoken up for you. Not least Detective Sergeant Korpanski.' A hint of softening of his lips before he continued. 'Unlike his wife.'

'Yes, sir.'

'This time we have decided to be lenient with you.'

'Yes, sir.'

Colclough ventured the tiniest of smiles, which she could not return.

Taylor continued. 'You understand that this will remain on your record for five years?'

'Yes, sir.'

'And that if there is a further problem you will be suspended or asked to leave the force?'

'Yes, sir.'

'We will not tolerate a repeat of this deliberate flouting of our rules.'

'Yes, sir.'

Taylor's lips softened. 'I think this time you mean, "no, sir".'

'Yes, sir.' She felt herself smile out of relief.

'You're free to go.' He couldn't resist one more score. 'And don't let me ever see you in a situation like this again.'

She escaped. And met Barraclough in the corridor. 'How did it go?'

'Well,' she said, 'I've still got a job.'

He grinned. 'And I've got some news for you.'

'Barra?'

'The skirt,' he said. 'There's a palm print on it. And guess what?'

'Go on?'

'It's Steve Shand's.'

Whatever she had been expecting, it had not been this. She didn't even have to ask whether he was sure. Barra was expert at his job. He did not make mistakes. If he said the palm print was Shand's then Shand's it was.

'There's more.'

She waited.

'The toxicology report's back. She was very drunk. But there's more still. She'd been slipped a drug.'

'What drug?'

'We're not sure.' He consulted his printout. 'It's a sort of benzodiazepine.'

She raised her eyebrows.

'A kind of tranquillizer. She'd have been right out of it.'

'So someone slipped her something.' She looked up. 'Our perp?'

'Could have been.' He hesitated. 'Or she took them herself.'

She was silent. 'Something's ticking away in the back of my mind,' she said.

'Like a little time bomb.' She stopped, tried to focus on what was giving her this uneasy feeling, and failed. 'I'm going to ring the hospital,' she said. 'But first . . .'

She made her way back to her office where Korpanski was sitting, staring fixedly into the computer screen. But knowing Mike as she did she didn't think he was concentrating. She moved behind him and put her hand on his shoulder. 'It's OK, Mike,' she said. He swivelled round in his chair, his relief tangible. 'I've just had a ticking off,' she said. 'That's all. Warnings and it'll stay on my record for five years.' She suddenly wanted to shout. 'But I still have a job.'

Korpanski nodded, smiled, stood up and kissed her cheek. 'Great news,' he said. 'Great news.'

For a minute they simply looked at one another, then Joanna

relayed Barra's findings – both the palm print and the initial toxicology report.

Joanna picked up the phone.

'You want me to leave the room?'

She shook her head. 'I'm only finding out whether Kayleigh has been assessed by a psychiatrist,' she said.

'I thought you'd be ringing Levin.'

'That too,' she said.

SIX

Thursday, 2 December. 11 a.m.

I t took a while to connect with Dr Bopari and Joanna had practically given up hope when her voice came over the telephone. 'Inspector Piercy,' she enquired politely.

'How goes the investigation?'

'It's progressing,' Joanna said. 'How is your patient?'

'Physically she gives us no concern,' Dr Bopari said.

Joanna picked up at once. 'But mentally?'

'A psychiatrist has assessed her and that does give us a reason to have some concerns.'

Joanna's ears pricked up. 'What sort of concerns?'

'It is not appropriate to discuss this over the telephone,' Dr Bopari said, 'particularly as Kayleigh herself deserves the right to confidentiality – but I can tell you this. There is evidence that she has been in the habit of self-harming.'

'Is it possible that I could speak to the psychiatrist?'

Dr Bopari hesitated before caving in. 'It might be an idea but I must get Kayleigh's permission. If she gives it I'll talk to the doctor concerned and if he is willing he will ring you back presently.'

'Thank you. Naturally I am only interested in that it might help us find the man who assaulted her. How long do you intend to keep Kayleigh in for?'

'I'm not too sure at the moment. We're waiting for further psychiatric assessment.'

Joanna thanked her and put the phone down, her feeling of disquiet growing stronger by the minute. Korpanski was watching her, waiting for her direction. She frowned. She needed to be active. But in which direction? She stood up.

'Right,' she said briskly. 'Has there been any response from the boards outside Patches?'

Korpanski shook his head. 'Nothing,' he said. 'I have the feeling that people will hold back. You know what it's like.' He shifted uncomfortably. 'People have secrets, don't they? Maybe *they* shouldn't have been there in the first place. Or they were there with someone they shouldn't have been with.' He grinned apologetically. 'Too much to drink then driving home. Drugs. The fact is that people don't quite trust the police these days, Jo. They think we'll use any way of exacting a conviction without necessarily being too fussy how we got the info in the first place. So it keeps people from coming forward,' he finished.

Joanna tut-tutted. 'A nice state of affairs.'

'We-ell.'

'So we're going to have to flush it out of them, Korpanski, aren't we? And maybe we'll start with Shand's "mates".' Her mind was starting to untangle. 'Hesketh-Brown will be talking to Kayleigh's father's two friends as well.'

Her frown deepened at Korpanski's puzzled look and comment: 'I can't see what he can have to do with it. He's been off the scene for years.'

She justified her actions. 'He broadly appears to fit Kayleigh's description of the rapist. I want to cover all aspects, that's all. Kayleigh herself is the key to all this.'

'Obviously.' Sergeant Korpanski was patently in sarcastic mood.

'I don't mean it in the way you think. I mean her character, her past, the story about her stepfather; truth or untruth? Her habit of self-harming.'

'OK. Whatever.' At Korpanski's side his telephone rang. He picked it up and listened for a while, then looked confused and covered the mouthpiece. 'Dr Afarim?'

For a brief moment Joanna, too, was confused. She took the telephone from Korpanski. 'Detective Inspector Joanna Piercy?' she said.

'I understood you wanted to talk to me about Kayleigh Harrison?'

Joanna's face cleared. 'Oh. You're the psychiatrist?'

'That's correct.' It was a polite, African voice. 'I am Doctor Zed Afarim, a consultant specializing in adolescent psychiatry. I have interviewed young Kayleigh at length and have formed some opinions.' He paused. 'But before I talk to you and explain her psyche I would prefer to spend a little more time speaking with her – if that is convenient.'

Joanna was intrigued. 'Are you suggesting that there is something you can tell me that might help this investigation?'

'I really would prefer to be more certain about her. But, Inspector, I can tell you this. Kayleigh Harrison is a complicated young lady with plenty of issues.' Another pause. 'It is possible that her personality does have a bearing on this case and on your investigation. If so I will be happy to help and Kayleigh, too, is anxious for you to get to the bottom of this assault, but I need to spend more time with her first. One more interview should do the trick.'

Joanna smiled. Like many colonialists Dr Zed Afarim had picked up on English idioms. She thanked him.

'I will be in touch,' he promised. 'Very soon.'

She looked at Mike. 'So what do you make of that?'

Korpanski looked uncomfortable. His neck flushed a dusky red. 'I'm keeping my opinions to myself these days,' he said.

This time it was a knock on the door that interrupted them. Sergeant Alderley peered round. 'I've got Andrew Crispin here,' he said. 'Came in of his own accord to make a statement.'

'Ah – the nightclub bouncer,' Joanna said, satisfied. 'That's saved us having to drag him in. Good – we'll see him in the interview room.'

Crispin was a beefy man – almost as beefy as DS Mike Korpanski, but he didn't have the sergeant's height. Korpanski was six foot three; Crispin barely five foot nine, at a guess. He came in awkwardly, walking with a rolling gait, and in spite of the freezing weather he was wearing bleached denims and a sleeveless T-shirt which displayed tattooed arms as powerful as a gorilla's. These men, Joanna reflected, didn't appear to feel the cold. Or was it simply bravado?

'Thank you for coming, Andrew,' she said politely.

Crispin looked at the floor. 'Chawncy persuaded me,' he admitted. 'He thought it'd be best if I came in of my own accord.' Then in a fit of candidness, he added: 'It was that or get the sack.'

'Quite,' Joanna agreed with a bright smile. 'Sit down, won't you?'

Crispin dropped into a chair – and still looked awkward.

'I take it you understand we're investigating an alleged serious sexual assault on a fourteen-year-old?'

Crispin nodded miserably.

'Who had first spent the evening at Patches,' Joanna continued smoothly.

Another curt nod from Crispin.

'I understand you were the doorman on duty on Tuesday night – the night of the alleged assault?'

Crispin nodded again.

'It might help you remember the girl if I tell you she was wearing a very short silver skirt, a black boob tube and high-heeled silver sandals.' Joanna waited. 'Do you remember seeing a girl who fitted that description on Tuesday night?'

The question provoked another miserable nod from Crispin.

'OK,' she prompted gently. 'In your own words.'

Crispin swallowed. 'I did see her. I think I saw her about nine-ish.'

Korpanski interrupted. 'Alone?'

Crispin shook his head. 'No,' he said. 'She was with someone. He had his arms around her as though he was keepin' her warm. She looked cold in her top.' He couldn't resist a cheeky grin. 'If you can call it that.'

Both Joanna and Mike ignored the comment. 'Did you check her ID?'

'Well, no. She looked –' He stopped. 'They just looked like a couple. The guy was obviously older than her but they looked OK together. I just took it he knew the rules. I mean, there's signs everywhere.' He sounded slightly aggrieved.

Korpanski stepped forward. 'Can you give us a description of the man?'

Crispin swivelled his head round to look Korpanski straight

in the eye. 'Tall – about six foot. Thinnish. Brown hair. I can't remember anything else.'

'What was he wearing?' Joanna sat back, letting Korpanski lead the questions.

Crispin squeezed his eyes shut. 'A leather bomber jacket, I think. Jeans – maybe.

'There's no dress rule on a Tuesday.'

'Did you hear him speak?' Mike pressed on.

That stopped Crispin in his tracks. He frowned and didn't answer straight away, instead thinking silently. 'I must have done, I suppose,' he mused.

'Was he a local guy?'

Crispin shrugged. 'I dunno,' he said. 'I'm really sorry but I couldn't tell you, mate. There was so much noise going on.'

'Had you ever seen him at Patches before?'

'No. Not that I can remember. I don't think I did know him. He's definitely not a regular.' He looked pleased with himself now.

'Did you see them leave?' Joanna asked.

Crispin shook his head. 'No,' he said, turning to her. 'I didn't.' He chewed his lip. Korpanski butted in again. 'Do you ever leave your post?'

Crispin didn't like the sergeant's question. It made him truculent and defensive. 'We-ell, I have to go for a pee break,' he protested.

'Apart from that.' Joanna reflected that Korpanski could sound very hostile when he wanted to.

'I generally clock off a bit early,' Crispin admitted. 'Have a couple of dances myself and maybe a pint or two.'

'So what time did you leave your post on Tuesday night?' Joanna asked silkily.

'Round about a quarter past one. No one comes in at that time.'

'And when you had had your "couple of dances" did you happen to notice Kayleigh in her silver skirt?'

Crispin nodded.

'Was she alone or still with the tall man?'

Crispin drew in a deep breath. 'She was with him but they were more havin' a laugh than flirting. They weren't necking or anything – just seemed to be having a good time.'

'What time do you close the club?'

'Two. We don't have a license for any later.'

Joanna nodded. 'When you closed the club did you see Kayleigh there?'

'Crispin thought for a minute then shook his head. 'No,' he said. 'I didn't. But I seem to remember they left together.'

'Thank you.'

'What time did *you* leave?'

'A bit after two. I have to see everyone off the premises and then supervise the locking up. It's part of the job.'

'OK. Is there anything else you can tell us about either the girl or the man that she was with?'

Crispin shook his head. 'Not that I can think of.' He looked from one to the other, searching for a smile he was not getting. It made him go the extra mile. 'If I do remember anything I'll get back to you. OK?'

'Fine,' Joanna said and couldn't resist pressing home her advantage. 'You do realize that we could prosecute Patches for allowing a fourteen year old to be admitted and drinking alcohol?'

Crispin nodded warily. 'I'd lose my job,' he said. 'I'll be lucky to keep it anyway after this.'

She actually felt sorry for him. 'Mr Crispin – Andrew,' Joanna said. 'You've come here today of your own accord and helped us as far as you can. For that we're grateful. I cannot promise that we won't prosecute or even close Patches but your help today has saved us time and money from having to dig you out. At the moment all we're interested in is the greater crime: the alleged assault on a fourteen-year-old.'

Crispin absorbed this information into the small eyes set in his puffy face. 'OK,' he said. 'I understand.'

'One more question.'

Crispin looked instantly wary.

'Are you in a relationship at the moment?'

To her surprise Andrew Crispin didn't seem to know how to answer this very simple question.

'I am . . . seeing someone,' he finally admitted.

'Her name?'

'Shula McIvoy.'

'She lives with you?'

'No – with her mum and dad.'

'Where does she work?'

Crispin looked even more uncomfortable. 'She doesn't,' he said, 'yet.'

And suddenly Joanna understood. 'How old is Shula?'

'Nearly sixteen.' And now his eyes were both wary and evasive.

'I see.' Joanna met Mike's eyes and knew what he was thinking.

'Well, that's all.'

Crispin didn't move.

'You're free to go,' Korpanski said.

'Thanks.'

And he was gone.

The minute the door had closed behind him Joanna said, '*Now* you can look him up on the PNC.' A few flicks of the keys and they were staring at Andrew Crispin's criminal record. Two convictions of ABH dated 2006 and 2008.

'I'm not so interested in the details of the 2008 conviction,' Joanna said, scanning the screen. 'Outside the nightclub; a couple of drunks. No weapon. Just a boozy punch-up. Part of the job, I suppose.' She grinned at Mike. 'Or should I say one of the perks of the job?' She scanned further. 'He would have got away with this except that the boy he assaulted had a father who was a criminal solicitor. Take away that one small fact and it would never have got as far as the courts. At most the club might have paid out a bit and got the boy to sign a disclaimer.' She scrolled down the screen. 'But the 2006 conviction is a bit more interesting. It's a case of domestic violence against his partner, who was a very young girl. Only sixteen at the time.' She looked up at Mike. 'How old is he?'

Korpanski clicked a few more keys. 'Thirty-eight.'

'So the girl was almost twenty years his junior.' Their eyes met. 'Like Shula. He likes his younger women, doesn't he?'

Danny Hesketh-Brown was enjoying himself. He had tracked Johnny Ollerenshaw via a mobile phone to the banks of the Caldon Canal where Kayleigh's father's erstwhile friend was fishing. Hesketh-Brown had recently taken up fishing himself and occasionally even took his son with him. Ollerenshaw had also been a farmer in the Staffordshire moorlands but had sold up a few years ago and was living off the proceeds. He was a plump, relaxed, friendly man with an open manner. After a brief preamble, mainly about fishing and bait, Hesketh-Brown settled down on the bank beside him. Ollerenshaw had erected a shelter, inside which were a couple of folding chairs. When they were settled, keeping an eye on his line, he poured him a welcome cup of tea.

'Tell me about Peter Harrison,' Hesketh-Brown said. 'You and he were good friends?'

'Yeah.Very.'

'What about his wife, Christine? Were you good friends with her too?'

'Not really.' Ollerenshaw dragged it out. 'I think she resented her husband going off with me, fishing, like. She'd have preferred him to take her shopping.' He gave a sly grin which exposed two missing top incisors that added an odd whistling sound to his speech. 'Very feminine sort of woman, she was. Liked pretty clothes and nice things and always wantin' sommat new for the house.' He spoke in a slow, Potteries accent. 'Bit of a romantic, she were, always wantin' kissin' and cuddlin' and reassuring that he loved her. Well, he did in his way but he couldn't take all that attention. All that need. Specially when little Kayleigh come along. To be honest,' he said thoughtfully, 'havin' Kayleigh didn't really suit either of them. Anyway, he went off when she were no more 'an a tot. Struck out on his own, as I understand.'

'When did you last see him?'

Ollerenshaw scratched his head. 'Years ago,' he said. 'Years ago. He's never even rang. We've kind of lost touch. Fishin', you see,' he said.

Hesketh-Brown was momentarily thrown. 'Sorry?'

'It was what we had in common,' Ollerenshaw explained. 'Once we'd lost that – well.'

He turned and grinned at Danny. 'See what I mean?'

Hesketh-Brown tried another tack. 'What about Terence Gradbach? Didn't the three of you used to go fishing together?'

'Aye,' Ollerenshaw agreed warily.

'See much of him, do you?'

'Now and again.'

'Does *he* see anything of Kayleigh's father?'

'Not as I know.'

'Do you happen to know whether Peter had any contact with his daughter?'

'Couldn't say. Doubt it.' He gave a throaty chuckle. 'Not very fatherly, you could say.'

'Do you have any photographs of Peter?'

'I really couldn't say. Happen I have.'

'If you do come across one perhaps you'd drop it into the station?'

''Course.'

Coincidentally, at this very moment, Peter Harrison was the subject of Joanna and Mike's exchange. Korpanski was curious. 'Why are you so interested in Kayleigh's father? He dropped out of her life years ago.'

'Background.' She paused. 'He fits the description she gave.'

'Well, it was a pretty vague description, Jo: tall and skinny.'

'There was more to it. Teeth, an accent. Somehow I felt a presence.' Without looking at Korpanski she knew he'd be rolling his eyes heavenwards. 'Besides, as well as entering the club with Kayleigh our perpetrator was happy enough to be seen in her company that evening and didn't try to conceal his interest in her. He was perfectly open.'

'What on earth are you getting at, Jo?' Korpanski was appalled. 'Are you suggesting Peter Harrison raped his own daughter?'

'He wouldn't have known it was his daughter,' Joanna said, 'if he hadn't seen her since she was a baby.'

Korpanski sat, scowling.

'As usual I don't really know. Just thinking aloud, Mike,' she said. 'Going over things in my mind. Our perpetrator probably wouldn't have dreamed that Kayleigh was only fourteen. He might naturally have thought sex would take place, particularly as she got more drunk. He might have thought he could persuade her into it or even force her without there being such consequences. She probably wasn't in much of a state to fight him off. She's a tiny little thing. But having been seen with her and possibly realizing she was very young or a virgin, perhaps by physical means or by the way she reacted he then panics, abandons her, leaving her to her fate. I can't get a handle on this man, Mike. What sort of a person is he?'

Though he knew she did not expect an answer, Korpanski couldn't resist. 'Person?' His look was one of surprise. 'I'd have thought, being a woman, you'd have used the word monster.'

She shrugged. 'It really isn't helpful. We need to understand his actions as a man. Careless, open, cruel. Sexually predatory but careful. Wise enough to use a condom, leaving no DNA. He's in a strange environment, in a town where no one knows him; presumably the geography's unfamiliar. Have our enquiries come up with anyone staying in Leek on Tuesday night?'

Korpanski shook his head. 'Not a soul.'

'So where did he go after abandoning Kayleigh?' Joanna was silent for a moment before adding, in a note of frustration: 'He must have gone *somewhere* on Tuesday night. It was snowing. Driving would have been difficult.'

'He could have driven back to London or Manchester or Birmingham – even Stoke.'

She couldn't argue with this. But she was still unhappy. The police often find it helpful to imagine the sequence of events. Piecing it together using forensic evidence from the scene and witness statements. This all seemed unpleasantly vague and out of focus. She needed to find some evidence or a reliable and memory-fast witness to sharpen the picture.

'I need to speak to Kayleigh again,' she said finally. 'And the psychiatrist.' She rather looked forward to meeting Dr Zed Afarim. She had liked the sound of humour which had bubbled through his voice in spite of the serious content of their conversation.

Having extracted very little of value from Ollerenshaw, Hesketh-Brown's second call was to Peter Harrison's other close friend, Terence Gradbach, who unlike Ollerenshaw had remained in farming. Danny tracked him down to a cowshed where he stood scratching his head over a tap from which sprouted a long, slim icicle.

'Costing me a bloody fortune, this weather is,' he grumbled as the DC approached. 'I don't know what happens out here. I've had that many bursts this year with the cold weather I'm keeping the plumber in bread and jam let alone bread and butter. And now I'll have to call him again. I've had him out nearly every day since early November.'

'Couldn't you lag it?'

Gradbach looked at him pityingly. 'I've done that.'

'No, I mean double lag it. I've had to do it at home. Just put two lots of foam around it.'

Gradbach studied him. ''Appen I will,' he said, 'when I've had it fixed this time. Now then – what did you want to speak to me about?'

Hesketh-Brown repeated his questions. Gradbach was turned away, still studying the tap, but Danny had the distinct impression that his shoulders had stiffened. 'Why do you want to know about that?'

'His daughter has been in a bit of trouble,' Danny said tentatively.

'Little Kayleigh?' Obviously Gradbach didn't know much about his friend's daughter; his benign response had been very different from anyone who actually *had* known her in the last couple of years.

Accordingly Danny had to choose his words with great care. 'She was assaulted outside a nightclub in Leek.'

Gradbach looked genuinely shocked. 'In Leek?'

'Yes, sir.'

It took a moment for Gradbach to absorb this information. When he had he said softly, 'Poor little mite. How is she?'

'Well, obviously I can't give you all the details, Mr Gradbach. She's in hospital currently but she'll be all right. Don't worry. Now, about Kayleigh's father, Peter. When did you last see him?'

'I don't know,' Gradbach said grumpily. 'Couldn't tell you.'

'Do you know where he's living now?'

'Nope.'

Hesketh-Brown had the feeling he should be asking more questions. Maybe more subtle questions but he felt that whatever the truth he would get no more from Gradbach. He had one more try; a stab in the dark. 'And Christine Harrison?'

Gradbach still kept his back towards him. 'Heard she got married again,' he said. 'And divorced.' A pair of bright blue eyes met his. 'Some women aren't too lucky in love, are they?'

This time it was Detective Constable Danny Hesketh-Brown's turn to shrug.

Thursday, 2 December. 4 p.m.

Molly Carraway was Christmas shopping on Stockwell Street with her best friend, Clara. There was a small jewellery shop halfway along what served as the high street which sold inexpensive pieces and Molly had spied a silver bracelet which would be just right for her cousin, Maisie, who at eight years old was becoming quite a child of fashion. She fingered it then turned to her friend. 'Clara,' she said, 'can you keep a secret?'

The fact was that Clara couldn't. In fact, telling her a secret was just like putting it on the front page of the *Leek Post & Times*. However, she looked at her friend and reassured her. ''Course I can,' she said, pretending to be insulted even to be asked. 'What is it?'

'I've met someone really nice over the Internet,' Molly confessed. 'He's just like Robert Pattinson from *Twilight*. He's just gorgeous. He lives in London. I think he might come up and see me.'

'You lucky thing.'

Molly moved a little nearer. 'Don't tell Mum and Dad, will you?' Molly's parents were well known for being strict with their only daughter.

Clara shook her head. 'As if,' she said scornfully. Then she put her hand over her mouth. 'Molly,' she said, 'be careful, won't you? Make sure it isn't one of those paedos.'

Molly laughed. 'I'm fifteen years old. Bit old for a paedo.'

Clara was a little more streetwise than her friend. 'There's still girls that get groomed and meet people. I mean it.' She put her hand on her friend's arm. 'Be careful. Don't go anywhere without telling someone.' She tried to make a joke of it. 'Even if it is just me.'

But her friend was irritated by her concern. ''Course. I'm not stupid.' She paused and couldn't resist a further airy comment. 'I might even go down to London to meet up with him. If I do will you cover me – say I'm at your place?'

Clara looked awkward. 'It'll get me into no end of trouble.'

'Please.'

Her friend was difficult to resist. 'OK.'

'Thanks. You're a brick. Now what do you think about this bracelet?'

SEVEN

Friday, 3 December. 7 a.m.

Joanna was standing in front of the calendar. The month was closing in on her. It would soon be . . . She felt a shudder of sheer dread, a sense of nausea and was suffused with an instinct of suffocating panic. She could not breathe. At the same time she was convinced that she would not be able to go through with this. It was as though a dark curtain hung between her life right up until 30 December – and beyond – was nothing. The next second, she was frowning. Whatever was wrong with her? She loved Matthew, didn't she?

On cue, he shouted down the stairs. 'Don't be late tonight, Jo, I've booked a table for eight.'

She still stood in the kitchen, willing the disturbing feeling to evaporate and for her emotions to return to normal but they didn't. She couldn't tell Matthew how she felt. She just couldn't. He would be both puzzled and hurt. And yet as she saw him rounding the top of the stairs, already dressed in casual trousers and a sweater, she had the feeling that he did know and to some extent understood.

He reached the bottom step, his eyes warming her. 'Jo?'

She managed a smile which didn't fool him for a second. In two bounds he was folding her into his arms. 'Jo,' he said, stroking her hair as though she was a cat or a pony. 'Hey.' He tilted her mouth up to meet his. 'Am I so very scary?'

Looking into those warm green eyes, beautifully crinkled around the corners from smiling so often, feeling his mouth both hard and soft on hers, the touch of his arms around her, she felt really silly. How on earth could she possibly doubt that she and

Matthew loved each other, that their life together would be anything but happy?

He was waiting for her response. She nestled against him, feeling the power of his arms around her and challenged him. 'Don't *you* think that making a commitment for the rest of our lives *is* just a little bit scary?'

He held her tighter then. 'Yes and no.' Then: 'We'll talk tonight. There really isn't the time now.' He kissed her again. 'Have a good day, darling. I'll see you later.'

She left in a fidget of nerves which only steadied as she reached Leek police station and pulled into her parking slot. She could not wait for the spring and to get back on her bike. That was one way to banish the spectres and ghosts raised by peering too far into the future. She sat for a moment, reflecting until she saw Mike Korpanski's burly shape disappear into the station. When, with a sigh, she finally moved.

By the time she reached her office Korpanski was already yawning into his computer screen. She hung her coat up. 'Late night, Mike?'

He barely looked up. 'Jossie was being sick all night, poor kid. I hardly got a wink of sleep.' He yawned again and rubbed his eyes.

'Poor Mike,' she sympathized and couldn't resist a quick dig. 'That's what comes of having children.'

'She's hardly a child, Jo. She's growing up faster than she should. But last night . . .' His face softened. 'She seemed a little girl again. Just wanted her daddy.' He looked pleased with himself. Smug as he basked in the adoration of his "little girl". Something Kayleigh Harrison had missed out on.

'Come on, sentimentalist,' she said. 'I suppose that means I'd better make the coffee this morning.'

'Thanks. You wait,' he called after her. 'It'll happen to you one day and then you'll be the sentimental mother.'

'I don't think so,' she said to the coffee machine.

As she handed him his Styrofoam cup he asked her what the plan was for today.

'I thought we'd track down Steve Shand's little party of men on the pull,' she said. 'One, two, three, four.' She held her fingers up. 'Also, I want to talk to Kayleigh's mother again and then I suppose we really should visit young Kayleigh herself. But after the bunch of "mates". We'll start with Shaun Hennessey, the guy who was celebrating his big three-o.'

There was a swift briefing where Danny Hesketh-Brown related his findings. 'Basically, Jo,' he said, 'I drew a blank. Neither of Peter Harrison's friends appear to have seen him since he left Leek twelve years ago.'

'Really?'

'Well – as Mr Ollerenshaw pointed out – their big hobby was fishing. Without that they didn't have a lot to share so I suppose it makes sense.'

'OK. What did they say about young Kayleigh? Did they know if she had any contact with her father?'

Hesketh-Brown made a face. 'They wouldn't know if she did.'

Joanna pursued her point. 'True. But as far as they knew?'

Danny shook his head. 'No.'

'OK.' Joanna scanned the room. Anyone else have anything to add?'

There was a sea of shaking heads.

'Right. Keep in touch.'

They tracked Shaun Hennessey down at one of the 'middle' schools in Leek where he taught a class of eight year olds. Not wanting to disrupt the class they waited until the eleven o'clock break. The head teacher had set a room aside but seemed concerned that one of his teachers needed to be interviewed by the police. Joanna spent some time reassuring him that the interview was simply a matter of pursuing a routine enquiry.

Shaun Hennessey was a tall, athletic, handsome man who wore an air of arrogance as comfortably as a well-fitting suit. 'Inspector,' he said, with a flash of even white teeth. 'Sergeant?'

'Hi, Shaun.' Korpanski gave Joanna an embarrassed grin accompanied by a lift of the eyebrows and a shrug of the shoulders. Joanna could interpret it perfectly.

I didn't realize it was him.

She could even guess where Korpanski and Hennessey had bumped into each other. Judging by their musculature both were men who "worked out". They'd have met at the gym, of course.

Hennessey had visibly relaxed when he had recognized Sergeant Mike Korpanski and Joanna took advantage of his composure.

'This is just an informal chat really,' she said, needing the birthday boy to be at his ease. 'I take it you know what happened outside Patches on Tuesday night?'

'Yeah. It's been in the *Post and Times*.'

'With a description of the person involved.'

Hennessey nodded.

'Do you know what the young woman was wearing?'

'Steve told me.'

'Did you see her in the nightclub on Tuesday?'

Hennessey didn't answer right away. He thought about it. 'I did,' he admitted after a pause, 'but I didn't take a lot of notice. To be honest . . .' He gave a swift glance at Joanna, as though wondering whether to proceed along this perilous path. 'She wasn't my type. She looked – yes, young. Too much make-up. I didn't like the way she was throwing herself around. She looked a bit – tarty, really.'

'Did you have a dance with her?'

Hennessey shook his head. 'I was at the bar most of the evening,' he said. 'Everyone seemed to be buying me drinks and I was enjoying chatting.'

'Are you married?'

'Next April. Tying the knot.' Again Hennessey grinned.

'And your fiancée didn't mind you spending your birthday evening with your friends?'

'No. Jen's really easy-going. Besides, I'm taking her out to dinner tomorrow night to a very classy restaurant.'

Joanna smiled at him. 'Is there anything else you can add?'

Hennessey shook his head. 'Sorry,' he said. 'I'd like to help but . . .' He gave his disarming smile again. 'The entire evening is a bit hazy – as you can probably imagine.' They left the school.

'Sorry, Jo, Mike apologized. 'I didn't realize I knew him.'

'It probably didn't make a lot of difference, Mike,' Joanna said. 'It's OK.'

Dr Afarim rang late in the morning. 'I've spent considerable time with young Kayleigh Harrison,' he said, 'and have formed some interesting conclusions which may or may not have a bearing on your investigation. Would it be convenient for you to come and talk to me at the hospital – in confidence, of course.'

Joanna was intrigued. 'Anything that will help take this enquiry further would be appreciated,' she said. 'When would suit you?'

'I am free at two o'clock,' he said.

'Fine.'

'If you can come to my office on the new medical wing?'

Again Joanna said 'Fine', and put the phone down.

'Change of schedule,' she said to Mike. 'Get one of the others to talk to Shand's mates. We've got other things to do. We'll talk to Christine Bretby. See if she's got anything to add. Then we'll see the doctor and Kayleigh as we'll be in the hospital anyway.'

Christine Bretby was no more pleased to see them second time around. She peered round the door, her lips tightening when she saw who it was. She even heaved a theatrical sigh as she stood back to let them enter. 'You're back, then?' Her resentment made her voice gravelly and coarse.

'We won't be here long, Mrs Bretby,' Joanna said. 'We just wondered about Kayleigh and her father.'

She looked surprised at that. 'I told you,' she said. 'Peter left when Kayleigh was two.'

'To your knowledge have they had any contact since then?'

She looked very puzzled at the line of questioning. 'I don't think so. Not that I know of. It's possible, I suppose. She probably wouldn't have told me. Ask her. Why do you ask?'

'The description of the man Kayleigh was with on Tuesday night matches that of your husband.'

'Ex-husband.' She put two and two together. 'Look, my ex was no saint but he wouldn't have assaulted his own daughter.'

'Would he have known she was his daughter?'

The question silenced her.

'Have you sent him pictures of her over the years?'

Again she was on the defensive. 'I didn't even know his address. How could I? Why would I? He never showed any interest in her.'

'What about the Child Protection Agency?'

'They could never find him. He never paid a penny towards

her upkeep. I just had to manage on my own as best I could. In a way I preferred it like that. A clean break. I didn't have to see him or have anything to do with him.'

'Right.' Joanna waited before changing the subject. 'Tell me about Neil Bretby and Kayleigh. How would you describe their relationship?'

'Leave him out of it,' she said wearily. 'The poor man's had enough trouble as it is. He must regret the day he met me.'

'Just answer the question, please.'

'She was jealous of him. She always was. She wanted all the attention for herself. She couldn't bear to share me. He tried. He really tried to be a decent dad to her but she was off him from the first.'

'Did they talk, laugh, go places together?'

'Sometimes.'

'Alone or with you?'

'For goodness' sake. Leave it, will you? He never touched her. I'm sure of it.'

'Were you working at the time?'

She nodded.

'Where?'

'I had a job at the hospital, cleaning.'

'What hours did you work?'

Christine could see exactly where this was heading. 'Evenings,' she said steadily. 'Five till nine.'

'I see.'

'Do you know where Neil Bretby is now?'

She drew in a deep breath and didn't answer.

'Do you have his address, please?'

Christine's face became hard, resigned; her mouth a straight, angry line. Without a word she left the room, returning with a piece of paper. 'Here,' she said. 'But I do mean it. Leave Neil out of this. I don't want him to have any more trouble because of us. Kayleigh's caused him enough grief already.'

'We won't bother him any more than is necessary,' Joanna promised. 'Thank you for your help.'

As they left she couldn't help noticing Christine's face: hopelessly bleak and sad. And now Joanna couldn't help wondering: who should she feel most sorry for? Kayleigh or her mother?

And was almost glad of the distraction of her own mother's text on her mobile phone informing her that Lara, her niece, had changed her mind and now did want to be a bridesmaid. Once in the car she rang her back. 'OK,' she said. 'You sort it. Colour, design, dress. You sort it, Mum. I'm just too busy. I'm on a rape case.'

Her mood was not helped by Mike Korpanski's bland smile, pretending not to be listening but staring straight ahead with a faint smile pasted on his mouth. He was getting his own back on her for his poor night's sleep.

Molly Carraway was sitting in her English lesson but she wasn't concentrating. When she had gone home after school yesterday evening she had gone straight on to the Internet and there had been a message from her 'friend'. She had stared at it for a few minutes before reading the text. 'I'm coming to Leek on Thursday on business.'

On business. It sounded so grown up. So rich. She read on.

'I'd really like to take you out, Molly. Please say you will. Please.'

She had typed in her answer.

EIGHT

Mike drove her to the hospital to meet up with Dr Afarim. They could kill two birds with one stone: speak to the psychiatrist and visit Kayleigh. On the way they stopped at a newsagents and Joanna picked up a couple of 'celebrity special' magazines, sure that Kayleigh would appreciate them.

Dr Zed Afarim proved to be a handsome African in his thirties with excellent English, impeccable manners, the whitest of teeth and a pair of dark eyes that sparkled with amusement as he greeted her. 'Inspector Piercy,' he said, holding out his hand. 'I was looking forward to meeting you. And Sergeant Korpanski,' he added, still in the same polite tone.

As they took a chair Joanna felt very relaxed in the doctor's company. She could understand how he would make a good psychiatrist with his bright eyes, measured tone and careful English.

He sat down behind his desk. 'Tell me how I can help you best,' he began, 'to unravel this sad tale.'

'We're interested in anything you have to tell us about Kayleigh's mental state,' Joanna said, 'whether or not you think it has any bearing on our investigation.'

'I shall endeavour to do that,' the doctor said, 'without using too many long medical terms. If there is anything you don't understand I will explain.'

'If it helps, Dr Afarim,' Joanna said, 'my degree is in psychology.'

Afarim's eyes gleamed with appreciation. 'Excellent. Well, then. Without further delay, you understand that I am not trying to solve your crime for you. I simply would like you to understand young Kayleigh a little better.' He leaned back in his chair and regarded them. 'Her mother and father were in all probability fairly neglectful in her early years and this has resulted in typical attention-seeking behaviour by exaggerating stories and events. She is a very insecure young lady and craves affection. These young ladies are frequently emotionally labile and this makes them vulnerable to approaches from the opposite sex. Kayleigh is textbook typical of these girls. Hysterical and prone to forming unsuitable or dangerous friendships in their desperate search for continuing human contact and approval. When her father abandoned her as a child it planted the idea that she was unlovable – that she would always need to demand it in one way or another. This only serves to irritate people, which makes the subject more needy. Her mother probably didn't want Kayleigh around when she married her new partner. This would have left Kayleigh in a very lonely state indeed. It was another rejection.'

'But her new stepfather, by all accounts, tried to befriend her,' Joanna commented.

'Ah –' the psychiatrist held his forefinger up – 'but at the cost of her mother's attention which she had previously had one hundred per cent.'

Joanna watched the psychiatrist talking and wondered, why

was he spending time telling her all this? Was he implying that Kayleigh's story was a lie? She tried to tease it out of him. 'Are you telling me that Kayleigh would fabricate stories simply to gain her mother's attention and sympathy?'

'She wouldn't see it as fabrication,' the doctor said. 'Merely extending or altering the truth.'

'Would she have a conscience about the consequences of her "extending or altering the truth"?'

Afarim was silent for a moment, his face troubled. He was patently deciding how best to answer this. 'Probably not,' he said. 'Unless it had an impact on her, such as, if it was found out and she lost face or friends by her falsehood.'

It was an old-fashioned word for a lie but Joanna approved. It seemed right to use the lesser word.

'Did you speak to her about her stepfather and where that story led her and her mother?'

'I touched on it.'

'And?' Joanna asked bluntly.

Afarim leaned back in his seat. 'She insists there is some truth in the story.'

'Some?' she queried. 'How much?'

Afarim shook his head sadly. 'Who can say?'

'Do you believe her stepfather had sex with her?' Joanna asked bluntly.

Afarim continued shaking his head. 'I can't say.'

'Do you think *anything* happened between them?'

'Probably not.'

She caught Korpanski's eye. His face was wooden, expressionless. Yet she thought she caught a hint of anger as he drew in a sharp breath.

'Was she a virgin previously?'

Zed Afarim shook his head. 'We don't know.'

'And the self-harming? What's the significance in that?'

'That's more interesting,' Doctor Afarim said, animated now. 'When I spoke to her about it there was a definite change in her manner. She appeared depressed. A little defeated. I detected self-pity but also guilt. Normally I would assume that the self-harming could be explained again by attention or pity-seeking – wanting to appear the injured child. But in Kayleigh's case this would not appear to be the case. She was *hiding* the marks. Not exposing them.'

Korpanski almost exploded. 'In a black boob tube?'

Afarim was unruffled. 'She'd put some make-up over the marks,' he said. 'She didn't want people to see them. A nightclub is a dark place. In this context she wouldn't want to evoke sympathy.' His eyes twinkled as he challenged Korpanski. 'I promise you sergeant that this is the case.'

Joanna decided it was time to try and pin the psychiatrist down. 'So what about Tuesday night? Did she fabricate the rape? Did it actually happen or did she pass out, drunk, and try and blame it on someone or something? Did she have consensual sex that night? Was she in a position to consent to sex? Or did she simply pass out because she was drunk and had had a cocktail of drugs? What's the bottom line here?' Joanna felt a burst of fury. 'What am I investigating, Doctor? Nothing but a teenage girl's desire for attention?'

For the first time Afarim looked uneasy. He frowned. 'I can't tell you that,' he said. 'Not for certain.'

'Her story was detailed and clear,' Korpanski said, looking at Joanna as he spoke.

'I suspect that the very clarity of the story makes at least part of it that. She'd had a lot to drink and on top of that had taken or had administered some sedative. Although she did not say this in so many words the implication was that the truth is that she remembers little of that night: certainly in the later hours. What happened is possibly as much a mystery to her as it is to you. She simply does not know. And yet . . .'

The two of them waited as Zed Afarim continued thoughtfully. 'There is something about that night that is deeply troubling to her. I don't know what it is. What is significant is that she wants to hide it from me. Ergo it is of importance. But, Inspector –' his eyes rested on her – 'if you have a degree in psychology, you will understand this. If someone is determined to keep something from you the signs are there but it can be difficult – if not dangerous – to force them to tell. And stupid to try and guess.'

Joanna nodded. 'Will you be seeing her again?'

'One more time – and then only if she wishes it. She has the right to refuse, even to discharge herself. I cannot force her to stay. In the end we have to let her go.'

'Where?'

'Home. To her mother. I have spoken to Mrs Bretby and she is in agreement with this plan. We will assess her in a month. If this fails she will be placed in foster care.'

'You wouldn't think of trying to contact her father?'

'It's a possibility,' Dr Afarim said. 'But we would have to see what she would feel about it. And her father too. Remember – these two are perfect strangers.'

Perfect strangers.

The phrase seemed important, significant. It lay, like oil, floating on the surface of her mind, swirling and indistinct, puzzling and polluting her thoughts.

She waited until they were outside before sharing her thoughts with Korpanski. 'So where do we go from here? We don't even know whether she was raped.'

'It's not going to stand up in court,' Korpanski agreed. 'We'll never get a conviction out of this. And if our friendly psychiatrist speaks up – well – he could almost be acting for the defence.'

'Then we drop the case, Mike?'

Korpanski looked troubled. 'I don't see we've got much choice, Jo. We probably won't even get a conviction of underage sex. She's fourteen and looked older. The CPS will only prosecute if the parents insist. And I can't see Christine making much of a fuss or the absent father. And the truth is that Kayleigh hardly knows what happened. Under the circumstances she's not going to make a good witness.'

She picked up the magazines from the passenger seat. 'So?'

Mike simply huffed out a big sigh.

'Come on, Mike,' she said. 'If this was Jossie . . .'

'But it isn't Jossie. If it was I would string the bastard up by his balls.'

She eyed him and knew it was true. 'Do you mind if I talk to her alone this time, Mike? I think I'll get more out of her if you're not there.'

'Fine by me,' he said. 'Do you want me to wait around or –?'

'Why not go and talk to the Newcastle-under-Lyme Police,' she suggested. 'There are lots of clubs round here. See if anything like this has happened before and what the outcome was.' She glanced at her watch. 'I'll meet you in the car park at three thirty.'

This time Kayleigh was watching television in the day room. She was wearing blue pyjamas with Disney figures on and had applied some make-up, lip-gloss and heavy, thick black mascara that contrasted with her skin and made it look even paler. She still looked tired but managed a smile as Joanna handed her the most recent *Hello!*, *OK* and *Closer* magazines.

'Thanks,' she said weakly, then looked up. 'What do I have to do to deserve these?'

'We need another talk.'

Kayleigh's mouth instantly twisted so she looked cynical and old. Without a word she stood up and led the way back to her room. Once there she closed the door behind them and sat on the bed facing Joanna, who had settled back in the chair.

'Kayleigh,' Joanna began by meeting the girl's eyes. 'You understand that a charge of rape is very serious?'

The girl nodded, chastened.

'And that while you almost died because you were left in the snow a rape charge will be a difficult charge to make stick as you don't really remember the details of that night and there is no specific evidence.'

A more hesitant nod this time accompanied by a cunning, wary look which disturbed Joanna.

'You also understand that a great deal of police time will be spent in trying to find this man who you claim,' she said carefully, 'raped you.'

Kayleigh's face changed. 'What are you tryin' to say,' she demanded. 'That I'm lyin'? You don't believe me.' Her face tightened and she tossed her head. 'Oh, well, I'm no stranger to people not believin' me. I've met it before – prejudice.'

'Ah, yes – your stepfather, Neil Bretby,' Joanna said. 'Tell me about him.'

Kayleigh moved her face so she stared straight at the wall. But Joanna could see her expression in the mirror over the sink. What she saw – or thought she saw – puzzled her. Kayleigh's expression was deeply sentimental.

So she spoke very slowly, fumbling her way, trying to tease

out the truth. 'You alleged he made inappropriate sexual advances towards you.'

Kayleigh nodded.

'Was that true?'

The girl's shoulders stiffened but she neither nodded nor shook her head. Simply sat still; her face sphinx-like.

Joanna repeated the question. 'Did he?'

Again there was no response.

'Kayleigh,' Joanna said finally. 'We don't have enough resources in the police force to go on to spend thousands of pounds investigating a story,' she used the word deliberately, 'if that's what this is. It's a criminal offence to waste police time.'

The girl's shoulders drooped. She was defeated.

'I'm sorry,' Joanna said, 'but we would need a statement from you, detailing exactly what you remember of what happened on Tuesday night. I suspect that the truth is you were drunk and don't remember.'

The girl's shoulders dropped even more and Joanna wondered, was she letting this child down? Was she right? 'The story about your stepfather was dropped, wasn't it?'

Kayleigh's head hung.

'This will come out in any trial. It will prejudice the jury against you.'

Tears began to roll down the girl's cheeks. 'I don't count, do I?'

Irritatingly Joanna felt herself torn. She felt sympathy for the girl but anger too. Her instinct for the truth almost made her want to shake it out of her. 'You do count, Kayleigh,' she said gently, 'but I have to make the decision whether or not to proceed with the investigation. And to continue with it I would need to be certain that I am likely to secure a conviction. Do you understand?'

Kayleigh nodded.

Korpanski, meanwhile, had chanced on Detective Inspector Sandra Johnson at Newcastle-under-Lyme police station. And Sandra, newly single after a very messy divorce, liked the look of the burly DS from Leek with his muscular frame, black hair and dark eyes, and made a quick decision. She would prefer to help him with enquiries than pursue her current, unpromising case: an octogenarian's body which had lain undiscovered for a number of weeks. According to the pathologist the octogenarian had died of natural causes and there were no suspicious circumstances – no forced entry into her council bungalow. It was simply a case of isolation and loneliness so time was not exactly of the essence.

She listened to Korpanski's questions before settling down in front of the police computer in the main office. Korpanski was not above using his personal charms to his advantage. 'Thanks for agreeing to help,' he said. 'I really appreciate it.'

Sandra's thin face lit up. She wondered if the DS was married. He wore no wedding ring, she noticed.

But she was not generally lucky in love. She gave a sigh and turned to peer into the screen. 'We did have a case,' she said, 'back in May. Whether it is connected with your current investigation, Sergeant,' she looked at him slyly, 'is kind of hard to be sure of but there are distinct similarities. A teenage girl who had recently had sex, we couldn't know whether it had been consensual or rape, was found unconscious outside a nightclub early the following morning, barely conscious. We got her to hospital but she died.'

Korpanski felt his pulse quicken – and so did DI Johnson. 'She actually died of a combination of alcohol poisoning and an overdose of a benzodiazepine.' She drew in a deep breath. 'We didn't secure a conviction, though we must have interviewed every person who was at the club that night. The man used a condom.'

She looked up at him. 'Don't they all?' She rubbed the back of her neck as though it was stiff. 'We made enquiries but finally dropped the investigation after three weeks. We never got to the truth of it but as the girl had died of natural causes and we had no other evidence we were never going to find out exactly what happened.' She met Korpanski's eyes and smiled. 'I've kept it on file, though. After all – someone out there knew what had happened.' She seemed to feel Korpanski's judgement weigh heavily on her and rubbed her neck again.

'I know,' she said resignedly. 'I know. Leaving him to do exactly the same again.' She sketched out a few more details.

'Can we have all your notes?'

'Sure.'

She flicked a few keys and finally handed him a memory stick. 'That's most of it. The rest you'll get by using the link.' She risked a flirtatious smile. 'Let me know how you get on, Sergeant.'

Friday, 3 December. 3.30 p.m.

Joanna listened to Korpanski's story with interest. 'Did they have *any* description?'

'Not really. Unlike Tuesday at Patches in a snowstorm this was Lymeys on a summer Saturday night. The place was packed solid.'

'*Lymeys?*'

Korpanski grinned. 'Newcastle-under-Lyme? A bit of a pun.'

Joanna couldn't resist a smile until she focused back on Korpanski's story. 'And the girl died? What was her name?'

'Danielle Brixton. She was fifteen.'

She thought for a moment; bent slightly forward in the car seat. 'You know what bothers me?'

Korpanski nodded. 'If they are the same man he's either local or he has visited this area more than once.'

'You know, Mike, it might help if I speak to Neil Bretby. Perhaps I'll understand a bit more then.'

NINE

It was almost six when they arrived back at the station. Joanna glanced at the clock as they walked in. If she was to get changed before dinner she didn't have much time but still she clicked on the computer until she found the Newcastle-under-Lyme case. She leaned her chin on her hand and peered at the screen, feeling the familiar tingling in her toes. The facts were startlingly similar. A nightclub, some sort of assault, a teenage girl very drunk, raped and left for dead. Only in this case the victim *had* died. Joanna felt stunned. All police know that a criminal leaves his identity behind in every crime scene. This unique fingerprint tells you when the crimes were committed by the same guy. A guy who was careful enough to use a condom to rape a drunken girl; careless enough to not even care whether she lived or died. It was sickening.

Joanna felt a shiver of apprehension. This was man at his worst. She sat and thought and pondered, oblivious to time passing.

Korpanski broke into the silence, looking over her shoulder. 'It *is* the same guy, Jo, isn't it?'

She looked up at him and read the revulsion in his eyes which must be mirrored in her own, then focused back at the screen. 'He's got away with it once, Mike; it was only in the summer and the case was dropped.' She was silent before speaking again because another thought had pushed in, unwelcome but it had to be voiced. 'What if,' she began, turning around in her chair to meet Korpanski's eyes again. 'You've read the article,' she said slowly. 'They're graphic and dramatic, headlines like this . . .' She indicated the image and writing across the *Evening Sentinel*'s front page: GIRL LEFT FOR DEAD AFTER RAPE OUTSIDE A NIGHTCLUB. 'What if Kayleigh read this article and . . .' She shook her head. 'No. Forget it.' But her mind was active, puzzling through things. She didn't know it but she was scowling. 'Why did she say he had a cockney accent?' She frowned. 'Where did that come from?' Then: 'I just don't get it,' she said finally. Tempted and frustrated, she glanced at the memory stick which held more data; maybe the key. 'Let's have a quick peep at that.'

'Thought you said you were going out tonight.'

She glanced at her watch again. Six thirty. 'Ten minutes,' she said. 'No more.'

It was almost exactly ten minutes later that Sergeant Alderley stuck his head round the door. 'I've got something for you,' he said, handing her a large brown envelope. 'I was going to leave it on your desk. I thought you'd be gone.' Joanna looked enquiringly at him.

'Chap called Ollerenshaw dropped it off.'

For a minute Joanna couldn't think who on earth Ollerenshaw was. Then she remembered. Peter Harrison's fishing mate. So presumably this was a photograph of Peter Harrison, Kayleigh's father. She drew it out. And stared. 'Just look at this,' she said, handing it to Mike.

The photograph had been taken on the bank of a canal, probably the Caldon. Harrison was dressed in an olive-green mac and wellies. He was grinning into the camera lens. Tall, slim, brown hair, large teeth. Joanna and Mike stared at it and wondered.

It was Korpanski who spoke first. 'Gives me the creeps,' he said. 'She could have been describing her own father.'

'But according to her mother they never met. She didn't even have a picture of him.'

'Mike,' Joanna said slowly, 'if you had never met your father do you think you'd be curious?'

Korpanski nodded.

'I think it might be worth talking to Peter Harrison,' Joanna murmured.

It was twenty to eight when she finally reached Waterfall Cottage. Matthew was peering out of the window. He hardly needed to say it but he did anyway, grumpily scolding as she walked in: 'You're late.'

'I know.' She could have pointed out that her job was hardly a nine-to-five career but she didn't. He knew that already. Instead she smiled and apologized. 'I'm sorry. I'm really sorry, Matt. I'll have a quick shower.' She tried a smile. 'I'll be down and spruced up before you can say . . .' She shrugged and tried again, harder. 'Here comes the bride?'

She didn't wait to see the grimace.

It was actually five past eight when they emerged from the cottage. Matthew had called the restaurant to warn them they would be late. He was silent all the way there. Not a good start.

However, as they sat down over a glass of wine, he smiled at her. 'I'm sorry,' he said. 'I get really twitchy about timing.'

He was hard to resist: flashing an apologetic grin, his eyes warm, his hand reaching across the table for hers. 'I know. I'm sorry too but you know, Matt, I can't just down tools.'

'It isn't that,' he said. He angled his face up towards the light. It caught the colour of his hair and gave it a rich golden look, rumpled and thick.

She waited as he touched his lips with his fingers – the

well-known gesture of editing your speech. 'I think it's a sort of jealousy, Jo. You're so absorbed in your work that when you're there I don't exist. Sometimes when I ring you I think for a second you almost wonder who I am.'

It was true but she felt she must defend herself. 'But you are absorbed in your work too, Matthew,' she pointed out.

'I am,' he said. 'But not to the same extent. I don't shut you out.'

She couldn't argue against this. So instead she diverted the conversation, knowing that if she confronted Matthew with a puzzle he wouldn't be able to resist trying to help. It was inherent in his nature that he would always search for answers. Maybe it was these two characteristics that had led him first to study medicine and then to specialize in pathology. 'The trouble is, Matt,' she said, 'this case is one of the worst I've had to deal with.'

He accepted the change of subject with a rueful grin and rose to the bait. 'How so?'

'I simply don't know whether to proceed or not. Whether there is a case to investigate. Should I throw everything at it and try and make some sense of the girl's story, even though I'm convinced she is a very mixed up young lady and I'm not at all sure we shall ever find out the truth? Certainly not through her. Plus I know I'll never get a conviction. And now this turn of events.' She told him about the Newcastle-under-Lyme case.

'I did the post mortem on that girl,' he said. 'Months ago.'

'May.'

'I remember quite well. Apart from a dose of a benzodiazepine – possibly Rohypnol, the so-called date rape drug, she was so way over the limit. Absolutely pickled in alcohol. The stomach contents were pure rum. The stink filled the mortuary for days.' He grinned and couldn't resist a black joke. 'Everything was cleaned and sterilized in the alcohol. No need to clean up the morgue.'

'Matthew,' she remonstrated and his face sobered.

She sipped her wine, glanced around the restaurant to make sure no one was near enough to eavesdrop. 'What did she actually die of?'

'The cause of death was inhalation of her own vomit. The milkman found her around six a.m. They got her to hospital but couldn't save her.'

'Had she been raped?'

'She'd had intercourse. It hadn't been particularly violent. She was just a kid.'

'So she died of natural causes. Not murder – if anything she died of neglect – just like Kayleigh would have done; only Kayleigh survived.'

Matthew nodded. 'It is a mirror image of your case.'

'Yes. And now I have to decide whether to proceed with the investigation. I can't afford to get it wrong as I'm persona non grata in the Leek police force.'

'Maybe you should speak to Colclough about it. Ask his advice – for once.' His eyes were gleaming with mischief. 'Break the habit of a lifetime?'

She nodded, smiling back at his good-humoured dig. 'Not a bad idea that, Matt.' As he had done before he had illuminated her case with a useful glimmer of light. 'You know, I think I will speak to Colclough. That's a good idea.' She met his eyes over the rim of her glass. 'I'll drink to that, Matthew.'

He smiled at her fondly, brushed her fingers with his lips and touched the black pearl which was her engagement ring. 'And now can we talk about us and the wedding, please?'

She leaned right across the table, smiling into his face. 'What a good idea.'

The evening passed pleasantly, a thaw gradually warming them both. As the main course arrived Matthew raised his glass to her.

'You look nice tonight,' he said. 'Really nice. I love your clothes. I love that dress. I love you. I shall feel very proud knowing that you are my wife.'

The words were so sincere that for a moment she could not match them with an answer. 'Thank you,' she said finally and aware that her words were far too banal for the occasion and the compliment. 'I'm fond of this dress myself.' She was wearing a claret coloured woollen dress, short, with knee-length black leather boots with tall, spiky heels. Both were local purchases from a small boutique in Stanley Street and were new.

'In fact,' he continued, 'you look so very attractive tonight,' he was grinning, 'that I'm going to give you another clue as to where our honeymoon is going to be.'

She would not rob him of his moment of fun. She waited.

'It'll be hot.'

'Oh, good,' she responded. 'I know we could have gone skiing or something, Matt, but there's been so much snow here and it's been so cold. I'd much rather go somewhere hot and flake out in the sun.'

'I knew it,' he said. 'And your wish is my command. I thought you'd prefer somewhere warm.' He hesitated. 'You know,' he said, 'it is good to have you to myself for once.'

She smiled at him, loving the rumpled hair, the intelligent eyes that were sometimes a little too perceptive, that square chin, which was slightly too long and square and denoted extreme stubbornness. Their life together would not be calm. 'Oh, Matthew,' she said impulsively. 'I do love you. I know I'm a pain sometimes and not that easy to live with; hesitant when I should stride forward, obsessed with my job, irritable and impatient, selfish and everything else, but I do love you.'

He grinned confidently back at her. 'I know,' he said, leaning back in his chair with an air of authority. 'That's why I think our marriage will work.' He took her hand. 'It won't be any different, Jo, being married.'

'So why all the fuss? Why have a wedding at all? Why not just have the honeymoon?'

He didn't answer her straight away. When he did his eyes locked into hers. 'Because I don't want our children to be bastards,' he said steadily, his meaning unmistakable. 'I want them to be legitimate.'

She felt a pang of disappointment and moved away from him. 'Is that what this is all about then – children?' He continued regarding her and the cold feeling of doubt was back, settling in her stomach again like thick, sludgy porridge. She had lost her appetite. Matthew continued eating, doggedly forking in the food.

Saturday, 4 December. 12.30 a.m.

'That guy keeps staring at me. Watching me.'

'You mean he's *stalking* you?' Clara couldn't keep the thrill out of her voice. She looked around the crowded nightclub. 'Which one do you mean?' She scanned along the bar. Plenty of men in Patches were looking at her friend.

She looked at Molly enviously. Apart from the reindeer head-dress she was wearing a red dress with shoestring straps which suited her olive skin. Her teeth gleamed bright white and, now the braces were off, were perfectly straight. Her hair, glossy, very dark and thick, hung almost to her waist and she tossed it periodically, sending out a waft of musky perfume. It wasn't surprising that someone was keen to be with her. Clara knew that she might wear the shorter skirts, the thicker make-up, the more fashionable and revealing outfits but it would always be Molly who attracted the gazes.

Saturday, 4 December. 8 a.m.

They were aroused by a fierce knocking on the door. The evening had been spoiled and Joanna had had trouble dropping off to sleep, worrying and fretting halfway through the night. This morning was one of those mornings when she wouldn't have minded sleeping in until 8.30 a.m. – at least. She groaned and rolled over. Matthew was still fast asleep; his breathing deep and regular. She heard the knocking again and sat up.

Then, to her blasting fury, she heard Eloise's voice calling. 'Dad, Dad – are you there? Hi, it's Eloise. Dad.'

Matthew sat up straightaway without there being anything between the states of deep sleep and wide awake. He was out of bed and across the room, fumbling with the window catch and sticking his head out before Joanna could even say the curse, *Eloise.* 'Eloise,' he shouted. 'Darling. Whatever are you doing here so early? Is something wrong?'

'I've run into a problem and wanted you to help me, Dad. Something I don't understand. I'm stuck.' Eloise had two voices: one a normal adult voice; the other raised by two pitches when she wanted to wheedle something out of her father.

Matthew chuckled. 'Is that all? I thought there was at least a fire or a death in the family. Hang on a minute. I'll be right down.' Quite unnecessarily as he shuffled into his dressing gown and slippers he explained to Joanna: 'It's only Eloise. She wants some help with her work.'

'Great.' As usual, Matthew chose to ignore her sarcasm.

So she lay in bed, alone; stared up at the ceiling and pondered.

Last night had ended frostily. There were two things in her imminent marriage that she felt would never be solved. One had been mentioned last night and the other was downstairs. When the chill came, usually as the result of one of these two taboo subjects, there seemed nothing either of them could do to thaw it. They could have done with finishing the conversation this morning but hey, it wasn't to be. Joanna sat up and not for the first time in her life heartily cursed Matthew's daughter, soon to be her very own stepdaughter.

He was in a dressing gown and scuttling down the stairs two at a time before she'd had a chance to speak a word. She heard them talking in the hall, gave up on sleep, stood underneath the shower and sulked. By the time she joined them downstairs they were sitting at the breakfast table, books scattered all over the place. Matthew was drawing a diagram of something. Joanna couldn't have guessed what. Both were drinking from large glasses of orange juice and talking nineteen to the dozen about 'radiological evidence for interstitial lung disease'. Neither acknowledged her entrance.

She was just about to make up a story and tell Matthew that she had to go down to the station to interview someone about the Kayleigh Harrison case when the telephone rang. She picked it up and was greeted by the stiff and hostile tones of Matthew's father. Great. Bonus number three. Last night which should have been a celebration ending in a cold war, Eloise's unexpected and ill-timed arrival. And now Matthew's father on the phone.

'Good morning, Joanna. Is my son there?' Without a word she handed the phone to Matthew.

Matthew's parents blamed her for the break-up of their son's marriage to Eloise's mother, Jane. In spite of the fact that Jane now lived in York, near her parents, had remarried a wealthy accountant and had recently given birth to twin sons, Matthew's parents still held her responsible and had not forgiven her. Everyone, it seemed, had 'moved on' except Mr and Mrs Peter Levin and, of course, Eloise.

Matthew was very fond of his parents and appeared blind to their rejection of Joanna.

'Hi, Dad.' He greeted his father enthusiastically, listened for a while then sucked in a deep breath. 'Great.' Next he suggested hotels in and around Leek, commenting on each one and finishing with, 'I think that would be the best and Rudyard Lake's a lovely place. It'll be a good break. OK, Dad, you book there.'

He listened again then told his father that Eloise was with them. Joanna listened with half an ear to a loud 'Harrumph' and Matthew answered what must have been a question.

'I've managed to get a flight from Manchester on the Sunday so we'll be around on Saturday until the evening.'

Joanna didn't catch Matthew's father's next remark but Matthew obviously did because he responded with a chuckle and said, 'Can't tell you that, Dad. It's a secret. Even Joanna doesn't know.'

There was the sound of another throaty chuckle on the other end and Joanna wished that things had been different, that Matthew had been unmarried when she had met him. Then there would have been no blame – and no bloody Eloise.

She glanced across at the girl with Matthew's blonde hair and green eyes but her mother's thin, spiteful face. *She* was talking to her grandfather now.

'Hi, Gramps.'

A few deep words followed, then: 'Yes, he's helping me. It's the lungs. For some reason I just find them really hard.'

Another comment down the line, then: 'Well, it's the CTs – interpreting them.'

Without needing to decipher the words she knew what Matthew's father would be saying. *In my day . . .*

He was a retired GP. Another medic.

She poured herself some apple juice and a bowl of cornflakes.

Saturday, 4 December. 10 a.m.

Clara had a big problem. Molly's parents were strict. They were against her going to nightclubs, so she had simply told them she was staying the night with her friend. But last night, at some point, Clara narrowed her eyes. They'd both had quite a bit to drink. Patches had been very crowded with Christmas celebrations and the music had been loud. She had got a thumping headache and had gone to the 'quiet room' only for a bit. But when she had emerged, Molly had disappeared. Clara had looked for her everywhere but after half an hour and with no response to her text she concluded she must have gone off with the guy who had been eyeing her from the bar, whichever one he had been. Now she couldn't find her anywhere. And so, disgruntled, she had taken a taxi home, having to pay the entire fare instead of only fifty per cent. She felt alone, sad and unattractive. And that made her angry with Molly so she railed against her. It wasn't fair. Why should Molly have all the gifts? She'd arrived home where, again, there was no sign of Molly. She paid the taxi man, slipped her shoes off and tiptoed upstairs. Her parents were lenient but even they didn't like her coming in so late. Breaking her curfew could mean she'd be grounded – in December! Half awake, half asleep, she'd listened out for her friend in case she called up at the window or knocked on the door, but in the end Clara had dropped off to sleep and Molly was not here this morning. She must have stayed the night somewhere.

In the past when they had been out together they had usually spent the following day together too, chatting, shopping, talking, playing with make-up, watching videos, washing hair, listening to their iPods, even doing some of their homework together.

Clara looked out of the window and worried. She wished Molly would come back or at least phone her. This was just plain selfish.

Then she had another thought. Maybe Molly had gone straight home last night. Unlikely but it was possible. What she could not do was ring Molly's home and ask to speak to her. What if she wasn't there? Her mother would assume they were together, as did her mother who looked surprised when she finally emerged from her bedroom on her own. 'Molly not with you?' Clara shook her head. 'She went home.' Saying this made her feel worse.

It wasn't her way to lie to her parents. She didn't like doing it. Bloody Molly had got her into this. She felt cross – and then worried. *Please*, she thought, *let her be at home safe and sound.*

TEN

Saturday, 4 December, 11 a.m.

It was obvious that Matthew and Eloise were holed up for the day. They were on the Internet now and she caught some of their unintelligible conversation. Matthew was running through something with his daughter; his finger tracing something on the screen. 'Look at the markings, darling. And see that thickening on the line? There.'

Eloise's response was lively and enthusiastic. 'I can see it *now*, Dad.'

Joanna gave up. It might be Saturday but she may as well see if she could talk to Colclough. She'd done this before – spoken to him, unofficially, at his home – but not since she'd 'fallen from grace'. She wasn't sure how she'd be received. His wife hated and resented it but in the past, Joanna suspected, Superintendent Arthur Colclough rather enjoyed acting as police consultant. She dressed casually in tight black trousers and boots, picked up a red woollen jacket and then rang Colclough's home number. To her relief it was Arthur himself who picked up the phone and she came straight out with it.

'What?' He was going a bit deaf. She repeated her request.

'All right, Piercy.' He sounded his normal, gruff self, not hostile at all. 'Though I'd have thought with only a few weeks to go before the wedding that you'd have other things to worry about.'

'I have, sir,' she responded, 'but it would help if I could have some advice.'

'All right, then. Come now and make it snappy.'

'Yes, sir.'

Though Matthew was obviously otherwise engaged he still made a fuss about her going out to do something connected with work. When he looked up briefly his eyes looked stormy. 'On a Saturday?'

'It's an opportunity to talk to him away from the station.'

Eloise's eyes bounced from one to the other. Taking it all in. No doubt to report back to her mother if Jane was still interested, which Joanna doubted.

'When will you be back?'

'Lunchtime. I have a fitting of the dress this afternoon.'

His face softened at that. Matthew was so predictable at times. There were 'encouraged' activities and 'discouraged' activities – basically anything to do with work was classed as the latter.

'OK. See you later, then.' He tried to make a joke of it, smiling now – or at least curving his mouth into the shape of a smile – but it was nothing like his normal merry grin. 'Well, I hope you won't be late for the wedding, Jo, because you're out there catching some villain.' He winked at Eloise. Underneath the light banter Joanna caught the hint of sarcasm and resented it.

She didn't even bother to say goodbye to Eloise. The girl looked up briefly; her eyes hostile. They flickered with a light as cold as winter before she bent back down over her book without uttering a word or even making the weakest attempt at a smile.

Joanna sighed. 'See you later,' she said to the room. Normally she would have kissed Matthew goodbye but in front of Eloise it would have seemed a deliberate act, so she simply smiled and left.

Clara checked her phone every few minutes, expecting at any time a text from Molly. She decided her friend was mean not to tell her where she was and where she'd vanished to last night. After all, Clara was putting herself at risk of trouble too. If her mother found out all the lies she'd told on her friend's behalf she'd be in the shit and grounded for weeks. Her mother and father were liberal and easy-going but they would not approve of the lies she told for Molly. Clara gave a loud, irritated sigh and texted Molly the questions again. Where r u now? Where did u get 2 last night?

Then she leaned back against her pillows.

Molly was probably still asleep. Somewhere.

Superintendent Arthur Colclough lived in a Victorian semi-detached house on the Buxton road out of Leek, practically the last one in the town, just before the road climbed and climbed and climbed towards a rocky crag known as The Winking Man which was part of the climbers' Mecca – The Roaches. Mrs Colclough let her in with a disapproving look, showing her into a pretty sitting room decorated in pale green with a circular Chinese carpet in the centre. Colclough was sitting in a deep, green armchair, wearing a cardigan and slippers and looking homey and relaxed. To her relief he gave her a warm smile as she entered. It was a smile which reached his eyes with a twinkle; a smile she hadn't seen for months. She was forgiven.

'Piercy,' he said. 'I'm glad you came over.'

So the awkwardness was over. 'Thank you, sir.'

'Sit down. Mrs Colclough will bring in tea and some biscuits. Now, then.' He settled back in the chair and gave her a benevolent look. 'What is it that's bothering you?'

She outlined the two cases of Kayleigh and Danielle and he listened intently, his bulldog jowls quivering with interest. She realized he'd never lost his love of being a copper and wondered whether her enjoyment of the job would last as long.

'And you think there might be more victims?'

'Possibly, sir, but the thing that is really bothering me most is whether to proceed with the investigation. Kayleigh is a young woman who exaggerates. Worse than that, she's not above fabricating the evidence.'

'But if her story is the truth I think you must,' he said gently. 'Someone is preying on young women and assaulting them, not caring whether they live or die.'

'The Crown Prosecution Service will think it unlikely we will secure a conviction on Kayleigh's evidence and there's no DNA,' she said. Colclough shrugged and reminded her that the force had solved crime and secured convictions well before the days of the wonderful DNA. They both looked up as Mrs Colclough entered carrying a tea tray and not even trying to disguise her disapproval of Joanna's mere presence. 'Don't forget we're taking Catherine to the birthday party,' she reminded her husband pointedly. He smiled and shook his head.

When she had closed the door behind her Colclough leaned forward and picked up a ginger biscuit, nibbling on it absently. 'Catherine will soon be the age of those young women,' he said quietly but with menace in his voice. 'These girls have mothers, fathers, grandparents. If anyone did that to my granddaughter I would think castration too good for him.'

Joanna nodded and drank her tea. Colclough recovered his equilibrium; his face returning to his more normal bland expression.

'You need to ascertain whether young Kayleigh's story is the truth,' he said. 'That'll at least be a start. If she is lying leave the previous investigation to the Newcastle-under-Lyme Police. After all, you say that girl died of natural causes?'

'Matthew told me she died from inhalation of vomit.'

Colclough made an expression of disgust, then smiled at her. 'Notwithstanding your recent . . . mistake,' he said, 'I continue to trust your judgement, Piercy.'

'Thank you, sir.'

'So my advice is to do a little research around young Kayleigh.' He drained his cup and set it firmly back on the tray.

She finished hers quickly, thanked the superintendent and left, returning along snowy, single-track lanes until she reached Waterfall village. As she let herself in the phone was ringing.

It was her mother.

Joanna let her rant on about being selfish, telling her that Lara, her niece, had changed her mind, yet again, about wanting to be a bridesmaid; that her aunt had managed to book a last minute flight from Sydney, that her uncle Bob was not going to be able to make it from San Diego and that Daniel would want to leave early as he'd been invited to a New Year's Eve sleepover. And she was worried about her hat.

Joanna listened impatiently, finally managing to squeeze in a few words. 'Mum, I have to go. Eloise is here and I need to make lunch. Then I have a fitting.' She thought that mentioning this would mollify her mother.

She was quite wrong. 'You're cutting it very fine,' she snapped.

'Yes, Mum.'

Her mother tried one more time. 'So what about Lara, dear?'

'Tell her to get a dress,' Joanna said. 'I'll pay. If she wants to do it, fine. If not that's fine too. OK?'

Her mother's reply was smooth and well rehearsed. 'We have time,' she said, 'to sort everything out.'

Something in Joanna snapped then. Her mother could always

manage to do this to her. 'Well, I haven't. I have a rape case on and it's complicated.'

'Darling, what could possibly be more important than your own wedding?'

There was no reply to that. Except . . .

The sitting-room door was open. Through it she met Matthew's eyes – surprised, disappointed, and Eloise's – smug and self satisfied.

She caved in and felt dreadful. 'OK, Mum,' she said, turning her attention back to the phone. 'That's fine. Yes, I'm happy with that. Lara would have made a beautiful bridesmaid. But if she doesn't want to do it I don't mind and at least she'll have got a dress out of it. And mum . . .'

Her mother's, 'Yes, dear,' was wary.

'Thank you. You're being brilliant. I don't know how I've had managed any of it if it wasn't for you.'

Even her mother couldn't quite respond to this. She simply said, 'Good practise, dear. Goodbye, Jo,' leaving Joanna wondering what on earth she'd meant by that.

She put the phone down and radiated a deliberately wide smile to Matthew. 'Looks like we just might not have a bridesmaid,' she said, then turned to Eloise. 'Sure you don't want to accompany me down the aisle?'

Eloise's reply was predictably frosty but impeccably polite. 'I don't think so, but thanks all the same, Joanna.'

Clara's mother thought her daughter was very quiet during lunch. She looked at her sharply. 'You haven't fallen out with Molly, have you?'

'No, Mum.'

'But she always stays after you've been out for the evening.'

'Not last night. She decided to go home.' Clara *hated* this lying and she hated Molly Carraway for putting her in this situation. She fingered the mobile phone in her jeans pocket, willing it to receive a text. Why didn't Molly ring – or at least text? She was beginning to get worried.

As Joanna drove to the dress shop she wondered why, if their rapist was not local, he had come to Leek in the first place. It was a small moorland town. A city would have been much safer. He would have had a better chance of staying anonymous. Instead he had come here. So was he local or a visitor? Did he come here in connection with his work? Was this a first-time visit? Was he from the Potteries in spite of the southern accent? Had he gone to Patches with a predatory intention? Or had he some other reason for going to the nightclub? In connection with drugs, maybe? Or had he simply been a lad out for the night, after a bit of fun and when the opportunity had presented itself he had taken advantage of a very young, very drunk girl? If, indeed, there had been a crime at all – apart from, as Korpanski had pointed out, sex with a minor. It was all to be chewed over.

She found a parking space in St Edwards Street and walked up the steep hill to the shop, passing mock Tudor Victorian shop fronts and the Indian restaurant on the corner.

The shop had an upstairs room set aside for private fittings. Her dress was hanging up, waiting for her. Joanna looked at it with mixed feelings. It was a beautiful dress, the fabric exactly as she had wanted and somehow the seamstress had understood the design which she had held in her head. But the day that she would wear it felt menacing as it loomed closer. They had opted for a civil ceremony in a hotel near The Roaches. She just hoped it didn't snow, although snow would really look beautiful in such a wild and lonely place.

The seamstress bustled up the narrow stairs to the bridal fitting room. 'Joanna,' she said. 'What do you think?'

There was only one response. 'It's lovely. Thank you so much.' Somehow happiness and some pride and passion took over as she looked at the dress. Foolish, wasn't it, to believe that, like a lucky charm, a dress could mend the cracks already formed in their relationship, but if any garment could this frock would. It was magical.

'Try it on, then,' urged the seamstress, pins in her mouth and at the ready to make any alterations.

Joanna slipped out of her jeans and sweater and let the dress slide over her head, feeling the satin slinky against her legs.

As she'd said to Matthew it was an almost perfect fit and yes, of course she was pleased with it. But it still felt strange to think that in a few short weeks she and Matthew would be married; bonded for life, joined to each other. She might still be Detective Inspector Joanna Piercy at the station but she would also be Mrs Matthew Levin. As she stared at herself in the full-length mirror she had the strangest feeling that she was splitting into two completely separate identities. She peered at herself. She could not be two women. That would be schizoid; a split and divergent personality. It was an uncomfortable and unpleasant thought.

'Ouch.' One of the pins had stuck into her waist.

The dressmaker tutted and spoke, her mouth full of more pins as she moved a seam in a little. 'You've lost a bit of weight here,' she said. 'Of course, most brides do coming up to their wedding day.' She concentrated for a while on pinning the seam straight before continuing. 'I do hope you have a nice day for it, Joanna,' she said. 'No more of that horrid snow but a little sharp winter sunshine. There . . .' She stood back. 'It's a spectacular dress. I don't think I've ever seen one quite like it, particularly in this colour. If the sun shines it'll catch all these crystals. Every one of them.' She smiled. 'And dazzle everyone. Now then; what about your hair?' she fussed. 'Your headdress?'

Joanna shook her head. 'I have an idea.'

Clara was part anxious and part angry with her friend. By five o'clock when she had worried herself sick at the lack of response to her texts she tried ringing Molly's mobile phone number. It rang and rang and rang until the answerphone chipped in with the usual cheery message. 'Hi, it's Mol. Sorry – can't get to the phone now. Please leave a message after the tone. And if it's Brad Pitt, yes, I am free tonight.' Giggle, flirtatious giggle. Clara had heard it a hundred times before.

'Molly, please ring me. I'm worried sick. Where did you get to last night? Where *were* you? Why didn't you get back to me? At least let me know you're all right.' She drew in a deep breath. 'If I don't hear anything in an hour I'm going to ring your home number. Molly,' she finished, 'this really isn't fair.' She ended the call.

It was dark when Joanna got home. And she was annoyed to see Eloise's Clio hadn't moved. It was still covered in thick snow.

Waterfall was in a frost pocket and although the snow was largely melting from Leek it hadn't altered much out here.

She let herself in and couldn't resist making a comment. 'Still here?'

Matthew scowled at her. Eloise didn't bother to answer and suddenly Joanna felt vicious. She was tired. She wanted to think and she wanted to be alone with Matthew, to voice her concerns and let him reassure her that everything would be all right. This was her home too and she hadn't invited the little minx to come here at all let alone stay here. Tomorrow was Sunday. They would only have three more Sundays before the wedding. She had another objection too. Matthew was different when Eloise was around. She'd always known that he was firstly Eloise's father and only secondly her fiancé. It wouldn't matter quite so much if the girl had not been so overtly hostile towards her. Sulkily she flopped into the chair in front of the fire: a log-burning stove which flickered and sizzled like a dormant dragon, but gave out plenty of welcome heat.

Matthew gave her a sympathetic look. 'How did the fitting go?'

She wanted to say that it had gone well, that the dress was a beautiful tribute to him, that she hoped very much that he liked her – loved her in it. She wanted him to tease her about the honeymoon destination.

She could do none of it with Eloise here so she simply said, 'Well, thank you.'

'Was he any help?'

'Colclough? Yeah,' she said, 'in a way.' Then, because she felt she owed it to him she added: 'Thanks.'

She badly wanted to talk to him about the case, wanting the benefit of his opinion. She did think about it. If there was one good thing she knew about Eloise Levin it was that she had already taken on board the rules of confidentiality. Joanna had discussed cases before in front of her – even *with* her at times, confident that the girl *would* never and *had* never breathed a word. It must be part of the medical training. She was completely trustworthy. And if she was anything like her father, which she was, Eloise would soon be a competent doctor. But tonight she just didn't want to talk about this case in front of her soon-to-be stepdaughter. If she and Matthew had been on their own she might have aired her feelings. A child damaged already by a broken home and a drunken mother. A child who was well on the road to delinquency and now this. She glanced across the room and as though sensing her emotions Eloise cued her in. 'What's your major case at the moment, Joanna?'

'The rape – or not – of a fourteen-year-old.'

Eloise made only one comment and that surprised and angered Joanna. 'Asking for it, was she?'

Joanna shook her head. 'I don't think so,' she said, recalling the face; white and frightened against the hospital pillowcases, the child underneath the bedclothes looking tiny in the hospital bed and very much alone. No mother, no flowers, no get well cards. No father. Nothing. Even trusting and accepting a police officer as a friend because there was no one else. Was there no one to speak for her?

She sat pondering this as Eloise and Matthew 'chatted'; now about the immune system, viruses and antibodies, a subject which seemed to excite the pair of them as much as a thrill on a white-knuckle ride. Joanna stayed silent, picking up the newspaper and scanning its contents, knowing that when they went to bed Matthew would make some comment about her 'adolescent sulkiness', meaning her rather than Eloise and 'why couldn't she make a bit more of an effort'.

She couldn't explain to him that when his daughter was around it was she who was the outsider; she who felt the odd one out. Eloise knew this and made the most of it.

Eloise, she thought as she glanced at her almost-stepdaughter's face, was quite capable of wrecking this marriage before it had even begun. She was a mischief-maker. And these negative thoughts took her right back to Kayleigh Harrison and Neil Bretby. Only in that case it had been the child who had been rejected. Joanna was silent as she watched father and daughter talking animatedly. No need to ask whether she intended staying the night. And not much point asking what her plans were for Sunday.

She made a pot of tea.

By 7 p.m. Clara was really worried. She tried her friend's phone again and left yet another frantic message. Half an hour later she made up her mind to speak to her mother. She sidled into the sitting room where her mother was watching *The X Factor*. 'Mum,' she said, 'I've got a problem.'

Her mother pressed the mute button on the remote. 'Go on,' she said steadily.

Clara dropped into the armchair, legs in the tightest of jeans, splayed out in front of her and large, fluffy lilac slippers on her feet, looking almost animal. She spilled out the whole story: the lies, the strict parents, the times when they – she and Molly – had omitted telling Molly's mother and father exactly where they were headed.

'I lost her in the club last night,' Clara said. 'And I've heard nothing from her all day. Not a single text. I've left messages but she hasn't got back. It isn't like her. I'm worried, Mum. And then there was that girl who was raped.'

Clara's mother took a minute or two to digest the story before coming to a decision. 'I'll try ringing her mother.'

'Thanks.'

'You've got the number?'

Her daughter read it out and Mrs Williams dialled.

Clara made a wish. *I wish that Molly herself would pick up the telephone.*

But that didn't happen. Her mother was eyeing her even as she spoke in her best telephone voice. 'Mrs Carraway . . . It's Rosa Williams here . . . Clara's mother . . . I wonder. Is it possible to have a word with Molly?'

Clara's heart sank as her mother spoke the sentence in an ominously quiet voice. 'She isn't?'

ELEVEN

Clara could hardly bear to listen to her mother's halting explanation. 'I'm afraid, Mrs Carraway, that the girls went to a nightclub together last night.' Without waiting for Molly's mother's response Rosa Williams hurried on. 'It was with our knowledge and permission. I assumed that Molly had told you where she would be.'

Clever that, Clara thought. It shifted the blame right away from them and on to Molly's shoulders.

But maybe it wasn't quite clever enough. Angry voices shouted down the phone. Apparently Molly's father had joined in.

Rosa Williams kept her calm, shrugged her shoulders and gave Clara a small, apologetic smile. 'That is between you and your daughter,' she responded calmly.

More angry noises down the phone then, even from the other side of the room, Clara could hear the question quite clearly. 'So where is Molly now?'

Rosa Williams gripped the phone very tightly, whitening her knuckles. 'I'm sorry,' she said. 'Apparently the girls were separated some time during the evening. When it was time to go home Clara couldn't find her. She assumed Molly had gone straight home, back to you. She didn't stay here last night.'

The next sound was a horrified, explosive, incredulous, 'What?!'

Rosa Williams repeated her last sentence very slowly. They were all beginning to see the implications.

'Let's get this straight.' Molly's father came on the line and he sounded livid. 'Are you saying not only that my daughter was at a *nightclub* last night but also that you haven't seen her since yesterday evening?'

Still Rosa Williams remained calm. 'Yes. Clara has been trying to get in touch with her all day but hasn't received a response. We wondered if you'd heard . . .' Her voice trailed away in the silence. A silence that was so thick and menacing that Clara scuttled across the room and went to sit by her mother. Rosa put her arm around the girl's shoulders.

'So where is she now?' Philip Carraway's voice was ice cold.

'That's what we're telling you, Mr Carraway. We don't know.'

In the background Molly's mother gave a sob. It made Clara feel much worse than Mr Carraway's bluster.

'Let me tell you,' he ranted on, 'that I hold you and your daughter responsible for anything that has happened to our girl.'

'I think that's a little unfair, Mr Carraway.' Clara could not but admire the way her mother was keeping her cool. 'Your daughter has obviously been deceiving you and last night she let my daughter down, too, leaving her alone in the club.'

Philip Carraway cleared his throat noisily but the words had their effect on him.

'Leave this with me, Mrs Williams.' Molly's father was now calm and a little worry was beginning to edge into his tone. 'I'll try and ring her. In the meantime if you *do* hear from her please, please get in touch.' Clara winced at the note of desperation in the man's voice.

He continued. 'If *I* can't contact her I shall be calling the police.'

'I shall wait for your call, Mr Carraway,' Rosa said.

'Just a minute.' Molly's mother was back on the line. 'Was the nightclub the same one where that girl was raped on Tuesday?'

Rosa Williams was nodding as she answered.

'Oh.' Molly's mother sobbed into the phone.

'I'm really sorry,' Rosa said and pressed the end call button. Then she looked at her daughter. 'I have to confess,' she said. 'I'm very worried.'

Clara merely nodded. She felt numb, dumb, responsible and terribly guilty. And then within a second her guilt was replaced by anger. Molly had dropped her right in it, hadn't she? She'd abandoned her, leaving her to sort out this mess. She wouldn't be in *her* shoes when she was reunited with her father. But she couldn't ignore the hollow feeling in the pit of her stomach.

At Waterfall Cottage Matthew and Eloise stopped their work for a supper Joanna had cooked: lamb chops, mashed potatoes, et cetera. Matthew opened a bottle of red wine, poured out three glasses and held his up to the light, admiring its colour. Then he proposed his toast with a wide and happy grin. 'To the two women in my life,' he announced. 'My clever daughter, who in spite of her cleverness will soon be another Doctor Levin. And . . .' He turned towards Joanna, 'to my almost-wife. I love you both so much.' They clinked glasses. Joanna took a swallow and felt almost mellow. She glanced across at Eloise and tried to smile. Matthew kept the conversation going throughout the meal, perhaps not noticing that 'the two women in his life' were not actually exchanging any conversation.

Once they'd loaded the dishwasher they passed the evening

watching a film and finishing the bottle of wine, then opening another.

At nine o'clock Philip Carraway called back to the Williams' household, this time getting hold of Clara's father, Mark. Luckily his wife and daughter had filled him in on the events and he had naturally taken his daughter's side. 'I can't see how it's your fault,' he'd said during the family consultation. 'Molly lied to her parents and then gave you the slip. She's a big girl, darling – not your responsibility at all.'

Clara had nodded. 'But Molly,' she said, 'is really naïve, Dad – not streetwise at all. I should have kept a better eye on her.'

Again her father had been defensive. 'She isn't your little sister, you know. She's your friend. You don't need to feel responsible, Clara.'

The girl had simply bitten her lip.

'Did you see her with anyone?'

'She looked really nice last night,' Clara said. 'I saw her with lots of guys. Practically everyone in the club seemed to want to dance with her.' There was a note of jealousy in her voice which didn't escape either parent.

Mark Williams was silent for a moment before he continued. 'You've read the description of the person who attacked that young girl at the beginning of the week, Clara. Was Molly with anyone who looked like him?'

The girl shook her head. 'Not that I noticed,' she said. 'Not particularly. She wasn't with anyone special. Just about everyone.'

So when Mark Williams listened to Molly's father he was sympathetic but also defensive about his daughter's role in the matter.

'Any news, Phil?' The two men knew each other very vaguely from being taxi drivers to their daughters – to and from school functions, mainly.

Molly's father sounded subdued, worried and upset. 'I can't get hold of her, Mark,' he said desperately. 'I'm going to call the police. I just wanted to let you know before I did.'

'If there's anything we can do to help.'

'No.' He sounded broken. 'Not at the moment. The police will want to talk to Clara, I'm sure.' Then the appeal came: 'What can have happened to her, Mark? Where is she? Has Clara said anything that might help?'

'Not really.' He felt he had to give Molly's father some ray of hope. 'But she didn't see her with anyone who looked like the person who . . .' His voice trailed off.

And now, needing someone to blame, Philip Carraway became hostile and angry. 'What could have possessed the girls to go there? When they knew what had happened only this week?'

Clara's father tried to mollify him. 'The rapist wouldn't strike twice in such a short time, Phil. There'll be a perfectly reasonable explanation as to why Molly hasn't been in touch. Her phone's probably out of charge or run out of credit.'

'We pay her phone bill,' Carraway said tightly.

'Itemized?'

'No. It comes in on line. We never really look at it.' He was beginning to sound defeated again. 'What am I going to do, Mark?'

'Get the police involved.'

At that the phone was put down. And even that act seemed heavy and weighted down with foreboding.

Saturday, 4 December. 9.20 p.m.

The desk sergeant took the call and did his best to calm Philip Carraway down. 'She's a young lassie,' he said. 'Probably knows she's in trouble. Don't you worry, Mr Carraway. Girls will be girls.'

But rather than being appeased at the attempt being made to comfort him the platitudes made Philip Carraway all the more livid. 'This is *my* daughter we're talking about,' he said tightly, 'who was last seen at the local nightclub where a girl was assaulted only this week and today appears to have vanished off the face of the earth. And you tell me not to worry?' he exploded.

'Leave it with us,' the sergeant said. 'We'll send someone round to speak to you. In the meantime keep trying to get in touch with her. If you do hear anything I'd appreciate it if you'd let us know.'

'I will.' The phone was banged down.

*   *   *

It fell to DC Alan King who was on night duty to speak to Molly Carraway's distraught mother and father. It was eleven by the time he arrived and he could have picked out which house was the Carraway home by the lights which flooded from inside it and the man standing at the front door in spite of the freezing night which misted the car headlights as he swung into the drive. For a second DC King, a gangly man with long arms, sat in the car without switching the engine off and wished that Mr Carraway would come forward and say the words, '*It's OK, Officer. False alarm. Molly's turned up. She's fine – a little sheepish and in big trouble – but she's OK.*'

But from the man's distraught face and immobility King knew that this would not be the case. He switched the engine off, opened the car door and walked towards the frozen man.

Sunday, 5 December. 8 a.m.

Joanna was dragged into consciousness by the telephone ringing. Her initial thought was, at least it can't be Eloise this time because she's already here.

She picked it up, listened to the desk sergeant's bald phrases and felt her heart drop. A girl was missing. There was a connection to Patches. She sat up in bed, ignoring Matthew's sleepy stare which, when he realized it was her work, changed quickly to petulant resentment. 'For goodness' sake,' he muttered and buried his head in the pillow.

Joanna ignored him and continued speaking into the phone. 'How old?'

'Fifteen. She was out with a friend, Clara, at Patches. They got separated. Molly Carraway, the missing girl, was supposed to be staying the night with Clara. Her parents are strict and don't approve of nightclubs so she always stays with her friend and omits to tell parents exactly how and where she's spent the evening. When Clara looked around for her friend at one a.m. she was nowhere to be found. She didn't go home; neither did she turn up at Clara's house. She's vanished.'

'Mobile?'

'Not even ringing. Straight through to answerphone.'

'I take it this is out of character?'

'Completely.'

'So where are you up to?' She was already sitting on the side of the bed, eyeing her clothes from yesterday.

'We've sealed off Patches but there's nothing there. Wherever she is she isn't lying freezing in the car park, like Kayleigh.'

'Mobile records?'

'It's switched off or out of range. We're getting the call records sent through. But you know what the coverage is like round here. Patchy to say the least.'

'I'll be with you in half an hour.'

What she didn't like about telling Matthew as he emerged from underneath his pillow was his look of anger. She hadn't organized this deliberately to get out of wedding plans or to escape from Eloise. It had just happened. And this girl was somebody's daughter. Like the pain in the butt in the bedroom next door.

She showered and dressed, went downstairs and poured herself some orange juice and a bowl of cereal. Matthew and Eloise came down together, as though they were jointly criticizing her imminent exit. As she explained that she had to go into the station in connection with her current investigation she noted a conspiratorial look pass between father and daughter. A kind of, *I told you so*, combined with Eloise's ill-concealed glee that she would have her father to herself for the day.

'Any idea when you *might* be back?' Matthew asked tightly.

'I'll ring you,' she said, equally tightly and then anger got the better of her. 'This is a fifteen-year-old girl, Matthew. Her family are distraught. It's bad enough that she's missing. But there's the added stress of what happened in the very same club less than a week ago.'

His response was a heavy sigh.

'Just imagine if it was Eloise,' she shot at him, and as soon as she had finished her breakfast she left.

Although it was a Sunday morning the station was buzzing with the electric tension that surrounds an investigation when something new has developed and she was greeted quickly by a worn out DC Alan King, contrasting with Danny Hesketh-Brown who looked disgustingly alert and wide awake. They filled her in on the bare details.

'Is Korpanski around?'

Hesketh-Brown answered. 'Couldn't get hold of him. He's probably at his son's rugby match. I've left a message on his phone.'

'Good. Right. Thanks, King. Are you on tonight?'

He nodded.

'Go home and get some sleep, then. And,' she added kindly, 'thanks. You've done well so far.'

'Right.' She looked Hesketh-Brown square in the face. 'It's you and me then, Danny boy. Let's get a plan of action. First I want you to dig out the pair of worms who run Patches and squeeze every last drop of information, every videotape, every description, everything out of them. I'll speak to Molly's parents and then to Clara and her parents.' She heaved a big sigh. 'For now we'll assume that the two cases are connected.'

'Right.' Not altogether displeased by the fact that they had been unable to track down DS Korpanski, Danny grinned across at her. He was more than ready to step into the sergeant's size eleven's.

Molly Carraway's house was on one of the more recent and upmarket estates, like Colclough's, on the Buxton road out of town. Worth five hundred grand, at a guess, Joanna thought as she drew up in front of the mock Tudor house. Five bedrooms, two to three bathrooms, study, conservatory – it would have the lot. Added to that, Roachside View wasn't really an estate at all but a 'select development'. Ten or so houses, each one individually architecturally designed; each one slightly different. This was the sort of house Matthew would have liked. What was generally termed 'a family home'. This early on a wintry morning the 'development' appeared deserted; its curtains drawn and cars frosted up, stationary in the drive. There was no sign of life except for at number eight from where two white faces peered out of a downstairs window.

The moment Joanna had stepped out of the car the front door was thrown open and a man came out, closely followed by a woman. The strain was visible in both their faces and neither looked as though they had slept. The woman, presumably Molly's mother, was finding it hard to keep her emotions in check.

Joanna spoke first. 'Mr and Mrs Carraway?'

They both nodded. She held out her hand. 'I'm Detective Inspector Joanna Piercy, Leek Police and this is DC Hesketh-Brown.' Mr Carraway gave them both a nod and a tight-lipped smile. He responded shortly. 'Philip and Beth. Look – it's freezing. Let's go inside.'

Joanna followed them into a smart sitting room, cream-carpeted with a soft-looking pale green sofa and an upright piano at the back. Through patio doors Joanna glimpsed a neat grey garden with furniture shrouded for the winter. It was all tidy and orderly. She returned her gaze to the room and Molly's parents.

Over the fireplace – a faux gas fire with a shelf over – hung a large photograph of a smiling girl in smart school uniform: grey skirt, a white blouse and maroon tie with a school crest on it.

Joanna recognized the uniform. Newcastle-under-Lyme Independent School. Her eyes lingered on the girl's bright, eager, sparkling eyes as she wondered what had happened to her. Where she was now? Was she dead or alive? Molly looked a cheerful girl; happy, with clear skin and clear eyes, long dark hair, neatly tied back and straight white teeth. Her face was scrubbed; innocent, beguiling. There looked to be no deceit in her. And yet . . .

Her parents followed Joanna's gaze to the picture and said nothing. But their shoulders drooped a little, hopelessly. Joanna sat down, both parents eyeing her expectantly.

'We had no idea she was going out,' Carraway began.

Joanna responded carefully. 'We've all done it,' she said, with tact. 'Been places we shouldn't. Played "economical" with the truth.'

'We certainly didn't know she was going to Patches,' Beth Carraway said, looking stricken. 'Especially after—' She stopped. Her husband took hold of her hand and held it tightly. His wife returned a sickly smile.

Mr Carraway drew in a deep and angry breath.

'That isn't the point,' Joanna said. She could not deal with this anger. Grief and worry, yes. That was to be expected. But not anger too. Not right now. It was too much. She was aware that they didn't even know about the Danielle Brixton case. She was also aware that if Molly didn't turn up, at some point she was going to have to tell them. Witness the change in their faces; watch their anger morph into terror.

'I am headmaster at Westwood School,' Carraway said, very carefully, 'and my wife teaches at Rudyard Special School. Molly is our only child.' His voice very nearly broke but he recovered himself with a quick shake of his shoulders and a mammoth effort, staring ahead of him as though challenging his eyes to let him down with the tears that threatened to spill down his face.

'Tell me about your daughter,' Joanna began gently. 'What is she like?'

Carraway bowed his head. 'She is taking her GCSEs this summer,' he began. Joanna shook her head impatiently. She had asked about their daughter as a person. Not about her academic achievement. Then she realized that to a pair of teachers academic achievement was all.

'As a young woman,' she prompted gently.

It was Beth Carraway who spoke. 'She was fun, a high achiever, full of adventure. And . . .' Here she eyed her husband and added, 'patently she is not above the odd deception.'

'You didn't know that she'd *ever* been to Patches nightclub with her friend, Clara?'

Beth Carraway shook her head and dropped her gaze. Her husband merely looked fierce.

'Do you know whether she has a boyfriend?'

A pause, then another shake of the head. 'Not as far as we knew,' Beth said with great and sombre dignity. 'But then we obviously didn't really know her, did we?' She looked up, puzzled. 'We thought she was concentrating on her studies, on getting a place at Uni. We thought—'

'Come on,' Joanna said, glancing at Hesketh-Brown. 'Just because she was a bit fun-loving it doesn't mean she wouldn't have worked to get into university. Was she allowed out at all?'

'Yes.' Both parents spoke together. 'She only had to ask.'

'What was she wearing last night?'

Beth Carraway smiled. 'Jeans,' she said. 'So tight she could hardly breathe, with a floating top over them. Then a ski jacket.'

Joanna nodded. From what she'd heard so far that was not the description of what Molly Carraway had been wearing when last seen. 'I'd like a list of friends,' she said. 'Her mobile?'

'We pay the bill,' Molly's father supplied.

'The number?'

Beth Carraway produced her own phone, flipped through the numbers, selected one and handed it to Joanna, who promptly tried it. As before the number went straight through to answerphone. She brought out a pad and copied the number down. 'And a photograph, please,' she added, 'as recent as possible.' She glanced up at the large photograph over the fireplace. 'Preferably not in her school uniform. Is there anyone else she might have stayed with? Another friend, possibly?'

'We've tried them all.'

Beth Carraway stood up, agitated, and left the room, returning a few minutes later with some paperwork and a photograph. She gave a long look at the picture before handing it, without a word, to Joanna.

Joanna looked at it. Ah, this was more like it. The true Molly Carraway: laughing into the camera and beautiful enough to have been a model. Shining, long dark hair; an inviting expression in luminous, large dark eyes, heavily made-up.

'She's lovely,' she said. Both parents nodded, the comment increasing their pain. In the hall the telephone rang and Beth Carraway jumped to her feet and was out of the door in the blink of an eye. In almost as short a time she was back, dropping into the sofa.

'It was Clara,' she said.

Joanna pressed on. 'Has Molly ever done anything like this before? Gone missing?'

Both parents shook their heads in unison.

'And you say she doesn't have a boyfriend?'

'There are a couple of lads she's friendly with at school,' Beth Carraway said, 'not what you'd call a serious boyfriend but we've already rung them. They haven't seen or heard from her.'

Joanna made an attempted to reassure them. 'In all probability she's just worried she's in trouble,' she said, 'and is reluctant to come home.'

The Carraways looked at her almost pityingly.

She tried again. 'It isn't likely that our attacker . . .' she couldn't say the word rapist, 'would strike again in the same place in such a short time.'

Philip Carraway shrugged. 'I suppose there's something in that,' he said grudgingly.

'Can I take a look at her room?'

It was Molly's mother who led the way up stairs.

'I wonder if you'd mind if I took a superficial look through her things?'

Beth Carraway nodded. 'Whatever will help you find her,' she said.

'Anything. Please.' She stood back to let Joanna enter the room.

As she had expected it was tidy and very modern, with an en suite bathroom. One Barbie-doll pink wall, the others white. It was stark, with one wall entirely taken up with pale ash fitted cupboards. She pulled open the doors. On the inside were a few pin-ups of stars: Robert Pattinson, Robbie Williams, Brad Pitt, Daniel Craig. The clothes were mainly jeans, trousers, school uniform; the shoes Doc Martens, wedges, boots. No miniskirts, no skyscraper heels. Joanna pulled open a drawer. It was full of underwear: M&S, but smart. At the back of the wardrobe was a suitcase. Joanna pulled it out, laid it on the bed then opened it.

Inside was the other Molly. All the fashionable clothes her parents would have forbidden. La Senza underwear; the high heels. And. most revealing of all, a few packets of the contraceptive pill, Loestrin 20. It was obvious that Molly had been taking them. Beth Carraway sank down on the bed.

'We didn't know our own daughter,' she said, dazed. Then, looking up at Joanna: 'This girl,' she wafted her hand towards the contents of the suitcase, 'is a stranger.'

There wasn't much Joanna could say. Which one was the real Molly? The almost saint-like, studious schoolgirl or this sophisticated and fashionable woman-about-town? Answer: both. Like most teenage girls there were two distinct sides to Molly Carraway. Light and shade, night and day, innocent and guilty. Joanna scanned the room. Which aspect of the girl had led to her disappearance?

Underneath the window was a desk on which sat an open

laptop. Involuntarily both women looked at it. 'I could do with taking this away,' Joanna said.

Beth Carraway held her hands up. 'Do what you like with it,' she said, her voice holding a touch of revulsion. She watched wordlessly as Joanna removed a hairbrush from the bathroom then followed her downstairs, still silent; part disapproving, part stunned at the revelations the scrutiny of her daughter's room had unearthed. Her husband was waiting at the foot of the stairs. Joanna looked at the pair of them as she and Danny faced them in the hall and she struggled to find the words to reassure them without sounding patronizing. 'Look,' she finally said, hearing the awkwardness in her voice. 'We will do all we can to find your daughter.' Molly's father's face was taut as a violin E string. It would have been insulting to trot out, 'I'm sure we'll find her' or 'believe me – she's all right'. Instead she handed them a card with her mobile number on as well as contact details at the station. 'As soon as we know anything we will be in touch.'

This was one of the most important aspects of the police investigation – keeping in touch, letting the family know that they were still beavering away with the police investigation.

Both parents managed to squeeze out a smile as Joanna and Danny left.

TWELVE

Sunday, 5 December. 2 p.m.

Clara was frightened. She was putting a brave face on it but it wasn't hard to read the girl's fear as she faced Joanna Piercy. To Joanna she simply looked young and vulnerable. And presumably her friend, Molly, stripped of her fashionable and seductive clothes and make-up would look very much the same. Joanna had tried to put Clara at ease but it was proving hard work. 'Were there any other friends of yours at Patches on Friday night? Could Molly have gone home with another friend?'

Clara shook her head and explained. 'Molly and I go to school in Newcastle-under-Lyme,' she said. 'There aren't many girls our age and from Leek at Newcastle.' She gave a hint of a smile. 'That's why Mol and I got so close.'

The girl was well spoken, articulate and, in the circumstances, quite self-possessed. Joanna tried the next question conversationally. 'Did you know many people who went to Patches?'

It sparked something in Clara. She looked worried and guilty. And her parents noticed too. Rosa Williams stood up quickly. 'Would you like a cup of tea, Inspector?' She turned to Hesketh-Brown. 'Constable?'

'No, thank you.' The distraction hadn't worked. Joanna repeated the question. 'So do you?'

Clara gave another swift glance at her parents. 'A few,' she said. 'Not many.'

Joanna sensed something. 'Clara; did you and Molly have a row on Friday night?'

Clara shook her head and shrugged her shoulders. 'No,' she said simply.

'Were you there on Tuesday night, the first of December, the night that Kayleigh Harrison was assaulted?'

Again the girl looked worried; her parents enquiring, but saying nothing.

Clara dropped her head and nodded slowly, then looked at her parents, 'Sorry, Mum; sorry, Dad.'

They merely nodded and gave her the look every teenager can translate into, *We'll talk about this later.*

'Did you know Kayleigh?'

Clara looked at them; frowned.

'She was wearing a silver miniskirt that night,' Hesketh-Brown put in helpfully. 'You might have noticed that.'

Clara blinked and thought for a moment; her frown deepening and then she nodded. 'Yes,' she said, 'I do remember someone dressed like that but I don't know her.'

Joanna leaned forward. 'Think,' she said. 'Can you remember anything about her? Who she was dancing with; who she was talking to. Did you see the same person talking to Molly?'

'She was assaulted and just left in the snow to freeze?' Her tone was shocked; disbelieving that anyone could treat a young woman like that.

Joanna nodded.

'When I saw her she was sitting at the bar, talking to a man,' Clara said slowly.

Joanna waited.

Clara had guileless baby-blue eyes. It was difficult to imagine that she would ever tell anything but the truth. She fixed these *truthful* eyes on Hesketh-Brown. 'He was tall and skinny,' she said, 'wearing a plain shirt, no tie. That's all I remember. Oh, jeans, I think.'

'What sort of age was he?'

She took in a deep breath. 'Not young,' she said, 'that's for sure. He was no eye-popper so I didn't really take a lot of notice.' Her confidence told Joanna that she was on safer ground here.

Joanna smiled and pursued the question. 'Thirties?' she prompted. 'Forties?'

'Somewhere round there,' the girl said. 'I couldn't be sure. I just thought he seemed a bit old for such a young girl.'

'Had you seen that man there before?'

'I don't think so.'

'Was he at Patches last night?'

Joanna had tried to ask the question casually but it didn't fool Clara. The baby-blues opened, flickered from Hesketh-Brown to Joanna and back to Danny. 'Oh, no,' she gasped. 'Not Molly. Please not Molly.'

Joanna repeated the question and this time Clara shook her head firmly. 'I didn't see him,' she said. 'If he was there I didn't see him but it was really crowded.' She was silent for a moment then she met Joanna's eyes. 'What do you think has happened to Molly?' Her voice held real fear.

It was a question impossible to answer. Joanna, too, feared the worst but she could hardly share that with this girl, this child. Instead she glanced across the room at Clara's parents and by the expression in both pairs of eyes she knew that they too feared the worst and dreaded their daughter's involvement. We all see things from our own perspective. At the back of their eyes, hidden right behind the concern, as they exchanged a fleeting glance with each other, Joanna read relief; that their own daughter was here, safe and sound.

'You're helping us very much, Clara,' Joanna encouraged. 'Now, can you remember any of the men Molly was with on Friday night? Was there anyone you particularly remember?'

Clara drew in a long sigh. 'She was with lots of blokes. In *her* get-up she attracted a lot of attention.' There was a hint of jealousy in her voice which did not escape Joanna.

'There was a guy: tall and slim – we've met before.' She screwed up her face. 'I think he was there the night that girl was assaulted but I can't be sure. I remember his hair. It was a little bit curly.'

'What sort of age?'

'Twenties, I think.' She frowned. 'I don't know his name but I've seen him at Patches a few times.' She bit her lip. 'Inspector,' she said slowly, 'Molly had met someone over the Internet.' Her eyes sought out her mother's, who looked stunned. 'After all our warnings, Clara?'

'It wasn't me, Mum – it was Mol. I don't think she was as open with her mum and dad. In a way, Mum, she was naive.'

Joanna listened and began to understand. 'Do you know anything about this man, Clara?'

'He was from London, he said. He was going to come up on Thursday and meet her. He said he had a business trip.'

Joanna met Hesketh-Brown's eyes. They'd better get on and search the laptop.

'His name?'

'I can't remember.'

'OK, Clara. We have Molly's laptop. We'll find out something from that if her Internet man is connected with her disappearance. Now can you remember any of the other guys Molly was with on Friday night?'

'No one special,' she said grumpily. 'When I last saw her – around ten – she was just flirting around.'

'We may want you to come in and look at some of the CCTV images,' Joanna said, taking pity on the girl. It wasn't her fault, after all.

Clara asked the next question timidly. 'What do you think's happened to her, Inspector?'

'We don't know – yet. Let's wait and see, shall we, Clara?'

The girl managed a brave smile.

Joanna stood up then. 'If you'll excuse me we have work to do.'

Rosa Williams saw her to the door. 'This is a dreadful business,' she muttered. 'Quite dreadful. I do hope you find Molly soon.' Their eyes met. 'And that she's all right,' Rosa finished.

Joanna was tempted to say much more to Clara's mother but she was an intelligent woman; she would have worked at least half of it out for herself.

Joanna and Danny drove round then to Patches where a methodical search was in progress; officers walking in formation across the area, combing it for any sign of the missing girl or a clue as to her whereabouts. Joanna and Hesketh-Brown crossed the car park and found Sergeant Barraclough directing the operation, keeping his ancient eyes trained on the proceedings. 'Found anything, Barra?'

'Not so far.'

She looked around her. It was a flat, grey scene; a typical winter's morning. Apart from the snow, not unlike the morning Kayleigh had turned up. She jerked her head towards the corner. 'The area by the bins?'

'We started there. And found nothing,' he said, then tried to make a joke of it. 'Hardly any rubbish, even.'

She could barely raise a smile.

Then there was a shout from the far end and everything froze, except Sergeant Barraclough, who had appeared at the lad's side.

One of the 'specials' was holding up his hand, excitement lighting his face. In a Hiviz jacket and uniform Jason Spark looked the part but he wasn't a police officer. He was a 'special' who was dying to join the force. But entry was difficult and Jason hadn't quite passed the required exams. Joanna watched him, amused and thinking that it was a shame that it was all down to exams. Young Jason, nineteen years old, was a born copper. He lived, ate, *breathed* the force, to the extreme annoyance of anyone who was a bona-fide officer. They found him too bouncy and enthusiastic. It would be *Jason* who found something. However and whoever tried to dampen his enthusiasm, it wouldn't work.

She wandered across.

Barra was holding a gold earring in his gloved hand. He slipped it into a specimen bag and handed the bag to Joanna. It was a large gypsy double hoop. Unusual, with the bit that pierced the ear still threaded and locked at the back and the catch still firmly fastened. Ergo it could not have dropped out of an ear so either it had been removed from the ear and then re-fastened or it had been torn out. Still holding it up to the light she fumbled in her pocket for her mobile phone and dialled the Williams's number. Rosa Williams picked up the phone on the first ring. Her 'Hello' was subdued and worried but the note of hope which lightened the tone didn't escape Joanna's notice. It was heartbreaking.

Joanna decided to ask the question to her, rather than speak directly to Clara. She didn't want to upset the girl any more than was necessary. 'Would you mind asking your daughter if Molly was wearing earrings on Friday night?'

Rosa was no fool. She didn't ask the obvious and was back in seconds. 'Gold double-hooped gypsy earrings,' she said. 'Apparently they were a present from her godmother.'

'And can you ask Clara if Molly was still wearing them later on in the night?'

Again Rosa Williams returned with the answer almost instantly. Her daughter must have been near the phone. 'When Clara last saw Molly she was still wearing them. Apparently they were quite expensive, nine-carat gold.' She paused. 'They were very precious to her. If she'd have dropped one she would have really tried to find it.' There was a pause. 'That's what my daughter says.'

Joanna thanked her and put the phone down, looking at the hoops of gold. They could get them tested for blood. Although she was teased amongst the force for copying some of Sherlock Holmes' practices she still carried a magnifying glass in her bag. She fished it out and peered through it at the catch. The wire was bent if anything, tightening the little hook that fastened it and locking it. She moved the glass a little nearer, peering through and saw what looked like a speck of blood. Her heart sank. She had been pessimistic about the fate of Molly Carraway from the first but put an earring torn out of an ear together with her disappearance and it looked as though her worst fears would be realized. In her heart of hearts she now believed the girl was dead; her body dumped somewhere with no more respect than the same perpetrator had shown for Danielle or Kayleigh. This had the mark of him scratched all over it. The same disregard for human life. Not all human life; the life of young girls who dressed provocatively and abandoned themselves to a fleeting nightclub encounter when they had had a drink or two. And what else? The other girls had been left in the car park. One dead, one alive. Why not Molly? Was it possible that their perp was learning something? Had he decided to remove the evidence to deflect the heat from himself? To remove his 'stamp'? Maybe to buy himself some time?

Hesketh-Brown was watching her. Without saying a word he closed the car door and they drove to 5 Roachside View. As soon as the car turned into the estate the door of number five opened and Beth Carraway stood there. In the brief period since they had initially met Molly's mother had aged another ten years. She stood and watched Joanna walk up the path and read correctly the small shake of the detective's face. She managed a smile and led the way inside without saying a word. Philip Carraway was sitting on the sofa; his face buried in his hands. He barely looked up as they entered.

Joanna showed the Carraways the contents of the specimen bag and knew the earring was familiar to them by the way their faces changed. It was tangible evidence of their daughter's presence – and absence. Beth clutched at her husband's hand before looking up and nodding. 'It's Molly's,' she confirmed. 'Can I look?'

Joanna didn't want her to see the bent wire, the tightened and distorted fastening, but she had no choice. She handed it over with a warning not to touch.

Molly's mother began to sob silently, the tears spilling out. She hardly breathed or moved. Her only movement was in the tears coursing their way down her cheeks. Her husband watched helplessly; unable, it seemed, to do anything – except put his arm round her, kiss her and join in her hopelessness. He simply watched as though his own misery was already more than he could take. The pair were in a state of suspended animation. Joanna had the feeling that when she had gone they would continue to sit there, unable to move or function in any normal way until they had news of their daughter, their only child.

There was so little she could say. 'We're doing all we can to find her.'

Beth Carraway turned tortured eyes towards her. She couldn't even voice her question. Her husband whispered it for her.

'Six months ago,' Philip Carraway said slowly, 'there was a report that a girl died outside a nightclub in Newcastle-under-Lyme.' He couldn't look at her to gauge her response. Joanna's heart sank. She had hoped this story would not become public knowledge quite so soon to join the frenzy of Molly's disappearance.

She did her best to console them. 'We don't know it's the same man. Only that the girl vanished from inside a nightclub. We had no description of the man who was with Danielle Brixton that night and she died of natural causes. She was not murdered.' She let the words sink in before adding: 'And Kayleigh Harrison is still alive . . .' She let the words hang in the air but Molly's parents did not look comforted.

Philip Carraway's voice was little more than a whisper. 'Surely *she* can give you a description of the man?'

The flicker of hope in their eyes was hardly there but it was there all the same.

'She doesn't remember much.'

She left the Carraways on the sofa, clinging to one another. It was enough to break the hardest of hearts.

She and Hesketh-Brown returned to the station.

Joanna was at her desk, staring into the computer screen, when her mobile rang. 'Home' flashed up. 'Hi, Matt,' she said heavily.

'Hi. Things all right?'

'No, not really.'

'Any idea what time you'll be home?'

'I may as well come back now,' she said. 'There isn't a lot I can be doing here. It's dark anyway. I'll just write up a few notes.'

'You sound down.'

'I am,' she admitted. 'The girl is still missing.' She paused, running her fingers through her thick, unruly hair. 'The longer she's gone the worse it is. I'm afraid . . .' She glanced around the office. Danny HK could have finished the sentence for her, as could Matthew. 'I'll be home in half an hour, darling.'

'Great,' he said. 'I thought I'd serve a roast.'

'Lovely.' But she had little appetite. She had a few more chores to do: photographing the earring, sending it down to forensics, organizing flyers with pictures of the fresh-faced schoolgirl. For a while she stared at the girl. *She was a beauty*, she thought. If she was still alive her life would surely be a success. She was bright, by all accounts; could go to university, enter a profession. She was certainly beautiful enough to be a model. If she was still alive. The worst scenario would be not to know. Never to know what had happened. She stood up. Time to go home.

She was back at Waterfall Cottage at four and even when she smelt the lamb found she could not concentrate on anything but the missing girl. Matthew must have had a word with Eloise because she was on her very best behaviour. She gave Joanna an almost beatific smile. Joanna did her best to respond in kind.

'How's your swotting gone?' She knew they did this; skirted around one another, never really finding a topic which was comfortable ground for them both.

Eloise grinned and flicked her blonde hair out of the way. 'I felt guilty,' she said. 'We did do some work but we went on a lovely long walk too.'

'Wish I'd been there,' Joanna said.

Matthew handed her a glass of red wine. 'You poor darling,' he said. 'What a shame for this case to crop up – and so close to the wedding.'

The wedding. The wedding. To Joanna it felt unreal. 'Yes,' she said quickly, and in as normal a voice as she could summon. 'Thank goodness for Mum and Sarah,' she said, reflecting on how Sarah, her older sister, was proving to be massive help alongside her mother with the wedding planning. 'Otherwise I'd be going stark raving mad.'

The phone rang. The three of them looked at one another. Joanna got up. As she had half anticipated it was her mother. They had a brief conversation; one sided, Joanna letting her mother talk about flowers and gifts and arrangements for guests. When she returned to the table she felt even worse. Matthew had put her dinner in the oven to keep warm but she hardly had the energy to eat it. She could not stop thinking about Molly Carraway.

Matthew and Eloise made desultory conversation but it was hard going and they finally gave up. Joanna wanted to ask when Eloise would be going back to her flat but she didn't. In the end Matthew came across to her and put his hand on her shoulder. 'In less than four weeks,' he said, 'you'll be in a bikini, with a cold drink in your hand and a ring on your finger, a husband sitting across the table and you'll say, "This is a wonderful place". Jo,' he said, 'I promise you.'

And at last she managed a smile.

THIRTEEN

Monday, 6 December. 8 a.m.

The trouble with the search for Molly Carraway was that they had so little to go on. Nothing, really. Where do you start when a girl is missing? Police protocol sounds simple and clear – at the place where she was last seen. You study any CCTV footage for clues and then spread out like a spider's web. They'd done all this and it had led nowhere. Sure, they watched Molly flirting, getting drunk, dancing showily – arms right up in there. Joanna made a face. Even the girl's armpits were beautiful. She made a mental note to book in for a leg, underarm and 'honeymoon' wax before the great day. When was she going to have the time?

Telephone calls to all of Molly's friends whose numbers Clara had supplied proved equally futile. Most hadn't seen her since her last day at school, Friday the third. Patches yielded no further physical clue other than the gold earring. Initial forensic tests on the earring had confirmed what Joanna had suspected: the presence of blood and a tiny piece of human tissue, which had been sent for DNA analysis. She hardly needed the 'analysis'. The blood and tissue would match up with Molly Carraway. The earring must have caught on something and had been torn out of her ear. Another person's tissue, blood, a piece of hair or a thread. That would have been something else. But DNA from Molly was not going to tell them anything they did not already know.

Joanna stared into her computer screen. In her heart of hearts she believed the girl was dead. All they needed to do was to find her body. And then . . .

She studied the facts on file. Clara's last sighting of her friend was somewhere around midnight, heading towards the ladies' toilets and the cloakroom, though neither girl had worn a coat. Frustrated and cross, Clara had finally left the club at one, unable to find her friend, though she claimed to have searched everywhere: the 'quiet' area, the dance floor, the bar, the toilets and the cloakroom area. Ergo Molly had disappeared from Patches some time between midnight and 1 a.m.

As she faced the investigating team, both plain clothes and uniform, Joanna persuaded them that their enquiries needed to fan out into the town. House-to-house, door-to-door, person-to-person. Even if they didn't know the significance of what they knew someone, somewhere, must know something.

Officers were checking Molly's mobile phone records and laptop but running through all the contacts would take some time yet.

More boards had been put up in the high street and outside the club. Thinking that as it wasn't so long ago that PC Phil Scott had been an eager young rookie himself, she thought he would be good for the eager young 'special' and accordingly teamed him up with Jason to talk to the cab drivers. In her experience they were an observant lot. And, more importantly, some of them were always idling outside nightclubs, ready to pick up fares.

Leek did have a few CCTV cameras scattered up the high street and she parked Timmis and McBrine in front of the screen to study the images, but two hours later they told her not one of them showed Molly, either alone or accompanied. Joanna absorbed the information, or rather lack of it. So the missing girl had not emerged into the town. Phil and Jason also reported back at lunchtime that they too had drawn a blank.

Joanna penned it all up on the board.

No taxi
No sightings on the streets of Leek.

Neither had her body turned up in spite of an extensive search in any of the quieter areas in the town. So it was time to extend it into the surrounding countryside.

And this was where they hit another problem. To the north, south, east and west, Leek is surrounded by vast tracts of countryside: empty, featureless moorland towards the north-east; rural farms to the east and west. Even to the south and the city of Stoke on Trent, there was a strip of a few miles which contained the tiny, scattered villages of Longsden and Endon, Stockton Brook and Horton. Then there was the expanse of Rudyard Lake and acres of boggy farmland which at this time of the year did not even have the human attention of a farmer tending his animals. They were all safely in cowsheds and barns. Searches in such an underpopulated and largely rural area would be futile and ultimately a squandering of both manpower and resources: the proverbial hunting for a needle in a haystack. The empty expanse was too vast. Bodies are small and weren't always found.

It had all happened before. Years ago a farmer who had gone missing at lambing time had not been found until harvest time, his shotgun at his side, in spite of extensive searches around his farm and the surrounding area. If a body was not on a walkers' route, a farm trail, or near a road, there was every chance that it would not be found – ever. It would simply lie there, decomposing. And in the meantime Molly's parents suffered, wondered, hoped and feared. The lack of *habeas corpus* was a serious impediment. With a body came forensic evidence, unless they were very unlucky and the killer very, very careful. So the sooner they found Molly the better – for everyone. At the back of her mind Joanna was aware that Danielle had died in May and Kayleigh had been assaulted in November. Molly had disappeared only three days after Kayleigh. If the same man was involved in all three events it didn't take much to realize his appetite and audacity were on the increase.

If only they could narrow down the area, just a little, they could rope in the RAF helicopter with its heat-seeking equipment. Even in these sub-zero temperatures Molly's body would decompose – albeit slowly. Decomposition produces heat.

Bingo.

All they needed was one tiny hint of a lead. That was all.

Joanna had already decided to involve the general public. In this moorland town there was a solid feeling of community. They were not short of volunteers, each supervised by a member of the force. The teams would keep in touch by mobile phone and the members of the public had strict instructions; if they found anything they were not to sully the crime scene but call for help.

Joanna briefed the officers so they all understood their role and the geographical area they were responsible for. In the meantime she and Mike were having a talk. 'The only real, tangible lead we've got,' Joanna said, frowning thoughtfully in Korpanski's direction, 'is Kayleigh. She's keeping something back. We have to try and get whatever it is out of her, Mike. She's our best chance.' She thought for a moment more before adding, with honesty, 'Our only *real* hope. We have so little to go on.' Korpanski eyed her, waiting for one of her flashes of inspiration. She was silent for a moment before adding, hesitatingly: 'I suppose *it might* be worth talking again to Steve Shand and his birthday mates. Perhaps one or two of them were at Patches on Friday night as well as the previous Tuesday.'

'It's worth a shot,' Korpanski agreed. 'As you say, as we haven't got any better ideas.'

'Mike,' she wheedled slowly, 'I wonder if you'd go back to Newcastle-under-Lyme and find out a little bit more about the Danielle Brixton case.'

He was puzzled. 'Such as?'

'I don't really know,' she confessed, 'but – you do agree, don't you, that it appears that the three cases are connected?'

'It's a big step, Jo, but yes, I suppose I do.'

'Let me just run this past you.'

'I'm listenin'.'

'OK. Stop me if you disagree with anything I'm saying.'

'OK.'

'Danielle was raped and left to die right outside Lymeys.'

Korpanski nodded, his dark eyes fixed on Joanna Piercy's face.

'The same with Kayleigh.' She paused. 'So if our perp is the same person why didn't he leave Molly to be found? That's the way he works. What changed?'

'Maybe he thought the heat was being turned up with Kayleigh being found less than a week before,' Korpanski suggested.

'Maybe. Then there's the time lapse.'

'Go on.'

'Six months between Danielle and Kayleigh. Only three days between Kayleigh and Molly Carraway.'

'What's your point?'

'I may be wrong,' Joanna said slowly, 'but I think he's an opportunist. A chancer.'

Korpanski frowned and she ploughed on. 'I want to know if anything else connects the three assaults apart from opportunity.'

'What sort of things, Jo?'

'Anything. Time of year, weather, what Danielle was wearing, who found her, at what time, how long she'd been dead, just stuff like that – general. I'll wander across to Patches and chat to our American friends; see if they remember anything more. Maybe the doorman too.' She heaved a great sigh. 'I shall have to pay Molly's parents a social call but I can leave that until later on this afternoon and I'll have another word with young Kayleigh.' She made an attempt at a smile. 'Maybe she's got her memory back, eh, Mike?'

Korpanski continued to look glum but he did nod and twist his mouth in a parody of a smile. 'We'll meet up here later,' she said, 'and swap stories.' She tried to smile too. 'Then we'll interview our 'birthday boys'. We should get some results on the earring by later on this afternoon but I can guess they won't take us much further.'

Korpanski picked his jacket off the back of his chair. 'OK, Jo, see you later.'

After Korpanski had left the room she sat motionless at her desk for a moment. She wasn't relishing any part of the day ahead. And underlying her unease was a fear that none of it would lead them to Molly, either alive or dead. She had a super-stitious feeling that this girl's fate might elude them.

Then she shook herself. Being spooked by a case was simply silly; letting herself believe that the Fates themselves would cover the truth. She wasn't paid to have 'feelings'; none of this was written in a horoscope somewhere. She simply had to get on with the job, piece these three stories together – if they were indeed chapters of the same book – and bang the perpetrator up for a suitably long time. She sighed and flicked through the case notes; picked out pictures of all three. Danielle had a clear gaze; a challenging expression. In spite of her youth she looked like a confident girl. One who was well able to look after herself; only she hadn't been. She was young. Too young to die. Joanna read through the police description. Pale complexion. Eyes: brown. Hair: brown. It didn't really begin to describe the living, shining silk that was Danielle's hair or the clear, young skin; the perfect teeth.

Next she picked up the picture of Kayleigh. Even in her clean school uniform Kayleigh looked different to the other two. Her mouth was small and thin, already twisted into an expression which whispered, '*victim*'. But at least she was still alive. Not such a victim, then. She had a mother; admittedly no father but she had had a stepfather who had cared about her. Maybe, Joanna thought, Kayleigh was just one of those people who are born to be on the underbelly of life.

Lastly she picked up the picture of Molly Carraway. Molly, like Danielle, looked supremely confident – of her social standing, her beauty, her popularity, a lifetime of success ahead of her. It was all waiting for her: university, travel, a career, boyfriends, a husband who would adore her, children to whom she would be a wonderful mother. It was all written in the girls' faces. What would be or what should have been. Joanna put the three pictures down side by side and gazed at them.

When she finally shook herself back to life she contacted the five birthday boys by mobile phone and arranged for them to call in to Leek police station in the afternoon. Fifteen minutes later she was back outside the nightclub.

Patches looked slightly less seedy this Monday morning, perhaps because a watery sun was doing its best to softly illuminate the scene. The wind had dropped and after the icy temperatures of the last few days it felt almost warm. Leek's Christmas decorations, strung across the street, gave the area a festive look. They had been switched on to great celebration and excitement over the weekend by a local celebrity – the owner of Leek football club; the nearest thing the town had to home-grown glamour. Even Patches itself had put up a Christmas tree – patently artificial and slightly tacky – white with huge gold baubles and pale lights, but it was an improvement of sorts. A huge banner draped across the windows wished *A Very Merry Christmas to you all,* and gave even this rundown area a festive feel. But as Joanna drew into the car park the festive feel washed right over her. Instead she had a depressing sense of déjà vu. Two assaults in less than a week. And no arrest. No one even 'helping the police with their enquiries'.

She sat in her car, studying the scene: the tall, square Victorian ex-mill with its overlarge size and numerous windows; the bleak, empty car park, scene of drama. Then she and Hesketh-Brown climbed out and knocked on the door. It was answered by a very glum-looking Chawncy Westheisen, who gave her a curt nod and said nothing. Behind him was a shorter, rat-faced man she took to be Marvin. She shook hands with them both while wondering whether they knew anything that would help them. Probably not, she thought, still in her depressed mood. Was there a connection with Patches or had they simply been unlucky?

'Crispin should be here in a coupla minutes,' Westheisen said, leading her back into her office. He indicated a chair and they sat down opposite, looking eager. 'Now, Inspector, how can we help you? You know we'll do anything to help you find the poor girl.' They were making a real attempt to be helpful. And keep their club from closing.

Joanna took out her notepad. 'Which one of you was here on Friday night?'

'We both were,' they answered in unison like Tweedledum and Tweedledee.

'OK. Take a look at these. She showed them the picture of Molly Carraway. 'Did you see Molly here on Friday?'

They both looked hard at the photograph of the fresh-faced, confident schoolgirl. 'Not looking like this. She looks around twelve years old. This is the girl that's missing?' Westheisen was spokesman for both of them.

'Yes.' Time to twist the thumbscrew. 'Molly Carraway was fifteen years old,' she said severely. 'She shouldn't even have been allowed in here.'

The two men squirmed.

'She was last seen between midnight Friday and one a.m. Saturday. No one has seen her since. She and her friend became separated. Her friend couldn't find her so went home, alone, hoping that Molly had gone straight home herself. She became alarmed when she heard nothing from Molly during the following day. She confided in her mother who finally spoke to Molly's parents on Saturday evening who, in turn, alerted the police.'

Chawncy, in particular, was scrutinizing the picture. 'I can't say that I do remember her,' he said. 'But girls look so different when they're all done up: make-up, clothes, everything,' he finished lamely.

Joanna laid the photograph of Clara on the desk in front of them, next to the picture of Molly. 'What about this girl?'

'This is the friend?'

'Yeah.'

Clara beamed over her shoulder coquettishly. It was a deliberate pose. 'Quite a looker, ain't she?' It was Marvin who showed appreciation.

Joanna nodded. 'They both are.'

Westheisen spoke for both of them once more. 'Sorry,' he said quickly. 'We kind of stay in the background. We don't see a lot of the kids in the club. Maybe Andrew will be a little more helpful.'

'We'll have to take some more of your tapes.'

They shrugged. 'OK by us.' Chawncy spoke for both of them.

He hesitated. 'It probably isn't fair to even ask you this,' he said slowly.

Joanna already knew what was coming next: a plea for mercy. 'The girls were underage,' she said severely. 'You know the rules. You're supposed to ask for ID at the door. Not let them in. But . . .' She looked from one to the other. 'You've cooperated well enough. It isn't your fault what's happened to the girls. I can't really blame the club for that.' She took pleasure in the fact that the two Americans were rattled. To herself she admitted that it would seem poor consolation if the only conviction to come out of this case was a prosecution of the owners of Patches for allowing in underage girls. In her low mood she reflected that if it hadn't been this girl and this club it might well have been another girl in another club.

As Chawncy and Marvin filed out she felt the visit had been a waste of time, right up until Andrew Crispin arrived.

He was a hefty man of medium height with a bullet head and the long-armed walk of an ape. He rolled in and sat opposite Joanna, fingering a recent bruise on his chin. Hesketh-Brown stood at the back of the room, legs apart, watching the proceedings but saying nothing. Joanna looked at him and smothered a smirk. He'd copied the stance from Mike Korpanski, she was sure.

'Sit down, Mr Crispin.' Again Joanna produced the photos, laying them down on the desk. Crispin pursed his lips and studied them. Then he nodded his head slowly. 'I know these girls,' he said, looking up. 'They're regulars.'

'Really?' Joanna already knew this but she'd decided to play dumb. 'How often do they come here?'

'Couple of times a week,' he said, meeting her eyes with a sudden frankness that both impressed and convinced her. He was a good witness.

'Always together?'

Crispin nodded.

'Do they leave together?'

'Whenever I've seen them leave. Most of the time I wouldn't notice.'

'Have you ever seen them leave with guys?'

He shook his head.

'Have you ever seen them with boyfriends inside the club?'

Crispin shrugged. 'I've seen them dancing with guys,' he said easily, 'having drinks. Girls like that attract the blokes like bees to a honey pot, but no one in particular. A couple of dances; a bit of flirting. Nothing heavy.' He shrugged. 'You know.'

Joanna nodded. 'What about Friday?'

'Oh . . .' He drew in a deep, sucking breath. 'It's difficult. Friday night was packed. They were like sardines in a tin. Christmas comin' up *and* a Friday night.' He counted on his two fingers. 'All adds up to standin' room only.' He made an attempt at a smile but Joanna wasn't smiling back. He raised his eyebrows. 'By eleven thirty I was turnin' them away.'

'But not these two.' Joanna had a thought. 'Was there anyone you turned away that was of special interest? Anyone seem particularly put out?'

'A bunch of guys,' Crispin said lazily, 'drunk as skunks; been at the pub all night. I couldn't let them in. They looked like trouble.'

'Do you know their names?'

'I know one of them. He was in here the night Kayleigh was attacked.'

'His name?'

'Gary. I don't know his second name.'

But Joanna did. It was Pointer. Gary Pointer.

'Did he seem angry?'

'Yeah. Kicked around a bit then finally left.'

'Any idea of the time?'

'Round about half twelve, I suppose.'

It was in the time frame. 'Did anyone else stand out in your mind on either the night Kayleigh was assaulted or on Friday?'

Crispin pursed his lips and frowned. 'There was a guy,' he said. 'I think I might have seen him once or twice before. Late thirties; maybe even older – early forties. He was on his own. Dressed quite smart, really.'

'What night are you talking about?'

'Friday.'

'So what did you notice about him? Why are you mentioning him?'

'I dunno,' Crispin said. 'He just seemed different. A loner.'

'Can you describe him?'

'Tall, skinny; wearing a leather jacket.'

Joanna leaned forward, frowning. 'You heard the description of Kayleigh's attacker.'

'But—'

'Did you see this man with Molly?'

'Yeah. But only talking.'

'Well, you wouldn't have seen what happened, would you?' Hesketh-Brown put in truculently. Joanna gave him a swift, warning glance.

'Hair?' she rapped out.

'Thinnish, light brown.'

Another swift glance at Hesketh-Brown. One thing would clinch it. 'Was he local?'

Crispin shook his head. 'I don't think so,' he said.

'Was he there the night Kayleigh was assaulted?'

'I – I'm not sure if it was the same guy. He might have been. I can't really remember. There's so many people. Crowds.'

'I want you to come down to the station and run through the CCTV,' she said. 'See if you can pick him out.'

Time to ease off a little. Joanna didn't want to put words into Crispin's mouth. 'I suppose in a club like Patches,' she said conversationally, 'you have your regulars?'

Crispin nodded warily.

'You know a good number of the people who come?'

Again he nodded.

'Hazard a guess,' she said. 'It being a Tuesday there were fewer people at the club on the night Kayleigh was assaulted than the night that Molly went missing. Off the top of your head,' she said airily, 'can you think of anyone who was there on both nights?'

Crispin was on his guard. 'I'd have to think about it,' he said.

She tried a shot in the dark. 'Did anything unusual happen on Friday night?'

The question appeared to rattle Crispin. 'What do you mean?'

Joanna was silent. The truth was that she didn't know what she had meant by the question. She was fishing around in the dark but to her surprise Crispin appeared angry. He was pressing his mouth together, breathing hard. 'Mr Crispin,' she prompted.

'There's always a couple of them,' he said. 'Kids trying to show off. Act big, like.'

'What happened?'

'They was just chinnin' up to me, acting stupid.' He fingered his bruise.

'Ah,' she said. 'But you didn't call the police?'

Crispin looked uncomfortable. He put his finger between his neck and the collar of his shirt. 'Didn't need to,' he muttered.

Hesketh-Brown shifted his weight between his feet. Joanna was thoughtful.

'Anything else you can add?'

Crispin shook his head.

'So you'll come down to the station?'

He nodded. Minutes later they heard him roar away on a powerful motorbike.

Once she and Danny had checked the back entrance and fire

escape Joanna left the club convinced that she was beginning to learn some but not all of its secrets. The videotapes were safely in her bag. She tapped them thoughtfully.

Next they drove round to Kayleigh Harrison's house. All was eerily quiet in the street. A few cars were parked up but there was no one in the road or on the pavement. It was odd. They caught sight of Pauline Morrison watching them through the window before the curtain was dropped back. Joanna knocked on the door.

FOURTEEN

A grumpy Christine Bretby opened the door and without a word led Joanna and Danny into the small lounge where Kayleigh was sitting, watching television. The girl continued to stare fixedly into the TV screen but Joanna knew from the stiffening of her shoulders that she was perfectly aware they were there.

'Hello, Kayleigh,' she said easily enough, settling down on the sofa. 'How are you today?'

Kayleigh was dressed casually in a loose-fitting white smock top and black leggings which emphasized her bony thighs. The room felt warm and was scented by a candle burning on the fireplace. It threw a strange light on to the Klimt, the flames catching the gold; the movement almost making it look alive. In this light it looked – not a cliché as Joanna had judged it – but beautiful.

'I'm OK,' Kayleigh replied, still staring pointedly into the screen. Her mother sat in the window seat, silhouetted against the glass and watching with scant interest.

The hatred between mother and daughter was palpable; visible and poisonous as mustard gas. The air between them was electric with tension, hostility and suspicion, yet as Joanna glanced from mother to daughter she realized that although Christine undoubtedly had her cross to bear, Kayleigh was the more vulnerable. Right up until she opened her mouth. 'I don't wanna see no friggin' shrink,' she said. 'I ain't nuts. *I'm* the victim here.' She scanned the room of its three occupants and challenged them. 'Don't you lot realize?'

Little Miss Harrison could stick up for herself, Joanna thought, her sympathy leaching away until she studied the girl and revised her opinion. Not always. There was a look in the girl's eyes: fright, bewilderment, vulnerability and, above all, a question. *Why me? Why do things always happen to me?*

The girl's vulnerability made Joanna alter her approach. She had come to the house quite prepared to bully Kayleigh Harrison into revealing whatever it was that she was holding back. Now she began more gently. 'Kayleigh,' she said, 'you do realize that a girl's gone missing from outside Patches?'

'What's it to do with me?' Her look was pugnacious now. She was wary and on the defensive, which made Joanna even more convinced that she was concealing something she knew was important.

Joanna kept her temper with difficulty. 'We don't know,' she said steadily. 'Maybe you're right and it is nothing to do with you. But look at it from our point of view. Same club; within a few days of the assault on you a girl goes missing. What would you think if you were me?'

It was a new police tactic; appealing to witnesses to look at crimes from the police point of view instead of their own. The approach took Kayleigh aback, as it was meant to do.

She tried, ''Spose I can see it's a bit of a coincidence, like.'

Joanna continued smoothly. 'Maybe Molly Carraway's disappearance has nothing to do with the assault on you but we are naturally suspicious that the person who attacked you is the same person who has abducted Molly.' She paused to give her next words their full effect. 'She's been missing since very early Saturday morning.' She aimed her glance at the leaden sky outside the window. 'It's freezing out there, Kayleigh. You were found *hours* after the assault. Not days. It was lucky for you that Steve Shand came back to collect his car.'

The sentence stopped her in her tracks. Luck? *Had* it simply been luck? Or had Shand returned to the scene of the crime to make sure that she was dead? Then why sound the alarm? No. That wasn't it.

'This girl, Molly,' she continued, 'has been missing for sixty hours.'

Now Kayleigh's truculent expression was replaced with one of cunning. It was just as ugly as the pugnacity but when she spoke her voice was as quavering as an old lady's. 'Wha-at makes you think it's the same person?'

'It's the same place.' Joanna kept her voice steady, though it was as much of an effort as holding a ship's wheel on course through a hurricane. Her emotions were surfacing.

She dropped the accusation as deftly as skimming a stone. 'You're holding something back, Kayleigh.'

The girl's stare dropped away but not before Joanna had read consternation, fright – and, surprisingly, guilt. Guilt?

She waited for the girl to speak. And she did. With difficulty, her eyes, the colour of mud, lifted to meet Joanna's. 'What?' she began then stopped. 'What do you think's happened to her?' Now she sounded no more than her fourteen years old. If anything even younger. Eleven. Twelve.

'We don't know. We have no idea. She's simply vanished.'

Kayleigh summoned up every inch of teenage bravado. 'People don't just vanish.'

'*I* know that.' Joanna knew she was using the voice of a teacher. An indulgent but firm teacher; the sort one always respects because they speak the absolute truth, never bending it for a story or altering the facts for expedience. 'But after Clara, Molly's friend, saw her around midnight, no one seems to have seen her. It's Monday today. No one has seen her for almost forty-eight hours. Where is she? Is she freezing, like you were?'

Kayleigh went rigid.

Joanna ploughed on, relentless. 'Or is she dead?' She deliberately aimed her glance outside the window, to the freezing, grey day. 'Is her body out there somewhere?' Interestingly it was Kayleigh's mother who flinched.

Joanna pursued her questions ruthlessly. 'Where is she?'

It had been a rhetorical question – she had not expected it to be answered but bravely Kayleigh tried to. 'She must be with *him*,' she said, and now her expression had softened.

Who is he? Who do you mean?'

Kayleigh licked dry lips. 'The bloke that went for me,' she said quickly.

'Who is he?'

A swift glance at her mother. 'I don't know,' she said. 'Honest, I don't.'

Joanna pulled out the picture of Molly Carraway. 'This is the missing girl,' she said. 'Do you know her? Have you ever seen her at Patches?'

Kayleigh's perusal of the photograph was wary, puzzled and cursory. 'I think I have seen her at the club,' she said. 'She's quite a good dancer.'

Which would have drawn attention to her.

Kayleigh kept her gaze on the picture then swivelled her gaze up to meet Joanna's. 'Pretty, ain't she?' There was a note of regret in her voice now.

'Yes, she is.' *Or was.*

Next Joanna showed her the photograph of Clara, which again provoked admiration from the less sophisticated Kayleigh. 'She's just gorgeous, ain't she?'

Again Joanna agreed. She watched the emotions cross the girl's face: grey clouds across a clear sky, and decided to change tactics. Impulsively she put her hand on the girl's arm. 'Kayleigh,' she appealed, 'please help us find her.'

The look of alarm on Kayleigh's face was obvious. Even her mother, who had sat, zombie-like, watching the interchange, was bound to say something, but being Christine Bretby it was neither comforting nor reassuring but aggressive. 'What 'ave you been up to, my girl,' she said. 'What hole 'ave you dug for yourself?'

Kayleigh practically cowered into the corner of the sofa. 'Nothin', Mum. I ain't done nothin'.'

Christine leaned forward. Slid a cigarette out of the packet and lit it before she responded to this. 'And if I believe that, my girl,' she said, 'I'll believe anythin'.' She wagged her finger at her daughter. 'You're up to somethin', Kayleigh Harrison.' She sucked in a long drag then wagged the burning tip in Kayleigh's direction. 'I don't know what it is but you're definitely up to somethin'. Probably lyin' through your teeth again.'

Wisely her daughter did not respond to this but lowered her eyes and muttered, 'No, I'm not.'

'Kayleigh.' Joanna appealed again. 'Please. Anything. A car, a smell, a sound. Something. Please. I want to find Molly.' In the doorway Hesketh-Brown shifted his weight from foot to foot. Kayleigh stared straight in front of her. 'All I can remember,' she insisted, 'is that he weren't local. He was tall and skinny. He smoked. I can't tell you anythin' more because I don't know it. It was cold. It was dark. There weren't much light in that 'orrible car park. I was frightened and that is it. There's no point you keepin' squeezing me for stuff I can't tell you 'cos I don't know.' Her eyes were begging to be believed but Joanna knew she was lying. It was the way she had just spoken: rehearsed, remembered lines. But not the truth. Which bit of her story was she hiding behind? She could not bully it out of the girl. There was a core of steel in Kayleigh Harrison, probably forged by years of dislike and contempt from her mother and complete neglect from her father. If Kayleigh did not want to tell she would not.

Well.

She stood up, ready to go, and fired her last question. 'Tell me, Kayleigh,' she said, in a sweet voice, 'do you think Molly Carraway is alive or dead?'

The girl looked straight at her. 'Alive,' she said. 'She's alive.'

Joanna said her goodbyes and, feeling confounded and frustrated, she and detective Constable Danny Hesketh-Brown returned to the station.

Afterwards Joanna would regret that she had not pressed Kayleigh harder but it would probably have got her nowhere, except perhaps in front of the Independent Police Complaints Commission. And she couldn't afford another brush with Police Complaints.

There was a briefing at lunchtime, partly to find out if anyone had any news and partly to hand out more flyers of Molly Carraway and revise the facts of her disappearance. Joanna looked at the map they'd pinned on the wall. There was not one pin stuck in, even to indicate a false sighting. There was no proof that she had been abducted – apart from the torn-out earring. She could have gone of her own free will. Joanna was well aware that teenage girls were capable of many things. There had been a disappearance a few years ago of a thirteen-year-old who had simply pinched some money out of her mother's purse and gone on a jaunt to Blackpool for a couple of weeks. There was another who had gone with a boyfriend to his home country of Morocco and could not find her way back. It was not beyond the bounds of possibility that Molly had been conniving. The four uniformed guys who had been scanning the CCTV footage had spotted Molly and Clara plenty of times but not noted any particular male interest – dances with various lads but no one fitting Kayleigh's description. There were other possibilities. Lured by promises of celebrity Molly could have gone to London to be a supermodel. There were victims of abuse who surfaced dead or alive but Molly was not one of these. No more than a high-spirited teenager. The real frustration of this case was her conviction that Kayleigh held the key, or at least could point them in the right direction.

Korpanski had enjoyed his morning at Newcastle-under-Lyme and was ready to report back to Joanna. She returned to their office to find him sitting at his desk, looking smug. She caved in. 'Go on, then,' she said, 'shoot.'

'Well.' Korpanski put his hands on his meaty thighs, grinned at her and took a giant bite out of his sandwich. 'They were pretty thorough. They took lots of statements, interviewed lots of people.' He shot a sneaky look at Joanna which she interpreted correctly. 'Sandra Johnson was really helpful,' he said. 'She went through them all with me,' he said. 'There are similarities to Kayleigh's case but you can't really say they're unique. There was a birthday party the night Danielle disappeared but it was a hen party; sixteen girls all dressed up with Playbunny ears, black frocks, high-heeled boots.' He grinned at her. 'I enjoyed looking at those.'

'Get on with it, Korpanski,' she said, knowing it was silly to rise to his bait but she was twitchy. Molly Carraway was missing and her wedding was looming, like a cross channel ferry, slicing through fog.

After a satisfied grin, Korpanski continued. 'It was a Tuesday night at the club so it was quieter than at the weekends. Danielle was doing a course at college, learning hairdressing. She was a real looker, into beauty therapies and stuff like that. Anyway, that night six of them had gone to Lymeys as it was one of her friend's birthday parties. She'd really tarted up in a gold sequinned dress.'

'Really?' Joanna felt a quickening of her pulse.

Korpanski looked smug. 'Apparently metallics are the in thing at the moment so she was well up to the minute.'

Joanna resisted a smirk. 'So glad you've swotted up on current fashion, Mike. Go on.'

'All night she'd been shimmying around, quite drunk, everyone noticing her and then – all of a sudden, her friends said – she just wasn't there any more.'

'I'm listening,' Joanna said, downing a mug of tea. 'Go on, Mike.'

'According to her friends' statements Danielle wasn't a virgin but she didn't have a steady boyfriend. She didn't want one. She'd told her friends she wanted to "play the field", which she did.'

'Do I sense a jealous boyfriend somewhere in the background?'

Korpanski's grin grew even broader. 'She'd been going out with a married man. There was a suspicion that it was a teacher at her college. One of her tutors.'

'Wait a minute.' Joanna crossed to the board. 'One of Shand's buddies is a teacher, isn't he?'

'Hennessey. But he teaches eight year olds,' Korpanski pointed out. 'Anyway, DI Sandra Johnson tells me the person who had sex with Danielle could have been just about anyone. He'd worn a condom. It was a rainy night; there was precious little good forensic evidence and plenty of forensic evidence – most of which would have had nothing to do with her. In the end, as Danielle died of natural causes the CPS and the local force decided not to pursue investigations. They could never know whether the sex was consensual or forceful.'

Joanna nodded. It all made sense. 'And how were her parents about this?'

'As you can imagine: not happy. In fact, they were furious. They made a complaint against Sandra, spoke to their local MP and took their story to the national tabloids, but to no avail. The case was closed and they've never learned anything more.'

They were both silent for a while. Joanna was picturing Danielle's parents coming to terms with their daughter's death and the sharp blow that the last person who had been with her alive had simply abandoned their daughter to her fate. Such an ignominious fate too.

'I think it's the same person,' Joanna said, 'that left Kayleigh. Little doubt about it in my mind; the same careful wearing of a condom but careless abandonment of life. It's like a modus operandi. Someone who preys on extroverted, intoxicated, attractive girls at a club: has sex with them and abandons them. This is our man. This is his psyche.' She paused. 'And then we have Molly, which is a different case altogether. He took her.' She was silent. 'What if it isn't the same person?'

'Bit of a coincidence then. Same area, nightclub, young girls.'

'It's too soon after the assault on Kayleigh.'

'Maybe that's the clever bit.'

She shook her head. 'It's six months since Danielle died. The assault on both her and Kayleigh are similar. They have the same stamp on them. An arrogance. No attempt to hide either the crime or the victim. No threats. The man just faded away, leaving them to their fate. Danielle died; Kayleigh lived. Our perp didn't care. He simply walks away. But not with Molly. She's nowhere to be found, Mike. We've made a cursory search of the surrounding area. We've spread out to a five-mile radius and been quite thorough, thanks to the help of the general public. She's been abducted; taken away and that makes it a different crime and I think it's been committed by a different person. Perhaps even a copycat.'

'Well, I don't agree and I'll tell you why,' Korpanski responded. 'DI Johnson was really helpful and let me look at all the files on Danielle. That night she was wearing a tiny little dress. Shining gold. According to her friends she was flinging herself all over the place, pissed out of her brains, wearing practically nothing.'

Joanna frowned. 'How long is it since you were inside a nightclub, Mike? All the girls wear practically nothing these days.'

'Yes, but – look at this.' With a flourish Korpanski produced a picture. 'This,' he said grandly, 'is a picture of Danielle ready to go out.'

It took Joanna aback because it could so easily have been Molly Carraway. The same shining brown hair, bold eyes, tiny dress which displayed to perfection a very slim figure. 'Well,' she said slowly, 'I can see the resemblance but you know, Mike, the girls these days could be cloned. They all look the same. They have the same hair, the same make-up, the same clothes.'

Korpanski looked so crestfallen Joanna almost felt sorry for him.

'I suppose,' she said slowly, looking up, 'what *you're* saying is that he goes for the same type?'

Korpanski nodded. 'Most men do,' he said, giving her a cocky grin. 'I've always liked brunettes with blue eyes myself. Don't ask me why.' Joanna laughed at his cheek, tempted to aim a punch at his torso but she didn't. The truth was that since the 'incident' she had not quite taken Detective Sergeant Mike Korpanski so much for granted. They were not quite as relaxed together as they had once been. The shooting had left a scar not only on Korpanski's shoulder but also on their relationship.

'Was there anything else? Did DI Johnson have any suspects? Any clues? Any idea at all?'

Korpanski shook his head. 'Not a sausage,' he said. 'She was stumped. She was getting nowhere.' He hesitated. 'She would love to have given the bloke a warning at the very least. If Danielle's parents had known who it was they might have taken things further but she didn't have a clue. She wasn't even sure that the guy Danielle had sex with was even in the club that night.'

Joanna ran her fingers through her hair. 'Oh, don't,' she groaned. 'Don't start that; widening the circle to someone who maybe wasn't even there that night.'

'Well, it's a possibility,' Korpanski pointed out sensibly.

'Mike,' she said, turning around, 'do you mind if I bounce a few ideas around?'

'Wouldn't be the first time.' The phrase was ungracious but she knew he was pleased.

'It's Kayleigh,' she said.

'Thought it might be.'

'When I spoke to her this morning her mother sat in. They are keeping something back. I can't work out why they would.

I even got the feeling that she was protecting someone, but why would she? She doesn't appear to have any particular relationship with any male at the club. The person was so callous towards her. Why would she protect them? She's given us a description of her dancing partners and the guy who maybe raped or had sex with her but she's still hiding something.'

Korpanski shrugged. 'No more than most girls of that age and wanting to go out for the night. If they were honest with their parents they'd all be locked up with chastity belts.' He gave a crooked grin that looked threatening. 'Wait till Jossie gets a bit older.'

'But I don't get the impression that Christine was exactly strict with her daughter. She couldn't have cared less.'

She thought for a minute, stumbling her way through, trying various angles and approaches. 'What about Danielle?'

Korpanski puffed his chest out. He was enjoying every moment of this. 'According to DI Sandra Johnson,' he said, 'Danielle's mum and dad didn't have a problem with her going out at night. They were very . . .' He frowned. 'What's the word?'

'Liberal?'

'Ah, that'll do.'

'But Molly's weren't. They would have gone mad if they'd known what she was up to. Molly was another liar, Mike. She'd deceived her parents very successfully. They saw her as whiter than snow.' She looked at him, wondering whether she was finding a way through; finally punching a hole through the blackness. 'What if this is another deception?'

'You mean she's still alive, just gone off somewhere?'

'I don't know what I mean,' she said uncomfortably. 'I'm just trying out ideas, Mike. I can't really imagine *anyone* being that careless or cavalier but it does happen.'

'What have we got off the laptop, Jo?

'She was having some sort of relationship with a guy but he's from London. They were supposed to meet up next week. There's no mention of Patches and no evidence that they ever met.'

'So what are you going to do to flush out Kayleigh's secret?'

'Dig around in her past.' She looked up. 'That, Korpanski, is what I'm going to do.'

'Fine by me.'

FIFTEEN

Monday, 6 December. 4 p.m.

Though Steve Shand's mates worked in different jobs, in different parts of both town and city, they arrived at the same time, trooping in together as though they were still at their birthday party. Joanna didn't like it because it smacked of collusion. They'd have had plenty of time to practise their statements on the way here. They certainly looked confident enough as they filed in but that could have a simple explanation; that they were innocent and had nothing to hide. It was up to the Piercy–Korpanski team to find out what was really going on. She addressed them collectively, sizing the five of them up as she spoke. 'You're going to be here for some time,' she said. 'Detective Sergeant Korpanski and myself will want to interview you – one at a time. OK?'

They nodded, shifting around on their feet, making a ragged line-up. She eyed them, one by one. 'Your names, please?'

One at a time they stepped out of line and she took stock, picking out the first one to move; the guy on the end, Gary Pointer. Her eye had landed him as he best fitted Kayleigh's description – right up until he spoke in an accent as unmistakably Staffordshire as a bacon-and-cheese oat cake. Tall and slim, he met her eyes without blinking, looking confident – if anything a little cocky. He was casually dressed in beige jeans and an open-necked checked shirt; his left hand anchored in his pocket.

'Gary Pointer, at your service,' he said with a frank and friendly grin and a mock bow. She would be starting with him.

Standing next to Pointer, Andrew Downey was short and plump with an impressive and mobile beer belly, which wobbled as he stepped forward and introduced himself. He had greasy black hair and pale skin, and was sweating profusely. Nerves? He gave Joanna a tentative smile showing rather nice, even white teeth and Joanna watched him thoughtfully. Out of the gang he was probably the nicest, the smartest and the one who was the most observant. She smiled at him and he moved back.

Next to him Clint Jones was powerfully built, stocky, around five foot eight. He gave a tight-lipped smile and a nod as he spoke his name then stepped backwards in line with his friends. Last of all, apart from Steve Shand, was Shaun Hennessey, the birthday boy, who was short and slim; much slighter than his friends, giving him an almost womanish air.

She organized coffees for the chums, sat them down and invited Gary Pointer to the interview room. He sauntered in behind them, swaggering slightly, cocky and confident. She and Mike sat down and checked his name. 'You are Gary Pointer?'

'Yeah.'

'Let's talk about the night of the thirtieth of November.'

As she'd anticipated Pointer had his answers off pat, ready to trot out in response. She might have to wait a long time for him to make a mistake.

She placed a picture of Kayleigh on the desk, taken on the night of her assault. The IT guys had enhanced the image from the CCTV and combined it with one of the photographs her mother had given them so her face was identifiable. In it she was wearing her silvery skirt.

Pointer's eyes lingered. Then he looked up. 'Yes,' he admitted. 'I did notice her. I had a couple of dances with her. She looked – well –' For the first time his gaze faltered but Joanna knew what he was about to say.

'Before you say anything,' she warned, 'Kayleigh Harrison was fourteen years old.' Pointer blew out a relieved breath and again Joanna read between the lines.

A narrow escape.

'Go on,' she prompted. 'At what time were you dancing with her?'

Pointer swallowed. 'Some time in the evening,' he claimed. 'Late-ish, perhaps around midnight I had a couple of dances with her but she was pissed. Well pissed. She was staggerin' around, talking a load of crap. It wasn't any fun any more. She didn't look sexy. She just kept fallin' around.' He made an expression of disgust. 'She was makin' a right tit of herself. Chuckin' herself at any bloke within twenty yards.'

Joanna frowned. She was getting a picture and it was an unpleasant one.

'What you're saying,' she said slowly, 'is that she was making herself look,' she chose the word delicately, 'available?'

Pointer nodded and looked away.

'So did you rape her?' Joanna asked the question very quietly, almost slipping it into the conversation. Pointer jerked. Their eyes locked. He was the first to look away.

'No,' he said, shaking his head. 'No, I didn't. I couldn't – do that. I just didn't fancy her. She could have stripped right off and lain on the floor. She wasn't turning me on.'

'She turned someone on.'

'It wasn't me.'

Joanna leaned back in her chair and regarded him from underneath lowered lids. By her side, Korpanski was sitting motionless. And although she wasn't looking at him directly she knew he would be staring Gary Pointer out. She looked at Pointer's regular features, 'honest' brown eyes. And even though all her police instincts were screaming at her not to be taken in by him she believed his story. This, she was convinced, was the truth.

But she was aware that she needed to direct the conversation towards the girl who was now missing. 'A few more questions,' she said casually. 'Do you ever go to a nightclub called Lymeys? It's in Newcastle-under-Lyme.'

'I've been there once or twice.' Now Pointer looked uncomfortable. Something had happened there that he was not quite so sure about.

'Were you there on the eleventh of May? It was a Tuesday,' she added helpfully.

Pointer stared. 'I haven't a clue,' he said. 'It's ages ago.'

'You might remember because a girl was raped and left to die outside the club that night,' Joanna said quietly.

Interestingly this made Pointer angry. He put his hands on the table, palms down, pressing on the wood. 'No,' he said firmly and deliberately. 'I don't think I *was* there that night and if I had been I wouldn't have had anything to do with anything like that. All right?'

Joanna smiled at him, trying to ignore the niggle of triumph that she had succeeded in rattling his cage. 'Thank you, Gary. Now, then. You might have heard that a girl who was last seen at Patches on Friday night has vanished.'

He nodded. 'Yeah,' he said. 'I've heard.'

'Were you at Patches on Friday night, Gary?'

Pointer looked from her to Korpanski. 'Yeah,' he admitted.

Right next to the photograph of Kayleigh Harrison Joanna flipped down the picture of Molly Carraway, smiling into the camera lens. The photograph of Molly had an effect on Gary Pointer. He looked down at it almost sentimentally.

'This is the girl, Gary. Her name is Molly Carraway. She's fifteen years old. Do you know her?'

He nodded.

'Well?'

Pointer licked dry lips. 'I've seen her around.'

'Gone out with her, had a dance, had sex?'

Pointer looked distinctly nervous now. 'I've danced with her,' he said carefully. 'I've had a few drinks with her. I've not had sex with her. She's just a schoolgirl.'

'She's been missing since some time after midnight Friday night,' Korpanski put in deliberately. 'Do you know where she is?'

Pointer shook his head.

'Let me put it another way,' Joanna said, resting her elbows on the desk so she could look straight into Pointer's transparent eyes. 'Do you know where she *might* be?'

'Not a clue.' Pointer shifted in his seat. 'Sorry. I wish I could help. She looks like a nice kid.'

'OK,' Joanna said. 'Thank you. You're free to go.'

Pointer hesitated as though he couldn't believe his luck.

'You can leave the station,' Joanna said and he bolted.

Next in line was Andrew Downey, entering carefully, as though he was worried the room might be booby-trapped. He was blinking behind large spectacles, his upper lip beaded with sweat. The armpits of his shirt held rings of moisture. He seemed very uneasy, possibly even a little frightened or simply intimidated by a police interrogation.

She'd get more out of him if he was at his ease; his guard and defences down. 'Sit down,' she invited and decided to open the

interview with a friendly 'chat'. Then she confirmed his name
and address and launched in.

'You married?'

Downey snickered and shook his head.

'A partner?'

A jerky nod.

'Male? Female?'

The way she'd phrased the question succeeded. It put Downey
at his ease. 'Male,' he muttered.

Fine. They'd got that out the way. Joanna shot Korpanski a
warning look which he pretended not to notice, gazing around
him with an assumed look of innocence.

Again Joanna produced the photos of Kayleigh – and then
Molly.

Now Downey was 'outed' he was much more at his ease. He
settled back in his chair, legs splayed, stomach overhanging
precariously as though about to drop to his knees. 'I did notice
Kayleigh,' he said easily, 'and guessed she was pretty young.
She was also very drunk.'

Joanna realized that, being gay, Downey would look at the
girls more objectively than the straight men in the club. She
would get more out of him. She leaned in. 'Who was she with
when you saw her?'

'Just about everybody in the entire club,' he said, 'but I did
see her talking and accepting a drink from a tall, thin guy that
I didn't know.' He frowned. 'I don't think I'd seen him at the
club before. He looked a lot older than her.'

Downey was a boon. Not only objective but also observant.

'What sort of age?'

'Forties.'

'Did you hear him speak?'

Downey shook his head.

'Did she call him a name?'

'She called him something.' Downey frowned. 'I didn't hear.'
He grinned. 'Have you any idea how noisy these places are?'

Joanna returned the grin and nodded. 'I know,' she said.

'They seemed to be pally enough.'

'Was he buying her drinks?'

'I think so. I saw him up at the bar, buying a couple of drinks.

I guess they were for her. You know what it's like in a club; disjointed. Lots going on. You don't really watch anyone in particular.'

'What sort of time was this?'

'Early on in the evening – before she got really pissed and started flinging herself around the place. She was relatively sober, just –' He fished around for the word. 'Normal.'

Joanna nodded. It was a fair description.

Next she produced the photograph of Danielle. 'This girl died outside a nightclub called Lymeys in Newcastle-under-Lyme, last May,' she said. 'Do you know anything about it?'

Downey shook his head. 'I never go there,' he said. 'If I'm out in Newcastle I would avoid Lymeys. It's not a good place for gays. If I go out in Newcastle I go to the gay bars.'

'OK.'

Finally she slapped the picture of Molly Carraway on the desk. 'What about this girl, Andrew?'

Downey looked up, his eyes troubled. 'This is the girl who's missing, isn't it?'

'Yes.'

'I wasn't at the club on Friday,' he said. 'My partner and I had a few mates round for dinner.' He smiled: a fat, happy, contented smile. 'We really like cooking. We did a fish pie and got some wine in. Had a great night.'

'OK, thanks.'

But Downey hadn't finished. 'I didn't see her then,' he said, fingering the picture, 'but I've seen her at the club other times, with her friend, a blonde girl. They're pretty popular.'

'With anyone in particular?'

'No. They just seem to be out to enjoy themselves: dancing, having fun, laughing.' He hesitated. 'I wonder what's happened to her.'

Korpanski answered for them both. 'So do we,' he said.

Clint Jones swaggered in and dropped into the chair, eyeing them with a bold, full-on stare. Like Korpanski, Jones was someone who 'worked out'. He pushed up the sleeves of his sweatshirt, displaying bulging biceps decorated with Chinese writing tattoos, and met their eyes without flinching. His

confident grin challenged them to a match. He'd had a dance
– or two – with Kayleigh, early on in the evening, he admitted.
He'd realized she was young – very young. Not his type. He
liked *women*. The way he spoke the word accompanied by
curving out a full shape with his hands together with the
appraising look he gave her made Joanna feel nauseous. He
was, she decided, probably the most boorish of the birthday
boys.

He denied having been at Lymeys the night Danielle Brixton
had been abducted, said he never went there but admitted he had
been at Patches on Friday night. 'Where else is there to go in
Leek?' He made a pretence of looking at Molly's photograph
then looked up, all innocence. 'Sorry,' he said shortly, 'I don't
remember her.'

'She was wearing a very short red dress with shoestring straps
and reindeer antlers.'

Jones simply pursed his lips and said again: 'Sorry.' Then he
grinned. 'I think I'd have remembered someone dressed like that.'

She gave him another chance. 'Maybe you've noticed her on
other occasions?'

Jones's eyes scanned the picture. 'No,' he said, 'can't say that
I have.'

When he'd gone Joanna turned to Mike. 'I can only think of
one reason why Jones would lie about noticing Molly and it sure
as hell isn't because he doesn't notice women.'

Korpanski nodded.

'She was pretty, with a good figure; extrovert, friendly. We'll
just have to delve a little deeper into our friend, Clint. See what's
so important that he can't even admit to noticing Molly. Take
another look at the CCTV. I could have sworn I saw him dancing
with her.'

'He doesn't fit Kayleigh's description,' Korpanski pointed out.

'True. But how reliable a witness is she? We have more than
one witness who's saying she wasn't just drunk. She was blind
drunk.' She looked at Mike. 'Blind drunk,' she repeated.

Korpanski shrugged. 'But as you keep saying, Jo, she's all
we've got.'

'Not all,' Joanna said, studying the wood grain on the desk.
'There's Clara. I'm sure she could give us more than she has.'

She gathered up the photographs again. 'And now all we have left is Shaun Hennessey, the birthday boy.'

Korpanski gave a yawn and stretched his arms up. 'This,' he said, 'is getting boring and I don't think it's getting us any nearer finding Molly.'

Joanna scowled. 'We don't know yet, Mike. We're learning things all the time. Anyway,' she challenged, 'you're giving me an idea of another direction, Mike, and I'll be happy to follow it. It's OK saying we're getting no closer finding Molly but how else do we go about it? I don't need to remind you. We have no leads and a very unreliable witness.'

Korpanski's face clouded. 'Maybe we never will find her.'

'Oh, don't be gloomy,' she appealed. 'If we don't find her it won't be for want of trying or giving up because we're disheartened. My point is, Mike, that Kayleigh is our best and only lead.'

'She was not only blind drunk but she's a little liar,' Korpanski protested. 'You can't believe a word she says.'

Joanna smiled at him. She loved it when he got angry. 'I'll let you into a little secret,' she said. 'I don't *believe* Kayleigh. At least – her story is not *entirely* true. But neither is it entirely *untrue*. The trick is to spot which are the lies and which the truth. And if she's lying, why?'

'Force of habit,' Korpanski responded grumpily.

'Well, we may as well see what Hennessey's got to say then pursue our other leads.'

'Which are?'

'Kayleigh's father; Kayleigh's stepfather. I want to speak to Clara again and her parents.' Her face changed. 'Then I shall have to call on Molly's parents. I'm not looking forward to that.'

Hennessey looked nervous and almost stumbled as he entered the interview room. Apart from the fact that he confessed to having been at Patches on both the nights in question and even at Lymeys on the night that Danielle had died, he didn't have a lot to add. When Joanna expressed surprise that he remembered a date so far back he'd looked uneasy. 'Well, you remember something like that, don't you?'

'I suppose you would.' She studied Hennessey more carefully

after that. The birthday he had recently celebrated had been his thirtieth. He looked much younger. Just a boy, really. She went through the same questions and got a mixture of the others' answers. Yes, he'd noticed Kayleigh in her silver skirt; yes, he'd 'fooled around' with her; no, he hadn't really noticed her with anyone in particular. Yes, he'd seen Molly Carraway on Friday and had noticed her before at the club and Clara, whom he'd had a bit of a crush on, and had asked out on one occasion. 'So did you go out?' Joanna asked curiously.

His face dropped then. 'No. She acted like she was too good for me,' he said. He dropped his eyes but not before Joanna had seen and interpreted the flash of anger that lit up his face and changed his features. She watched him, still curiously. When he was angry he looked like a completely different person. The only really surprising turn came when she asked him whether he had seen Kayleigh on the Tuesday night she had been assaulted. He leered back, 'Who could miss her? Hardly any skirt. No knickers.'

'How did you know?'

'She was on show, I can tell you.'

'Did you have sex with her?'

'Little slapper like that? I don't think so.'

Joanna got angry then. 'I wasn't asking you whether you *thought* so,' she snapped, 'I was asking you whether you *did*.'

'No.'

'And you're engaged.'

'I've already told you – I'm getting married in April.'

'Congratulations,' she said sarcastically.

Joanna was glad to see the birthday boys go. She now needed to analyse their statements and work out whether or not they had contributed anything helpful. Surely one of them had said something useful?

Korpanski was watching her, understanding both her moods and her thought processes and realizing that his irascible, unpredictable but always loyal colleague needed time to think . . .

And think.

But when she looked up he understood that she was still puzzling. 'Where the hell is Molly?' she asked, suddenly unbearably frustrated.

Korpanski shrugged.

'Is she dead or is she alive?'

Again he shrugged.

She dropped her face into her hands. 'Mike,' she appealed, 'this is hopeless. I wouldn't mind,' she began, 'if I had one single decent lead to go on. Things we can work with. A name, some DNA, some forensic evidence, a car number plate. A sighting. Not this big black piece of nothing.' Her shoulders dropped and she looked up and caught the concern in his dark eyes. I know it's not rational but I don't want to walk up the aisle in a little over three weeks' time with uncertainty over a girl's life and an unsolved rape at my back. I don't want to come back from my honeymoon –' she almost managed a smile – 'whatever part of the world it is in – to stare back into that void, to see those parents' empty, hollow grief. I couldn't bear it. Not to know is the worst thing. And we haven't got a fucking clue.'

In a sudden squall of emotion she thumped her fist on the desk, causing a few of the marauding officers to turn around in surprise, wondering if they were about to witness 'a scene' between the two colleagues – however close their reputation was reputed to be. They collectively held their breath.

But they were in for a disappointment. Korpanski's hand rested on her shoulder. 'Keep heart, Jo,' he said awkwardly. 'Don't lose your fighting spirit.'

She managed a segment more of a smile. 'I'll try not to. But it's Kayleigh who holds the key and I strongly suspect she's not going to swing the door open for us. She may have her reasons or she might simply find it as easy to lie as to tell the truth. We don't know and even clever police work might not winkle the truth out of her.'

When Korpanski merely fixed her with a stare she pursued the point, adding softly: 'What we have to work out is what's she got to gain by keeping mum?'

SIXTEEN

Monday, 6 December. 5.30 p.m.

The visit to Molly's parents was one of the hardest things Joanna had had to do. She could have requested a junior officer to call in but she knew it would have been cowardly. It wasn't her way. She was the senior investigating officer. It would win her no respect and set a poor example to her team to have delegated this task. In the future they would have to learn how to deal with difficult situations; the grief of families and the anger against the police force who were failing to solve a crime, convict a criminal, obtain what they considered a fair sentence. But this was no learning exercise. She could only hope that the lull in the investigation would prove to be the calm before a squall; the motionless doldrums before the wind took their sails and they found out what had really happened to Molly Carraway.

She found Beth and Philip Carraway quietly dignified with tightly reined in emotions. They sat together, motionless, on the sofa while she tried to convince them that the investigating team had had a productive day. It didn't fool either of them; least of all her. And yet. And yet. She couldn't tell them but those last interviews had unearthed something. They simply listened as she said her piece, their eyes numb.

Philip Carraway set his mouth tightly against any display of grief. 'Is there anything *we* can do, Inspector?'

'Not really. Sit tight. Let me know if you remember anything that might have some significance.'

She didn't even bother adding, *And let me know if you hear from your daughter.*

'What sort of thing?' He was still being polite.

'Any hint of a relationship you recall, any ideas you might have. Have you checked all her friends and family?'

'Yes, yes,' Carraway said impatiently. 'Of course we have. But even if we hadn't they would have rung.'

'Her mobile?'

'Off. Straight to answerphone.' He was sounding angrier now. Joanna looked at him in surprise. She had assumed the emotion they had been reining in so tightly was grief, anxiety, desperation, even. But now she looked at them closer she understood that there was another component. They were still angry with their daughter for her deception.

Molly's parents looked at each other. This time it was Beth Carraway who spoke. She cleared her throat first. 'Inspector,' she said, in her soft voice, 'we don't know that we can help you.'

She dabbed her eyes with a tissue while Joanna waited for her to explain. 'You see –' She shot a look at her husband. 'We've been wondering,' she almost whispered, 'whether we really knew Molly at all.' She made an attempt to explain and Joanna wondered what on earth was coming next. But even she was unprepared for the bombshell. 'We thought she was serious,' Beth continued, 'about going to university, concentrating on her studies and work. Now we find that she was lying to us all the time. Clara tells me that they were going out a couple of times a week, to that horrible club. We thought she was spending time with Clara, studying. Her grades at school were nothing like as good as she told us. And she didn't give us the letter about the latest parent-teacher meeting in the middle of November. We're finding out, Inspector, that Molly, our daughter, was deceitful. We're finding that almost as hard to come to terms with as her disappearance.' Beth's eyes were pale blue and met Joanna's with a look of complete confusion and hurt. 'We gave her everything,' she said, echoing the cries of so many middle-class parents. 'Every advantage. She had a stable and comfortable home life, a private education. Everything.'

Joanna could hardly believe her ears. Was this another, new manifestation of grief? So she found herself in the bizarre situation of defending the missing girl. 'Molly's just a normal, average teenager,' she said. 'I wouldn't think too badly of her. She's not the first to lead her parents up the garden path.'

Besides, she thought, feeling the unreality of the situation, *she's probably dead. No university. No swotting, no parent/teachers' meeting; just a bloody funeral.*

That was when Philip Carraway lost it and Joanna saw inside the life Molly Carraway must have led. 'Up the garden path?' he exclaimed furiously. 'Up the garden path? What you mean, Inspector, is that our daughter was a liar. A liar,' he almost screamed. Out of the corner of her eye Joanna marvelled that Beth Carraway's hand was stealing *into* her husband's. She obviously condoned his outburst of righteous indignation. Carraway's eyes were bulging. 'Had my daughter been honest,' he said, 'she would be here, with us. And you, Detective Inspector Joanna Piercy, would not.' There was real venom in his voice.

Aghast, Joanna sat very still, now pondering a new angle. Was this an extreme manifestation of Philip Carraway's grief and worry? Or was it something else? Had Molly Carraway so disappointed her parents that . . .?

It seemed incredible. And yet.

Joanna left with a heavy heart and a sick misgiving after giving them her mobile phone number. Her mind was frantically disturbed, tracking outwards furiously, in a new and terrible direction. Had she been barking up the wrong tree? Should she have looked a little closer to home for the missing girl? Were the three cases all part of the same picture – or not?

She looked at her watch. It was seven o'clock. Korpanski would be back home. She was tempted to drop by his house and talk this over with him but Fran Korpanski would not welcome her. She had resented Joanna from the first and now had a new reason for hating her. Joanna had put her husband's life in danger.

She drove home through a space invaders' display of swirling snowflakes which gave her the illusion she was travelling through time itself. Two teenage girls, both now labelled 'liars' by their parents. No, in the case of Kayleigh, only one parent. So what did her stepfather and natural father think of her? She hadn't pursued this angle of enquiry perhaps as much as she should. She rang the station from her car phone and asked them to fix up an interview with Neil Bretby on the following day and made a note to ask Hesketh-Brown if he was any nearer tracking down Peter Harrison. While they had no leads on Molly she may as well put the heat on Kayleigh. And what about Danielle? she wondered. What would she have been able to contribute to the investigation had she lived?

It was late when she finally drew up outside Waterfall Cottage, parked and walked up the path. Eloise's car was, hooray, gone. Matthew had left the curtains open though she had warned him about this on numerous occasions. 'You're a sitting target,' she'd said but he'd merely laughed. 'Who on earth would want to target me, Jo? We're in the Staffordshire moorlands, not the middle of Johannesburg. It's safe enough out here.'

The trouble was that in spite of his work as a forensic pathologist she and Matthew inhabited different worlds. Hers was populated by thieves and liars, cheats and people who believed the law did not apply to them so they could do what they liked: rape, torture, steal and kill. Most of Matthew's post mortems were on people who had died in their beds of natural causes. Even he rarely met the victims of crime and *never* talked to their damaged families. Like most pathologists much of Matthew's day was spent peering down a microscope at tissue samples.

She peeped in through the window and smiled. While he might pretend to be watching BBC *News 24*, in reality he was lying stretched out across the sofa fast asleep, his breathing peaceful and regular. She let herself in quietly and woke him with a kiss. For just a moment he looked sleepy and confused, his blond hair tousled like a child's. She felt overwhelming affection for him and relief that they were again alone. His face broke into a smile as he fed her the usual line. 'I wasn't asleep,' he said, just as she'd guessed he would. 'I was just dozing until you came home.'

'I bet,' she challenged, then gave him another kiss – on the mouth this time, feeling warm with affection when, without warning, a thunderbolt hit her and she spoke her truth without thinking. 'I wish we didn't have to go through all that stuff,' she said, settling down beside him.

Matthew sat up. 'What do you mean, *all that stuff*?' There was a razor edge to his voice which should have warned her.

'Oh, you know,' she said. 'The wedding. I wish we could just go on as we are. Why can't we?'

He was silent and still and she knew, too late, that she'd upset him – again. 'I'm sorry,' she said and clumsily tried to rectify the situation. 'What I mean is – the *actual* wedding. Just that, Matthew.' She reached out for his hand. 'I don't mean I don't want to be married. It just seems such a lot of palaver for basically nothing different. Know what I mean?'

'Not sure I do, Jo,' he answered slowly. 'Not – quite – sure.'

She could think of nothing that would heal the situation, so kept quiet.

Matthew sought neutral ground. 'Any news about the missing girl?'

She shook her head. 'Though I had a rather unpleasant insight into Molly Carraway's home life today.' She related the conversation the Carraways had had with her.

Matthew's eyebrows rose a fraction.

'Now I'm wondering whether she's taken off, perhaps with a boyfriend.'

'Surely her friend, whats-her-name, Clara, would know if Molly had had a boyfriend?'

'Mmm. Not necessarily. I'm beginning to realize that Molly could be quite cleverly secretive. A devious little thing, really. Maybe I should go into the school and speak to some of her classmates. What do you think, Matt?'

'The school won't like that. It's not the best of publicity for an independent, having the police in.'

'Maybe. But if it helps us find out what's happened to her it's worth ruffling a few feathers.'

Matthew smiled. Then his face changed. 'So what's bothering you?'

'The father,' she said simply. 'He was so – unforgiving. So – censorious, so prepared to reject his own daughter because she told a lie about where she was going. She'd have told her parents the truth if she could have, I'm sure.'

'And?'

Now she could voice her concern. 'What if he found out about the lies, followed her to Patches, laid in wait outside and then . . . took her?'

'That's a terrible accusation, Jo.'

'I'm not making an accusation at all,' she said. 'I'm just going over things. Exploring possibilities.'

'But what could Philip Carraway have had to do with the other girls?'

'Mm,' she said. 'See what you mean. Nothing.'

She sneaked a glance at him, realized she had all his attention, and risked it. 'Matthew,' she wheedled, 'you did the post mortem on Danielle Brixton?'

'Yes.'

'Can I ask you something about it?'

'Anything you like,' he said indulgently, stretching his legs out in front of him and giving her a smile that warmed her right through.

'Did she need to die?'

'Sorry?'

'If she had had medical treatment is it possible she would have lived?'

'Oh, yes,' he said. 'Undoubtedly. Hospital, antibiotics, oxygen; all a few hours earlier. She could have made it. She was young and healthy.'

'So, in a way, it was murder.'

'Well, manslaughter – though you probably wouldn't get it past the CPS.'

'Mmm. Was she a virgin?'

'It's hard to tell these days; probably not.'

Their conversation was interrupted by the telephone's intrusive and insistent ring. Joanna was tempted to leave it but Matthew always worried it might be Eloise. Besides, he 'remembered' when he was almost picking up the receiver that her mother had instructed him that Joanna call back 'the very minute' she got home. He handed her the phone with a rueful grin.

It was her mother. A one-sided conversation followed: about Lara who was still vacillating about whether she wanted to be a bridesmaid at all, about long lost relatives, a ticking off for concentrating so hard on work when there was still so much to do before the wedding, being so late back when she had a fiancé waiting for her. Give her mother her due, Joanna thought, she could really talk. By the time she had rung off Joanna felt exhausted – and guilt ridden.

Matthew held out his arms. 'I can think of something that'll cheer you up,' he whispered into her ear. 'Close your eyes. Now think blue sky, white sand, hot, sunny, fabulous beaches, surf rolling, white as snow, sea so clear you can see your feet beneath you. Lovely, lovely food, sweet fruit and drinks, all fresh. Keep your eyes shut,' he ordered. 'Keep thinking. Swimming in a sparkling blue sea, underneath a perfect sky with no clouds, diving coral reefs and snorkelling, fish streaming through your fingers if you splay them out, birds of paradise screaming through the trees. Think paperbacks by the pool; think honeymoon. And now you can open your eyes.' His eyes were bright and warm and his smile very broad. He was laughing. And now she was too.

'Oh, Matt,' she said. 'Surely our honeymoon can't hold all that?'

'It had better,' he said, 'or I shall want my money back.' He paused, before adding in a different tone, 'and it's less than four weeks away.'

Tuesday, 7 December. 8.30 a.m.

The day began awkwardly. As soon as she arrived at the station she was summoned by Chief Superintendent Arthur Colclough to 'update' him on the current case.

'How are your investigations going?'

'Slowly, sir.'

'I take it you have some leads?'

She shook her head. 'Not a lot, sir, I'm afraid. I've got ideas and there's a lot that doesn't fit together.'

'You have a girl alive, though, Piercy.'

'Yes, sir, but she's not a very reliable witness.'

'Why not?'

'She's brought apparently spurious allegations against her stepfather and was very drunk at the time of the assault.'

'Any other lines of enquiry?'

'I'm a little uncomfortable about Molly Carraway's parents' attitude towards her frequenting nightclubs.'

'A little uncomfortable doesn't sound a lot to go on, Piercy.'

'No, sir.'

'Anything else?'

'The gang of men who were celebrating the thirtieth birthday would benefit from further scrutiny.'

'Mmm. So what's on the agenda today, then?' he demanded. She explained that she had arranged to meet up with Kayleigh Harrison's stepfather and they were hoping to track down Kayleigh's natural father to try and ascertain how much her stories were to be believed. But as soon as the words were out of her mouth, Colclough frowned. 'Why aren't you concentrating on young Molly Carraway? She's the one who's missing – and getting all the headlines.'

'Because I don't have a lead and I believe that Kayleigh Harrison is capable of leading us to Molly's abductor, sir.'

'You do?'

'Yes, sir.' At one time Colclough would have simply asked for updates and not questioned her integrity. Perhaps, she thought, he had put too much faith in her abilities.

Maybe this was more realistic.

'How are you proposing to proceed, Piercy?'

There was only one way to play this. 'Do you have any suggestions, sir?' she asked innocently.

'Find some more of Molly's friends,' he said. 'Don't just rely on that Clara creature. She might not know everything, you know. Young girls can be very clever,' he finished. 'Clever, indeed. My little Catherine is small but by goodness she's manipulative.' He beamed proudly. 'Typical female.'

'Thank you for your advice.' She responded with a smile. 'I'll work on it.'

Only not today, she thought. *I have other fish to fry.*

'How long until your wedding?'

'A little over three weeks.'

'Hmm. Not long. You don't want to go on your honeymoon leaving loose ends, Piercy.'

'No, sir.'

'Right. Well, it's nice to have had this little chat. Keep me informed, won't you?'

'Yes, sir.'

'Go on, then.' He was practically pushing her out of the door.

She and Mike Korpanski had tracked Neil Bretby down to Stafford where he was now working as a self-employed plumber. As his business premises were basically his home they had arranged to interview him there.

As Mike drove her down through Stone, Joanna related the interview she had had with the Carraways the night before and shared her misgivings about Molly's parents, in particular her father. Korpanski's response was much the same as Matthew's. It couldn't link in with the other two nightclub assaults.

It didn't fit. She knew that – and yet she wasn't quite ready to reject the idea before testing it.

Much to her surprise she liked the look of Bretby. He was a strong-looking fellow with muscular sun-tanned arms, dark hair and a blunt-featured, honest-looking face lit by a ready grin. He was wearing a green sweater with its sleeves pushed up to the elbows, black jeans and Vans.

Joanna revised her preconceptions and wondered even more about Kayleigh. What had really been her objection to this man as her stepfather? Was her mother possibly right? Had her allegations been sparked by jealousy?

She introduced herself and Korpanski. 'In your own words, Mr Bretby, tell me about Kayleigh.'

'Do I have to?' he groaned. Joanna could give only one answer. 'It might help us,' she said. 'You know that Kayleigh was assaulted – *alleged* she was assaulted,' she corrected quickly, 'outside a nightclub in Leek two weeks ago?'

'I'd heard,' he said.

'And now another girl has gone missing from the same nightclub?'

'I heard that too,' he admitted. 'I've kept up with my friends in Leek – apart from Christine,' he added bitterly. 'Things got so bad between us.'

Joanna waited.

And Neil Bretby talked. 'You've no idea how good it was to meet Christine,' he said. 'My first wife and I had divorced a few years back. She'd met someone else – at work and that was that. We'd no children. My first wife was a "career" woman.' He sneered at the words. 'When I met Christine – and Kayleigh – and realized we all got on so well, it sort of wiped the slate clean, made everything all right. It was great,' he finished frankly.

'Really great, at first. I know she drinks a bit now but she was really lovely. Good fun. She tried so hard to make us a happy family. You've no idea.'

'And then?'

'It was when me and Christine got married,' Bretby said. 'Kayleigh changed towards me. I'd been like her friend.' There appeared an honesty and simplicity about him that was appealing – *would* have been to Christine and *should* have been to Kayleigh. If Bretby was to be believed.

Joanna turned to see how Mike was taking this story. He was holding his habitual expression – sceptical.

Bretby was frowning. 'I just don't know why Kayleigh changed and said those things,' he said. 'I've never understood it.'

'I'm sorry,' Joanna continued, 'but I have to ask you this. Is there any truth in the allegations she made?'

Bretby shook his head. 'No,' he said. 'If anything I was trying to be a dad to her. She was desperate for a dad. I thought I could be it but it backfired. And then Christine . . .' He dropped his face into his hands. 'I'd see her looking at me and wondering. I couldn't stand it. She's a lovely girl,' he said. 'She's had a hard life but it hasn't made her bitter. Christine's really sweet-natured.'

Joanna and Mike exchanged glances. This was not a description of the Christine Bretby they knew. The Christine Bretby he saw was a different woman.

'You miss her?' Korpanski asked.

Bretby nodded. 'I'd have her back tomorrow,' he said, 'if I thought it could work. But with Kayleigh there,' he said, 'it won't and I'm not fool enough to think it would.'

'Why did you marry Christine?' Joanna asked curiously.

'I loved her. We wanted children,' Bretby said. 'I really wanted kids of my own.'

Maybe, then, that was the reason for Kayleigh's resentment – a fear of being replaced.

SEVENTEEN

Tuesday, 7 December. 10.55 a.m.

Now there was only Peter Harrison to track down. She rang Johnny Ollerenshaw and after much humming and hawing he produced an address in Fulham and a mobile telephone number.

Harrison answered on the second ring, with a jauntily Cockney, ''Ello?'

Joanna introduced herself and received a wary, 'Ye-ah?' Again there was that upwards, questioning inflection.

'We would like to interview you.'

'What about?' He was sounding wary.

'It's concerning your daughter.'

'My daughter?' Harrison sounded astonished, as though he hadn't even known he'd got one.

'Yes – Kayleigh,' Joanna confirmed.

There was a brief silence before, 'I can't think what you can want to see me about Kayleigh for. I haven't seen her in years. I wouldn't know her if I passed her in the street. What do you want to speak to me about her for? Is she in trouble? What's she done?' His voice held genuine astonishment.

'When *did* you last see her, Mr Harrison?'

'Goodness knows. How old is she?'

'Fourteen.'

'Well, then.' He was quiet for a minute before answering, 'It's probably twelve, thirteen years ago that I last saw her. As I said – I wouldn't know her from Adam. Or do I mean Eve?' Untroubled, he chuckled. 'She's practically a young lady now then, ain't she?' Another pause. 'Although I very much doubt *my* daughter's a young lady. Now that would be a turn up for the books.'

Joanna waited for Harrison to ask what she was ringing him about but curiously he didn't. It was left to her to move the conversation forward. 'Look, Mr Harrison,' she said patiently, 'I really need to speak to you face-to-face.' She glanced at her watch. It was still only eleven. 'We can drive down and meet you later today.'

'Is it so important, Inspector? I can't understand what it can have to do with me. She may be my daughter but I don't know her. I don't know anythin' about her.'

'Please.'

'Yeah, yeah.' Harrison caved in, probably realizing he had no choice. 'All right. If you insist. I can meet you later today. How about somewhere near the Edgware Road? The Travelodge.'

It was about 140 miles. If the motorways were clear they should get there in three hours. They allowed four and arranged to meet at three o'clock, Joanna giving him a mobile contact number in case of delays on the motorway.

Tuesday, 7 December. 3 p.m.

The motorway behaved itself. They even had time to stop for a coffee and at five to three Joanna and Mike were walking through the doorway of the Travelodge on the Edgware Road.

Harrison spotted them straight away and lifted his hand in greeting. He was a tall, slim man who bore more than a passing resemblance to his daughter. He shared Kayleigh's expression, looking at the same time both streetwise and vulnerable. As they drew closer Joanna saw that he also had Kayleigh's cow-brown eyes that changed from warm toffee to cold mud in an instant. And he had his daughter's small, slightly prim mouth. But he differed from Kayleigh in two significant ways. Her crowning glory was her long, shining hair; her father had practically none – and what he did have had been shaved off and replaced with a tattoo, interestingly saying, *Sod 'em all*. The second big difference between father and daughter was Harrison's teeth. Kayleigh had the milky teeth of the young. Her father's were large and yellow. They were predatory or 'wolfish'. In fact, the description Kayleigh had given of her attacker fitted him like a glove. It was, to say the least, disconcerting. Joanna studied him carefully and he was quite well aware of her scrutiny.

She ordered a tray of tea and the three of them sat down

together; she, Korpanski and Peter Harrison, in an unobtrusive corner of the Travelodge.

Initially Harrison was friendly. 'I knew you was cops the second I saw you,' he confided cheerfully. 'Funny how you stick out, ain't it?'

'Yes, funny,' Korpanski echoed, his dark eyes missing nothing as he studied Peter Harrison. Joanna knew he would later be sharing every single thought that passed through his mind. She smothered a smile. She knew perfectly well that her sergeant didn't quite know what to make of Harrison. Yet.

Peter Harrison glanced at them both in turn. 'Now what's all this about my girl?'

Joanna poured them all some tea then took up the questioning. 'You say you haven't seen your daughter since she was one or two?'

Harrison crossed his legs, took a noisy slurp of tea and met their eyes comfortably. 'Not for years. She was a baby when me and her mum split up. I was never really one for marryin'.' He thought for a moment. 'Shouldn't have done it, really.' He gave a brief, cynical laugh. 'Only did it to give the kid a name. It seemed important at the time – don't know why,' he said reflectively, blinking. Then he grinned. 'Probably wouldn't bovver now. Anyway, not long after Kayleigh or Little K,' he smiled, 'or Special K, as we called 'er, was born, I 'opped it back down to the Big Smoke. I can't breathe out there in the countryside. All that mud and stuff. Stinks. Give me good ol' car exhaust any time. And bloody freezin' too, even in the summer. Nah – once a Londoner always a Londoner, that's what I say.'

Joanna watched him. Harrison didn't seem to be a bad bloke, just not the marrying, fatherly kind. A little like her own father, who had not done responsibility, either. And very unlike Matthew Levin, who almost seemed to need it.

Harrison was watching her. 'So what's 'appened to 'er, then?'

Joanna didn't answer the question straight away but chose a circuitous route. 'You knew that her mother had remarried?'

'Yeah. I was glad about that. Poor old Christine. She was a romantic. Wanted flowers and chocolate and stuff.'

'Yes,' Joanna agreed, thinking of the Klimt on Christine's wall.

'I was sorry it broke up,' Harrison added frankly.

'You heard about that?'

'Yeah. Me and Johnny 'ave kept in touch.' Harrison grinned. ''E keeps me informed.'

'What's your opinion of the *reason* they broke up?' Joanna asked delicately.

'What – that Christine's new bloke touched up my little daughter? Look,' he said earnestly. 'I don't know the bloke. Right? I don't know my daughter either so I can't really comment, can I?'

Joanna shrugged. It was fair enough but most men would burn if they thought another man had sexually assaulted their teenage daughter. Even if they had little to do with that daughter. Obviously Harrison had no paternal feelings for Kayleigh at all.

She felt a tinge of pity for the girl and scrutinized Harrison's face. No feelings? And yet . . . *something* was there. She just couldn't work out what it was.

Harrison drew in a deep breath. 'You still haven't told me what Kayleigh's been up to.'

'She has made an allegation that she was sexually assaulted outside Patches nightclub on the night of November thirtieth,' Joanna said baldly. 'She was found on the following morning, in the car park. It was snowing and she was suffering from hypothermia.'

'Oh my –' Harrison looked genuinely shocked.

'She was lucky to survive,' Joanna said, adding, for effect: 'the doctors said that if she hadn't been found she would have been dead in an hour.'

'Poor little thing,' was Harrison's response. But it struck Joanna that his statement was no more impassioned than he would have voiced over any female. Not especially his daughter.

'You keep in touch with your Leek friends?'

'No, not really. Only Ollerenshaw.' Harrison spoke casually but his eyes flickered away as he spoke. Together with Kayleigh's description of her attacker, which was so obviously a description of her father, it alerted Joanna. She shot Korpanski a swift look and leaned forward, asking silkily, 'When *did* you last see your old pal Ollerenshaw?'

'Couldn't tell you exactly.' His response struck Joanna as deliberately vague.

So she pursued it. 'In the last six months?'

Harrison looked uncomfortable now. 'Possibly.' This was at variance with Ollerenshaw's statement.

'In Leek?'

Harrison looked even more uncomfortable. He shuffled his feet then looked up. 'I was there about a week ago,' he finally admitted.

'Let me get this straight, Mr Harrison,' Joanna said very slowly and deliberately, beginning at last to see a glimmer of light. 'You were in Leek on November thirtieth, weren't you?'

Harrison nodded.

And now the soft breeze of the truth was blowing and the fog was lifting. 'You went to Patches, didn't you?'

Harrison paled and looked as though he might choke. Joanna looked at Mike and gave a tiny, triumphant nod as she asked her next question. 'Do you own a leather bomber jacket, Mr Harrison?'

'No.' He chewed his lip then confessed. 'Yes.'

'You went to Patches alone, or with someone?'

'On my own.' Harrison nodded stiffly, as though he knew all further questions were going to lead to a place he had no wish to visit.

'You danced with some of the girls there; had a drink?' Joanna spoke chummily. She gave her quarry an easy smile. But her glance was predatory, her eyes glued to Harrison's face as his shoulders dropped, defeated.

She flipped two photographs on to the coffee table. 'Did you dance with either of these girls on that night?'

Harrison's eyes glided over the two photographs before he looked up, frowning. 'This is Kayleigh, ain't it?'

Joanna nodded. 'Did you see Kayleigh on that night?'

Harrison shifted uncomfortably and tried to lie. 'Like I said, Inspector, I wouldn't have known my daughter from – well, Eve.' He tried the smile again.

Harrison's story was full of itty bitty holes. It didn't take a trained detective to spot them. 'But you recognized the picture of your daughter now?'

Finally Harrison admitted it. 'Yeah,' he said.

Joanna indicated the second photograph. 'And these girls?' She flipped to the picture of Molly Carraway, then Clara Williams and lastly Danielle Brixton.

Harrison's face was a blank. He looked up at Joanna, then at Korpanski and shook his head. 'No. I don't know these other girls. Who are they?' Harrison risked the lamest of jokes. 'Not more daughters I don't know about?'

'This girl's name is Molly Carraway. She's missing.'

'Never heard of her.' Harrison's voice was confident.

'She's a schoolgirl who went missing from Patches last Friday night and hasn't been seen since.'

Harrison still held on to his jauntiness. 'Can't 'elp you there, Inspector. Sorry.' He grinned.

'This girl is Clara: her friend who was the last person to see her.'

Harrison nodded. 'Pretty little thing, ain't she?'

'She is. And this . . .' Joanna flipped the last photograph down on the table, 'is Danielle Brixton. She was raped and left to die outside a nightclub in Newcastle-under-Lyme back in May.'

'Seems like crime's worse up there than down here,' was Harrison's comment.

Joanna couldn't be bothered to pursue this subject. 'It would seem so.'

Korpanski took over the questioning. 'Have you been in Leek *since* the night of November thirtieth?'

Harrison shook his head.

'You weren't there last Friday?'

Harrison looked relieved and exhaled loudly. 'I weren't anywhere near Leek last Friday,' he said. 'I was down here at a restaurant on the Fulham Road, in full public view.'

'Can you give us the name of the person or persons you were with?'

Harrison was patently on safe ground now. He visibly relaxed and nodded quite comfortably, even leaning back in his chair and resting his big hands on his stomach. 'Of course I can. There was a whole bunch of us.'

'But you were in Leek and at Patches the night your daughter was assaulted?'

Harrison looked paralysed. He tried to say he hadn't known it, but the words stuck. Joanna knew she would be better served by doing this properly, with legal representation present, or at least the offer of it.

The words, when she uttered them, were an absolute inevitability. 'We're going to have to bring you in for questioning, I'm afraid.'

Harrison nodded, resigned. But he hadn't quite lost his fighting spirit. 'I'm not under arrest, am I?'

'No. Not at the moment.'

'I can come up to Leek in the morning,' he conceded, 'with my solicitor.'

Again Joanna nodded, steadily, holding back the feeling of triumph which was seeping through her. She had to remind herself she was not there yet.

'In that case you're free to go now, Mr Harrison,' she said. 'But if you wouldn't mind coming to Leek police station tomorrow and making a statement – under caution?'

Harrison nodded.

'What did you make of that, Mike?' They were safely back in the car, had taken the North Circular and were heading back up the motorway.

'I don't know.' Korpanski's answer was predictably non-committal.

Joanna was frowning. 'I can't work out what's going on,' she said. 'I'd really like to speak to Kayleigh and her father at the same time.' She turned in her seat to look at Korpanski's profile; the thick neck, the bullish expression, 'Mike,' she said tentatively, 'the word collusion seems to pop up in my mind. What's going on?'

'Collusion?'

'Yes.' Joanna slowly nodded. 'Between Kayleigh and her father. They met that night. He recognized her photograph.'

'So what's it got to do with Molly, then? Is it going to lead to her?'

'I don't know. There's some connection. Perhaps – perhaps not. But –'

'What?' Korpanski grunted.

'Nothing. A stupid thought.'

Korpanski grinned and swerved to avoid a lorry which had swung out after one swift flash of his indicator. 'Bastard,' he grunted. Then: 'How stupid?'

'I wonder if the crimes really are – no; it is a stupid thought.'

She fell silent then but her mind was skipping around the odd assortment of half facts she had so far.

It was a long, slow journey back to Leek and she and Korpanski were tired when they turned into the police station. 'Sure you wouldn't rather drop me off at your house?' Korpanski enquired politely.

'No.' She turned to him. 'I shall want my car in the morning, Mike, but thanks anyway. And I don't want to take you out of your way.'

'All right. See you tomorrow.' He smiled at her. 'At least the snow's held off.'

She managed a smile and held up her index finger. 'One good thing.'

'No. Two,' he said. 'We have found Kayleigh's—'

'Stop right there,' she said softly. 'Right there.'

Matthew was already in bed when she turned in but she was too exhausted to sleep. Molly was still out there. When she closed her eyes she saw the girl's face: laughing, happy, safe.

She punched her pillow and lay back, her arms reaching out to touch Matthew's shoulders as they rose and fell. He murmured something in his sleep.

But instead of her matching his restful, peaceful sleep her dreams were vivid and disturbing.

Little Red Riding Hood was opening the door of the cottage. Someone was sitting up in bed.

'Oh, grandmother, what big teeth you have.'

She knew what the implication was of the encounter between father and daughter.

EIGHTEEN

Wednesday, 8 December. 7.15 a.m.

Another day marked off on the calendar towards zero. She stood very still and stared. Three and a bit weeks before the wedding. It felt like time was running out; life was closing in on her.

She wished it was spring and she could at least enjoy the bike ride through the moorlands, into work. But it would be at least a month after the honeymoon that she would be able to resume her daily cycle ride.

Waiting on her desk were the forensic results on Molly's gold earring. She scanned it through. Just as expected. Molly's blood; Molly's DNA on the tiny piece of tissue caught on the catch. No one else's. She tossed the report aside. It hadn't told her anything she hadn't already guessed.

It hadn't told her how Molly came to *lose* her earring. Had it been torn from her or had it simply got caught in something? Girls lose earrings all the time. Joanna fingered her own pierced ear, half closed her eyes and imagined.

Someone's fingers closing round the hoop. Tearing, fighting, a struggle, pain, a stifled scream; blood, the tinkle of gold as it hit the floor.

She sat up as the obvious hit her. Blood. Earlobes *bleed* profusely. She remembered Matthew telling her so once in one of his little 'tutorials'. 'Earlobes are vascular, Jo. Plenty of blood around.' He'd given one of his bright grins. Matthew knew she was a little – just a little – squeamish. He'd never quite forgotten her puking up in the sink after her first post mortem. And every now and again, when he wanted to score points, he'd remind her.

But she knew *why* the vascularity, to use Matthew's word, of the earlobe was important. Somewhere there was a crime scene and it would be spattered with Molly's blood. She only had to find it. Here there was none.

She rested her chin on her upturned palm, waited for the computer to fire up and stared at the familiar icons, unfocused. Where was Molly? Joanna was cop enough to know that the longer the girl was missing the less likelihood there was of finding her alive. But for her to have vanished so completely from a crowded nightclub? Not even a sighting. How? Joanna gave a cynical grimace. Not even a fake sighting: boarding a plane to Sri Lanka, in a coffee bar in Hanley, waiting for a bus in Uttoxeter. Nothing had turned up. It was almost as though she had never really existed.

Joanna leaned back in her chair and half closed her eyes. It was a terrible thought, that someone could be so obliterated that their fate was never known. Her mind drifted, like a bubble in a light breeze, bobbing around aimlessly, occasionally finding a solid surface but mostly simply bobbing. And then it found a solid surface on which to rest before the bubble burst and she was left with nothing.

It was something Gary Pointer, one of the birthday boys, had said; something about Kayleigh and what she had been saying. Joanna hadn't taken enough notice at the time but now she recalled it.

'*She was talking a load of crap.*'

What sort of crap? What had Pointer been talking about?

How long had he spent 'talking' to her?

With the background din of the club how could he tell what she had been saying?

Unless he had been in the quiet room or outside.

She reached out and picked up the telephone.

She had so many questions buzzing around her head now that she was hardly able to put them in order of priority. But now her mind began to tangle with the anomalies of the case of the three girls and slowly she began to sort out truth from untruth and begin to put them in order of relevance to her task: find Molly.

The telephone rang. 'Am I speaking to Detective Inspector Piercy?' It was a crisp, business-like voice on the other end.

'You are.'

'I am David O'Connor.'

She didn't recognize the name.

'I represent Peter Harrison.'

Ah. Now it was making sense.

'I understand you wish to interview my client?'

'That's correct.'

'And you would like him to attend the police station at Leek?'

'I would. I did speak to him yesterday and he volunteered to attend here today.'

'We can be with you for twelve o'clock.'

She sat up, alert. 'Good,' she said. 'That's fine. I shall look forward to seeing you both. Thank you for your cooperation.'

'My pleasure,' the solicitor said sarcastically.

Korpanski had just walked in when the phone rang for a second time.

Feeling that she had already had her one welcome phone call of today, she answered without enthusiasm. 'Hello, Inspector Piercy here.'

Philip Carraway's voice came down the wire so loudly and angrily that she held the receiver away from her ear. 'Have you any news of my daughter yet?' His voice was ragged. Whatever she had thought, whatever impression Molly's parents had given, this man was suffering.

'I'm sorry. We've nothing definite. We're moving on with our enquiries, Mr Carraway. That's all.' She added the platitude. 'These things take time, you know.'

There was a deep, angry sigh on the other end of the line before he added, brokenly: 'The strain, you know, it's terrible on my wife and myself. We want an answer. We *need* an answer.' Then, with a touch of hysteria: 'We *must have* an answer.' He was close to breaking point.

'We all want an answer, Mr Carraway,' she said quietly. 'I do sympathize with you but you must let us proceed with our enquiries at our own pace.'

The man was beyond politeness. He simply groaned.

'Mr Carraway, just for the record, where were you on Friday night?'

He lost his rag then. There was a long, angry silence on the other end of the phone. All Joanna could hear were his heavy snorts of fury before he exploded. 'I don't believe this. I really don't. So because you've made no headway in the case of my daughter's disappearance you turn on me. Well, it won't work, Inspector. I'm not some drivelling fool that you can intimidate, you know. I am a professional, intelligent man and I know a bodged case when I see one. And don't think you can falsify evidence against me. I'm up to you.'

Quite calmly Joanna repeated the question. 'Where were you on Friday night, Mr Carraway? It's just for the record,' she repeated.

'I was at home here with my wife.'

Even Joanna didn't quite have the nerve to ask whether his wife would be happy to verify this but she didn't need to. Beth Carraway came on the line, speaking quietly and with dignity. 'My husband was with me on Friday,' she said, in a low voice, 'all evening. We listened to the play on Radio Four until ten and then went to bed.'

'Thank you,' Joanna responded. 'I'll be in touch as soon as I hear anything.'

As she put the phone down she reflected that anger was an effective cure for grief.

After a moment's thought, Joanna checked her watch. Break time in school. She dialled a mobile number. 'Clara, I'm going to want to talk to you about Molly again, I'm afraid. Yes, yes. Down at the station. I want to ask you some questions.'

The girl was naturally wary and neither agreed to attend nor disagreed. Instead she said she'd ring her mother. Two minutes later Rosa Williams's steady voice came down the line. 'What do you want to talk to my daughter about?'

The truth was that Joanna didn't really have a clue, except that Clara was the only link she had to Molly. 'I simply want to clarify a few details; that's all.'

'What time do you want us to come?'

That was when the pinprick of an idea gave Joanna hope. 'Twelve o'clock?'

'We'll see you then. I'll get her from school.' Clara's mother was polite but distant. The truth was, Joanna guessed, that she wanted her daughter to have as little to do with the police as possible. Damage limitation.

Korpanski eyed her. 'You're up to something, Jo.'

She nodded. 'Oh, yes.'

'And knowing you you're not going to tell me, are you?'

She simply smiled before adding: 'I don't *really* know what I'm up to, Mike. That's why I can't share it with you. I just know I'm heading in the right direction.'

He grinned across the room at her. 'Have I ever told you you're the most annoying person to work with?'

'Frequently.'

'That's all right, then.'

She picked up the phone again, dialled another number. Unlike Clara, she was pretty sure Kayleigh Harrison wouldn't be at school. She was right. It was Kayleigh who picked up the phone. 'Hello, Kayleigh. Is your mother in?'

Christine came on the line and Joanna asked her to attend the police station at twelve thirty, with her daughter. Naturally neither of them seemed exactly enthusiastic but they agreed.

'And so, Mike,' she said, 'the trap is set.'

A briefing had been planned for nine thirty. There was a lot to get through – a mountain of paperwork, running through the results of interviews, mobile phone print-outs, CCTV footage. So much detail it threatened to swamp them. The job of a senior investigating officer needed someone with a clear head; someone able to take an overview but at times with so much extraneous evidence it could be hard.

Clara and her mother were the first to arrive. 'Is there any news of Molly?' Clara's mother's face held a mixture of concern and frustration.

Joanna shook her head. 'Not a word.'

'Her poor parents. It must be awful for them.'

'Yes.' Joanna could only agree. She turned her attention on Clara, who was looking pale and frightened. Joanna guessed she wished she'd never befriended Molly Carraway. 'Did you wear coats to go out, Clara?'

As expected, after a quick glance at her mother the girl shook her head. 'You have to queue up for ages for a coat and they charge a fiver,' she said, adding: 'It's a rip-off but if you just leave it around someone'll nick it for sure. We'd rather be a bit cold. But what's that got to with Moll?'

'Just gathering facts,' Joanna said kindly. 'I'd like you to run through the CCTV footage of that last evening with Molly. We've edited the bits with her in. It might jog your memory,' she said, in answer to the girl's enquiring glance. 'Look over them very carefully and see if there's anyone you particularly recognize.'

'OK.' Clara nodded. She and her mother sat, motionless, saying nothing, eyes fixed on the screen. Joanna stood behind them, observing their body language. Sometimes a psychology degree came in very useful. Clara's mother sat a little apart from her daughter. No friendly arm around her shoulders. No hug or reassurance. Rosa Williams was annoyed with her daughter.

The bit came when Molly was talking to someone silhouetted against a lit hallway. She was leaning in towards him, her body language suggesting she found him attractive. Clara's head whisked around.

'You know him?'

'I think I do,' she said dubiously. 'I think I've seen him talking to Molly before. I think she already knew him.' It was as though the realization had just hit her. *Thump.*

'Thank you.'

Joanna and Mike peered at the picture then gave up. It was Korpanski who voiced both their opinions. 'It could be anyone, Jo. You couldn't get an ID on that.'

Joanna was forced to agree. But: 'He's around six foot tall, of slim build. He has dark hair, is wearing light coloured trainers, a dark jacket, jeans.' She peered closer. 'He has his right hand in his pocket. Face turned away so features unidentifiable.' She looked at her sergeant. 'We don't have nothing, Mike.'

She asked the Carraways if they would sit in the waiting room and arranged for coffee to be brought.

Peter Harrison turned up a little after twelve accompanied by a weasely-looking man in a grey silky suit. He was in his thirties with thinning blond hair. Harrison introduced him as his lawyer, David O'Connor.

Lawyer to the mob was almost tattooed on the man's forehead; he looked such a wide boy with daintily shaped and filed fingernails and abnormally white teeth. He draped his jacket over the back of the chair and he and Harrison took their seats gingerly, Joanna and Mike opposite.

Harrison's forehead was beaded with sweat, as though he was nervous, but his hands were steady and Joanna had the feeling that he was actually quite in control. She watched him curiously.

O'Connor spoke first. 'My client,' he said with a nervous and apprehensive look at Harrison, 'wishes to make a statement.'

'We're all ears.' Joanna spoke for both of them.

Harrison's voice was unsteady but he kept his hands on the table in front of him, palms down, as though they steadied him. 'I hadn't met Kayleigh since she was tiny,' he said. Then his voice gathered confidence. 'I'm not much of a dad, Inspector,' he said frankly. 'I admit that and I didn't really think much about her. I just forgot I had a daughter. I carried on with my own life, girl-friends, mates, work, jobs. That was my life. As you know I kept in touch with a couple of my old mates up here: Ollerenshaw and Gradbach. Sometimes I'd come up and we'd go fishing. Johnny told me a couple of times about Kayleigh but –' here his mud-coloured eyes looked straight into Joanna's – 'I wasn't interested. She didn't seem like anything to do with me. Understand?'

'Perfectly,' Joanna said.

'I was up here the last weekend of November but I didn't go straight back down to London. Johnny was quiet on the farm and we thought we'd do a spot of fishing. Trouble was I got a bit restless so thought I'd go out on the Tuesday night. I'd scouted round the town like and seen this place, Patches, and thought I might just see what was around.' His eyes were now looking decidedly shifty as he bounced a glance off his solicitor.

Joanna took the opportunity to exchange a look at Korpanski and knew he was wondering what they would hear next.

Harrison cleared his throat with a rasping noise.

'You've got to understand,' he appealed. 'I hadn't met my daughter since she was in nappies, a Babygro and a shawl. And the lights in the club – well, they're dim. It's hard to see who's who.' He made an attempt at a smile and failed. 'I, um . . .' he was finding this bit hard. 'I does a bit of flirtin', like . . .' He looked at the floor. Even more shiftily, he continued: 'I sort of . . .'

Joanna could guess but she wanted him to have to admit to it.

'I was sort of –' Harrison was squirming – 'flirtin' with a girl I took to be – I don't know – eighteen or something.' He couldn't resist passing the buck. 'They ain't supposed to let 'em in under-eighteen,' he protested, 'so I thought I was safe, didn't I?'

'Naturally,' Joanna responded drily and could guess the rest – in part.

As Harrison squirmed, at his side O'Connor was sitting rigid. He scraped his throat, obviously in preparation for a warning to his client to keep his mouth shut, but Harrison was flying alone now and wouldn't have taken any notice of warnings, however wise. 'She seemed a nice kid,' he pushed on, 'young but I didn't have no concerns she was *too* young, like.' He was focusing on Korpanski now. Maybe he thought he'd get a bit of matey, laddish sympathy from the sergeant. 'Right up till we went out for a fag and she started talking to me about her dad and sayin' stuff.'

'So when did you twig that the girl you were flirting with and probably hoped you'd end up in bed with was your daughter?'

'I don't know.' Harrison stared straight past her. 'I don't know. There was somethin' sort of familiar about her. But I never thought about it. I never twigged. And I didn't rape her.' He stared at Joanna with his toffee eyes. 'I absolutely swear on my mother's life I never raped her. I asked her a couple of questions about her dad and got some bad vibes. I asked her how old she was. She said eighteen. Then I asked her name and I knew exactly who she was. So I knew she was younger. Quite a bit younger. I told her to go home then. I gave her money for a taxi and said she should go home to her mum. I left. I was a bit shocked. I went back to Johnny's place. I was home by midnight and the snow was falling.' He put his head to one side. 'It was a beautiful night,' he said. 'The snow was soft and sort of warm, like a blanket. Not drivin and freezing. Not blowin around. Just fallin'.'

They were simply words – almost clichéd. But they painted a scene in everyone's head – well, maybe not O'Connor's – but everyone else's.

'Where was Kayleigh when you left her?'

'Going back inside. To phone for a taxi, she said.'

'I suspect,' Joanna said slowly, 'that the money you gave her for a taxi was actually spent at the bar.'

Harrison shrugged. 'You can't blame me for that,' he protested. 'I'm not responsible for what she did with the money. I thought she should just go home. In fact, I couldn't understand how Christine could allow her out like that – and so young too.'

Much you did about it, Joanna thought. 'Did Kayleigh know who you were?'

Harrison looked less certain now. 'I'm not sure,' he said. 'I didn't tell her but I got the feelin' she might have guessed. When I gave her the taxi money she said I was just like a dad. Spooked me that did, I can tell you.'

I'll bet, Joanna thought. Then she ploughed on. 'Mr Harrison, where were you on the night of May the eleventh?'

Harrison frowned. 'That's ages ago,' he said. 'I haven't got a clue. Why?'

'Because another young girl was left outside a local nightclub to die.'

Harrison practically jumped out of his chair. 'Hang on a minute,' he said. 'I didn't leave Kayleigh to die and I wouldn't have left any other young girl to die. What sort of a bloke do you think I am?'

'I'm just pondering that very question,' Joanna said coolly. 'Have you ever been to a club called Lymeys in Newcastle?'

Harrison shook his head, looking genuinely vague. 'Don't know the place,' he said.

There was a knock on the door; a nod from the desk sergeant. Kayleigh had arrived.

'I'm sorry but I'm going to have to interrupt you,' she said, giving Korpanski a straight and meaningful look. 'Would you mind sitting in the waiting room?'

Korpanski caught her eye and she knew he'd understood her actions – perfectly.

As Harrison and his solicitor took their seats in the waiting room, she observed the responses. Clara looked up – and right through him. There was no acknowledgment at all. Surprisingly Kayleigh even didn't appear to recognize her father until her mother spoke. 'Well, Peter,' she said sarcastically. 'Come to look after your little girl at last?'

That was when Kayleigh studied her father shyly and ventured the tiniest of smiles. 'Hello,' she said. Harrison grunted a greeting back. Joanna watched the three of them: mother, father, daughter and read: surprise, curiosity and recognition.

Harrison gave his ex-wife a tentative smile. 'Hiya, babe,' he said.

Her response was not so friendly. 'What are you doin' here?'

Kayleigh was pressing herself into her seat, trying to become invisible. Hardly breathing. But her eyes were taking it all in.

Her mother turned towards her. 'This 'ere,' she said sourly, 'is your dad what you're so intrigued about.'

Kayleigh studied the floor. 'I know,' she said.

Clara and her mother were watching the interchange with interest but not with recognition. Though Clara's glance lingered on Kayleigh, as though wondering where she had seen *her* before, it appeared Harrison was a complete stranger.

Christine jabbed Kayleigh in the ribs with her elbow. 'Say 'ello to Daddy,' she mocked.

Peter Harrison moved a little closer and addressed Kayleigh. 'How yer doin' then, love?'

'Not bad, thanks.' She answered in a small voice.

'Did you tell your mum we sort of bumped into one another at the nightclub the other night?'

Christine was watching warily. 'No, she didn't tell me that,' Christine said sarcastically. 'Did you, darlin'?'

'Didn't seem important with what 'appened after,' Kayleigh responded sulkily. 'I sort of half forgot.'

Harrison settled down on the seat beside his daughter. 'Sorry to 'ear,' he said.

They left them to it.

Joanna called Clara and her mother in next. 'Clara,' she said. 'The people outside: did you know any of them?'

The girl hesitated.

'Or *think* you knew someone?'

'I think I've seen the girl somewhere,' she said, frowning. 'Probably at the club. She looks familiar but I can't be absolutely sure.'

'And the man?'

Clara shook her head. 'Not that I remember. Sorry,' she said helpfully. 'I wish I could help to find—'

'It's all right,' Joanna said. 'It's OK. Really.' She smiled. 'I promise.'

Rosa Williams spoke next. 'Have you any better idea what's happened to Molly?' She glanced at her daughter. 'This is awful for my daughter. She feels responsible.'

'We're following a few leads,' Joanna said.

'Surely you've got CCTV footage?'

Joanna sighed. 'Cameras are seen as a panacea for all evils,' she said. 'The easy solutions to all crimes, but the images weren't brilliant and haven't helped us as much as we'd hoped. Is there anything,' Joanna appealed desperately, 'that you can remember? Anything you can think of that'll help us move forward?'

Clara shook her head. 'I've tried really hard,' she said. 'I've gone over and over and over that night – and other nights, but I can't think of anything else. I'm sorry.'

'OK. You can go now.'

When they rejoined Kayleigh and her parents the air was still a little frosty and O'Connor was looking bored. But Kayleigh's eyes were sparkling. Joanna noted that now Harrison's arm was slung casually round his daughter's shoulders. But the situation didn't suit everyone. If Kayleigh looked a bit more animated and Harrison a little less sheepish, Christine looked positively po-faced. In fact, father and daughter appeared to be getting on rather better than mother and daughter ever had, considering . . .

NINETEEN

Thursday, 9 December. 9.25 a.m.

Joanna hadn't really wanted to visit the school, but Molly was still missing. Clara had failed to provide another lead. Someone, somewhere out there knew something and the person Molly was most likely to have confided in would have been a school friend; probably a girl. So she was pulling the dragnet via the school assembly. She was not above using every weapon at her disposal, so she'd brought Korpanski along with her. Young girls were bound to be susceptible to his rugged good looks and powerful frame. Besides, she needed him for moral support. Her own memories of school were not good. She had been bored, frustrated, disruptive and frequently in trouble through her high spirits. In fact, truth be known, she was dreading this return to the chalkboard. Even now, years later, the thought of going into a school made her feel queasy. But she had no option. She must explore all avenues. So at nine thirty, she stood, facing rows of scrubbed faces, and could almost read some of them reflecting her own cynicism towards the educational system.

Using a laptop she made a presentation with photographs of Molly, Clara; stills of Patches et cetera et cetera.

She used the usual line, addressing the entire school in a specially convened late assembly.

'As you probably know, Molly Carraway, one of your school-fellows, disappeared from a nightclub in Leek on Friday night and hasn't been seen since. Another of your school friends was with her at the club that night but they lost sight of one another during the evening.' Joanna moved the picture on to a few grainy portrayals of Molly dancing with various people; sometimes alone, in a dreamy, jerky movement, hands describing vague floating gestures; sometimes stamping and shaking her body around then later walking shakily underneath a tall chandelier, and she continued. 'Obviously we are concerned about Molly and very much want to find her.' She looked round the faces. She had all their attention. They were hardly blinking and the room was still and very quiet.

The question, as she looked from face to face, was did anyone have any useful information? Now she was here she wasn't quite so sure that it was such a good idea. The faces looked so honest, so without deceit. She continued. 'If any of you knows anything that might help us find Molly or wants to make a comment in private Detective Sergeant Korpanski here,' Mike gave the room a big, friendly grin, 'and myself will be waiting in the rooms along the corridor. Your head –' a glance at the man sitting motion-less on the platform – 'has allowed you time off from classes.

Please help us,' she appealed. 'We don't have a lot to go on and as every day goes by we are more and more concerned for your schoolmate's well-being.'

Again Joanna surveyed the ring of faces. They were bright kids. They would be able to read between the lines and know there was an above average chance that Molly Carraway's body was lying somewhere, as yet undiscovered.

It seemed the pupils of Newcastle school were only too anxious to help. An orderly queue had formed outside the doors even before Joanna and Mike had reached their allocated rooms. Most, it turned out, had little of significance to add, but after three quarters of an hour hearing various bits of tittle-tattle, Joanna hit a vein of pure gold.

Salena Mistry was a petite Indian girl; very smart with a long black plait and a short grey skirt, spotless white blouse and maroon tie. She knocked on the door and walked in, a shy smile lighting her face. She was neat and very pretty.

'Sit down,' Joanna invited. The girl sat almost primly and Joanna waited for her to speak. When she didn't, she prompted: 'You are a friend of Molly's?'

'Yes, I certainly am.' The girl had an attractive voice with a singsong intonation.

'Your name?'

'Salena Mistry.'

Joanna waited but the girl still hesitated. 'Salena,' she prompted, 'what can you tell me?'

The girl blinked. At first she said nothing. Then she leaned forward and fixed Joanna with a stare from large liquid-brown eyes. 'I wouldn't dream of telling you anything,' she said primly, 'except that Molly is in big trouble. She must be or she would have texted me or something.'

Privately Joanna agreed. This was nothing new. But she sensed there was more. 'What is it, Salena?'

The girl leaned forward further and pushed a strand of her hair out of her eyes. 'Molly was seeing someone,' she said.

'She had a boyfriend?'

'Sort of.'

'Do you mean the guy she was flirting with over the Internet?'

'No. Not the guy from Young Hearts. Another one.'

Joanna leaned forward. 'And Clara didn't know?'

'She wouldn't have dared tell Clara in case they bumped into him.'

'Where?' She already knew the answer.

'Patches,' the girl said simply. 'Molly would have been frightened that they might have bumped into him there. It was supposed to be a secret,' she added.

'Why?'

'Because he was married.'

'Married? How old was he?'

'I don't know exactly but quite a bit older than her,' the girl said correctly.

'How did she meet him?'

A moment of doubt. 'At Patches, I think, or one of the other nightclubs.'

The other nightclubs. Joanna could have smacked her forehead for her stupidity. 'Did Molly ever go to Lymeys?'

'A few times, yes. We went there together a couple of times and then she stayed over at my house.'

'Did you meet him?'

'I met him once,' the girl said, 'but it was at the club in Newcastle. It was dark and noisy. I couldn't swear I'd know him again.'

'OK. Just as much as you remember.'

'Tall, slim . . .' Salena's description ticked all the boxes.

'How long has it been going on?'

'At least six months that I know of.'

'Were they sleeping together?'

Salema lifted her heavy lashes and nodded. 'Yes,' she said, protesting. 'I did warn her but Molly – she's a law unto herself, that one.'

'What do you know about him?'

That was when the disappointments began. 'Very little, I'm afraid.'

'His name?'

Salema shook her head. 'She wouldn't tell me.'

'Was he from Leek or the Potteries?'

'I think Leek but I'm not sure. Molly thought Clara would

disapprove and that is one of the reasons why she did not confide in her.'

Joanna looked at the girl curiously. 'Clara was supposed to be her best friend. Yet she didn't confide in *her*?'

Salena shook her head.

'But she told you? She thought *you* would – approve?'

'I am not judgemental,' Salena said with dignity.

Clara hadn't struck Joanna as being judgmental either but she let the matter drop.

'Can you remember anything else? Anything,' she emphasized. 'Any small detail?'

'No,' Salena said flatly.

Joanna smiled. The girl was holding something back but pursuing it would not prise it out of her. She was going to have to bide her time. 'Thank you.' She stood up and gave her a card with her telephone number on it. 'If you remember anything else please do get in touch.' The girl returned a beautiful smile as she left. 'I certainly will.'

Salena proved to be the last in her queue and there was no one standing outside Korpanski's door so Joanna knocked and went in. He was talking to a geeky-looking youth with a pointed chin and pale intelligent eyes.

'This is Kieran,' Korpanski explained. 'He's in Molly's class.' The youth grinned at Joanna. He had an eager, engaging face.

'Hi, Kieran,' Joanna said. 'Here to help?'

The youth nodded. Joanna raised her eyebrows to Korpanski, who gave a weak smile and a faint shake of his head. He stood up and slapped the boy on the shoulder. 'Thanks, Kieran,' he said. 'Really appreciate it.'

'You think I've helped?'

Korpanski was too honest. 'Bit soon to say yet, mate, but well, hey.' Another clap on the shoulder. 'We'll see. OK?'

Kieran grinned at him, smiled at Joanna and scuttled off.

Korpanski watched him go with an indulgent smile. 'He wants to join the police when he leaves school – or college,' he said. 'Nice lad – but a bit fanciful.'

'In what way?'

'I think he's making things up.' Korpanski turned his dark eyes on her.

'What sort of things?'

'A telephone conversation he "overheard". '

'Oh?'

'Molly arranging to meet someone – he thought it was a bloke – at Patches on Friday night.'

'Really?' It was the missing thing Salena had kept to her chest.

'You look as though you've come up with something, Jo.'

She related the conversation she'd had with Salena and saw him smile. 'I wondered if there was something like that,' he said. 'I just wondered. I mean, Molly was an attractive, available girl.'

'Was?' she quizzed.

'OK, *is*, if you like, but we both know there's a distinct possibility that she's a corpse. What do we know anyway?' He hesitated. 'Actually I don't want to sound a wet blanket, Jo, but a "married man", well, it doesn't exactly narrow the field, does it?'

'Doesn't it?'

Korpanski gave a blokish grin. 'There must be lots of married men going to Patches on the razzle.'

She simply gave him a disappointed, quizzical look before saying, 'It gives us a lead – and possibly a reason – for her disappearance other than a connection to the other two assaults.'

'If you like, Jo.'

She went outside into the corridor and asked one of the teachers if she could speak to Clara again.

'With a teacher present, of course,' the teacher said severely.

'Of course,' echoed Joanna.

A minute later Clara was ushered in, a female teacher at her side. Joanna waited until the girl was sitting down before she dropped her bombshell. 'Clara, one of your schoolmates has told us that Molly was seeing a married man. Did you know anything about this?'

The girl's eyes widened. 'No, I didn't. Who told you?'

'I can't tell you that.'

'I don't think it's true. She would have confided in me.' She tried again. 'Who told you?'

'We're not at liberty to tell,' Joanna said, 'but do you know anything about it?'

'She went missing a couple of times before,' the girl admitted, 'when we were at Patches. Once or twice it was for ages. An hour or so but she always said she'd been just chatting to someone.'

'Have you any idea who it was?'

The girl put her hands up in a defensive gesture. 'How can I know,' she said, 'if Molly, my best friend, didn't tell me?' Her face changed. 'But I don't approve. If she'd have asked me I'd have told her married men who cheat are cheats.'

Joanna gave a weak smile. 'Tell me a bit more about your nights out.'

Clara made a face. 'It was all a laugh, really. We made a pact. We didn't want boyfriends. We were set on going to uni so if boys made a pass at us we'd just laugh it off. They were just local yobs as far as we were concerned. Chavs.'

Joanna was surprised at the girl's snobbery. 'So if they were "chavs" why would Molly have been seeing one of them?'

'I haven't the faintest idea.' She put her elbows down on the desk with a stroppy thump. 'We went because we were bored. We had to have something to do apart from school and schoolwork.'

Next to the elbows Joanna put on the desk a couple of grainy photographs of Molly with various dancing partners. 'Do you recognize anyone here? Did you ever see Molly talking or spending much time with any of these blokes?'

Clara gave the pictures a thorough look. 'No,' she said, puzzled. 'I don't know any of these guys.'

'Look again at these.' Joanna placed a couple of photofit pictures from descriptions the public had given them.

The girl looked instead at Joanna and snorted. 'They're a bit vague, aren't they?

'The photofits? Yes. They're not brilliant but they give a general idea and a sort of picture, stance, clothes et cetera.'

Clara just laughed. 'They don't even look human, Inspector Piercy. More like someone from *Dr Who*.' She laughed but it quickly turned to tears as she put a hand on each of the photofits. 'You think one of *these* has her?'

Joanna put her hand out. 'We don't know,' she said, 'yet.'

The girl's face looked sad and hopeless and Joanna saw that underneath the bravado, the snobbery and the front Clara was

worried, unhappy and now hurt because Molly, her friend, her
best friend, had not confided in her. She felt a wash of sympathy.

'OK, Clara,' she said softly. 'You can go now. But I just want
to say something.'

The girl lifted her eyes.

'This isn't your fault, you know.'

'No?'

'No. Whatever Molly did, it isn't your fault.'

The girl gave a meaningful glance at the teacher, which Joanna
interpreted correctly. 'You want to speak to me alone?'

'Please.'

The teacher was short, plump; in her forties with a calm, intelligent face. 'If that's what you want, Clara,' she said, 'that's fine.'
She smiled at her pupil, then at Joanna and left the room.

When the door had shut behind her Clara spoke. 'There was
one guy,' she said. 'He was there on Friday and I have seen him
before.'

'Was he there the night Kayleigh was assaulted too?'

'I think so. I couldn't swear to it, though.'

'Did he look like any of the pictures?'

'Not really. But he was sort of confident, a bit older and he
asked us if we wanted anything.'

Joanna lifted her eyebrows.

'I thought he meant drugs, Ecstasy or something like that. I
looked at Moll and I shook my head but she didn't. Later I saw
her talking to him and I was worried.'

'What did he look like?'

'Brown hair, tallish, slimish. He had a sort of cheeky face and
a confident smile.'

'Age?'

'He was about thirty, I think.'

'Would you know him again?'

'I don't know.'

'What was he wearing?'

Joanna risked a look at Korpanski and gave a slight nod. This
was her man. Not shadowy or insubstantial any more. It was a
solid lead which Clara had kept back until the affair with a
married man had come out. Then her loyalty had snapped. She
thanked the girl, resisting the temptation to ask her why she had

kept this important detail back for five whole days and she and
Mike left.

They picked up some sandwiches at the BP filling station
and arrived back at the station. Joanna shut the door on their
office. She wanted to speak to Korpanski alone.

'Mike,' she said slowly, 'I'm beginning to understand why this
case is proving so difficult. Three young girls: teenagers, all of
them clubbing. One dies, another is found almost dead, the other
one is currently missing. Naturally we have threaded the three
cases together.'

Korpanski nodded.

'But what if they are not connected, not even three crimes –
rather three separate incidents, the only connection being the
obvious ones: girls, clubs, alcohol, sex. Should we have dealt
with it like that?'

Korpanski frowned. 'It was a natural way to go, Jo,' he said.
'So will it lead us to Molly?'

'Oh, I think so, eventually. We'll get there, Mike, in the end.
A few phone calls, a few more interviews, some surprises, some
shocks. At the end of this case,' she said prophetically, 'some
people will be happy, even, while others will be sad.'

Korpanski eyed her sceptically. 'You can't know all that, Jo.
You're not a prophetess.'

She laughed. 'No, I'm not, but I can pretend.'

Korpanski took advantage of her mood. 'Still dreading the
wedding?'

She shook her head. 'Not any more.' She reached for the
phone, dialled and waited until she heard the voice at the other
end of the line. 'Mr Ollerenshaw, you should have told me that
Peter Harrison had been visiting you regularly in Leek.'

'I couldn't see what it could have to do with that but I knew
you'd try and make a connection.'

'I have, Mr Ollerenshaw. Believe me, I have. But it would
have helped us if you'd come clean with us from the first.'

After she put the phone down she looked at Mike. 'Fancy a
trip to the Potteries?'

He grinned. 'Do I have a choice?'

For answer she unhooked her coat from the hook.

'Are you going to tell me where we're headed?'

'I thought we'd visit Danielle Brixton's mother. I've rung her and she's agreed to speak to us.'

Korpanski was silent for most of the journey into the Potteries but eventually he couldn't resist asking, 'Whatever for?'

She took her eyes off the road. 'Wait and see.'

There was a prolonged, further grumpy silence before Korpanski said, 'You're not supposed to do that, Jo.'

'Do what?'

'Keep me in the dark.'

She gave him a sideways glance. 'I'm keeping you in the dark, Mike, because I am. Not because I'm playing some sort of a game.'

'Right.' Accepting that he folded his arms and settled back in his seat.

Danielle had lived in a sold-off council estate in Knutton, an area of Stoke-on-Trent which years ago had supplied miners to the nearby Silverdale Colliery. Now the area was rundown and slightly depressing.

Danielle's mother proved to be a small woman with faded blonde hair and a coarse expression. But she still looked too young to have had her daughter die in such a way.

Joanna introduced herself and Mike, flashed the obligatory ID and Shirley Brixton led them inside a small room scented with plug-in fresheners which barely masked the smell of cigarettes.

Joanna opened the interview. 'Mrs Brixton, I'm sorry for your loss.'

Shirley Brixton managed a tight smile. 'I'm getting used to it,' she said, 'believe it or not. When bereavement counselling told me I would I didn't believe them. But it's true.'

'Did Danielle have a boyfriend?'

The woman sniffed. 'My girl's dead,' she said in a flat, wooden voice. 'What good can any of this do now? She wasn't murdered Inspector; she just died of neglect.' She sniffed. 'No one even cared enough to get her to a hospital.'

There was no answer to this.

Shirley Brixton continued gently. 'I can't see how it'll help you find your girl, Inspector.'

'Maybe not,' Joanna agreed. 'We'll see. Thank you for your time.'

Danielle's mother smiled. 'It's OK,' she said. 'I did warn her, you know. I told her she was too young to go out clubbing.' She paused. 'And she was, wasn't she? She weren't up to the sophistication of the men there. They was older. She didn't understand what she'd got herself into. Alcohol, maybe drugs.'

There was no fair answer to that so Joanna simply nodded non-committally.

She glanced at Korpanski. He was sitting with a wooden expression on his face, staring straight ahead of him. Then he turned his head, caught Joanna's glance and made an expression of resignation together with a twitch of his hands. It was his way of asking, *So what have we achieved, coming here, raking over cold ashes?* She smiled back at him.

'We're getting close, Mike,' she said on the way home.

'The thing is, Jo, do you believe Harrison's story?'

'Call me naive,' she responded, 'but yes. I do. I think it's the truth. Rather strange; a bit of a coincidence, but the truth.'

He nodded and made no comment.

'And Salena's story?'

Korpanski looked enquiringly at her and she gave him an explanation – of sorts.

'The married man thing is a great way to stop your girl talking, Mike. It makes monkeys out of the women. They give them sex, everything, and get nothing back. It keeps them secretive and the man safe.'

'Ah,' Korpanski said.

'Let's get the birthday boys back in – all of them – separately. And we'll start with Steve Shand, finder of the body.'

TWENTY

Steve Shand sauntered in, hands in pockets, attempting nonchalance but only succeeding in looking shifty and very uneasy. He spread his hands palms downwards flat on the table and bent forwards. 'I know you're going to try and pin this on me,' he said, 'just because I was the one who found Kayleigh.

But I don't know anything about Molly Carraway. I promise.'
He spoke earnestly, his eyes meeting Joanna's full force. His
expression might be bland, she reflected, but there was a
suppressed anger too. He smelt faintly of a rather pleasant spicy
deodorant which emphasized his very maleness.

Joanna had already decided to give the birthday boys a rough
ride. A very rough ride. 'But you were there on the night Molly
disappeared?'

'Yeah, but I was with my girlfriend.' A wry smile. 'She wasn't
going to let me out on my own again so I had to take her along.'

True love, Joanna thought. *And an alibi.*

'Do you remember Molly on Friday? She was wearing a very
noticeable bright red dress.'

'I've already said I remember her.'

Joanna smiled and caught Korpanski's eye.

'So let's return to Kayleigh Harrison, shall we? You danced
with *her* the night she was allegedly raped.' She was aware that
the bald statement sounded very like an accusation.

'I've already admitted that,' Shand muttered sulkily. 'She
danced with just about everyone that night. Not just me, you
know.'

'And Molly?'

Shand looked surprised. 'Was she there that night?'

'Yes.' Joanna looked down at her notes, 'wearing "jeggings"
and a white crop top.'

Shand looked half interested. 'I do remember somebody
dressed like that,' he said. 'She wasn't half going it on the dance
floor.'

'Alone?'

Shand frowned. 'Sort of. She didn't seem to be with anyone
particular. There was just a crowd of people all dancin', not
necessarily together.'

'Did you dance with her that night?'

'I don't know. I don't really remember whether I did or not.
I don't keep a tab on every girl I have a dance with. You kind
of move around the room. And Claire was there.' His brow was
wrinkled as he eyed Joanna dubiously. 'Know what I mean?'

'Yes.' She hesitated. 'Can you answer me something, Steve?'

Shand looked wary.

'When you first noticed Kayleigh, the morning you found her, did you recognize her?'

Shand shook his head. 'No,' he said. 'A girl shimmyin' around the dance floor in a silver skirt looks nothing like a half-dead body slumped by a bin, half her clothes missin.'

'But you saw the silver skirt?'

He nodded. 'I still didn't make the connection – not until later.'

'And when you saw her that snowy morning, was your first thought that she had been raped?'

'I don't know.' He obviously hadn't thought of this. 'No. Yes.' He met Joanna's eyes. 'I really don't know,' he said. 'She looked – abandoned, rather than sexy.'

She smiled at him. 'OK,' she said, 'Thanks. You can go.'

'So who's next, Mike?'

Shaun Hennessey was finding it hard to contain his anger. He came blasting in, all guns blazing.

'What's the idea, dragging me in here again? I don't know nothing about this bird who's gone missing. Understand? I didn't even know her.'

'Think again, Mr Hennessey,' Joanna said icily, making no attempt at politeness or even civility. 'Either you or one of your buddies has something to do with this girl's,' she jabbed Molly's picture, 'disappearance. So either you tell me what you know or we shall keep you here for as long as it takes. Understand?'

Hennessey was not intimidated. 'I understand perfectly,' he said. 'But we weren't the only guys there that night on the prowl, you know. I don't know why you keep coming back to us.'

'Well, it was one of your buddies who discovered Kayleigh,' Joanna said smoothly.

Hennessey was dismissive. 'That doesn't mean anything,' he said contemptuously.

'You can't pin anything on me or my mates. I saw the girls. OK? I had a few dances with the one you call Molly, the girl in the red dress, but I did not abduct her or rape her or anything else.' He spread his hands out wide. 'I didn't even know her name until the story broke.'

'And what about Kayleigh Harrison?'

'What about Kayleigh Harrison?' Hennessey's lip curled. 'She was a little slapper. Pissed as a fart and offering herself to all and sundry. I wouldn't be surprised if any one of the fellows there that night would have raped her. She was so –' his face made an expression of disgust – 'available. You can't blame a guy for takin' what's offered to him on a plate, you know.'

'And abandoning her?' Joanna felt her anger brewing up. 'Leaving her to die?'

'It wasn't me,' Hennessey said, quiet again now, as though he sensed her hostility.

Joanna leaned back in her chair. 'So who was it?'

'I don't know.'

'OK, let's leave it at that and move on to something or someone else, shall we? We have a witness who says that Molly Carraway was having an affair with a married man.'

Instantly Hennessey looked wary.

'You're almost married,' Korpanski put in – right on cue.

But Hennessey merely shook his head. 'I wasn't having an affair with Molly Carraway or Kayleigh or anyone else,' he said baldly.

'So who was?'

'Why are you picking on me and my mates?' he asked again. 'There were plenty of other guys in the club that night. Why us?'

'A feeling,' Joanna replied. 'Just a feeling.'

Hennessey met her eyes without flinching. 'You're never going to make a charge stick on a "feeling",' he jeered. 'You're police. Not bloody clairvoyants.'

Joanna ignored the jibe and changed tack. 'Molly Carraway's parents are going spare,' she said quietly. 'They don't even know if their daughter's dead or alive. Have some pity on them, Shaun.'

Hennessey responded to her appeal. His face changed. Like frost in the sun his anger melted away. 'I'm sorry,' he said. 'I'm really sorry but I can't help you, Inspector.'

The three of them sat still, each wrapped in their own reflections. Joanna studied Hennessey's face and knew they would get no more out of him.

'You can go,' she said.

Hennessey didn't move.

'I said,' she repeated, 'you can go. You're free to go.'

Hennessey stood up, looked as though he wanted to say something, then walked out of the door.

Joanna looked at Mike. 'So what do you make of that?'

'He's either telling the truth or—'

'A half-truth, Mike,' she said, adding, 'and what's the first rule of an investigation?'

He grinned. 'Everyone tells lies?'

'Exactly.'

He made a face at her. 'Or I think what you once told me was that everyone tells at least one lie. They may not see it as a lie but it deflects us from the truth.'

'Right.'

'So who's next?'

'I didn't ask Andrew Downey to come in,' she said. 'As far as I'm concerned he's off the hook. And Pointer's arranged to come in tomorrow. So, Clint Jones.'

Jones had a rolling gait, long arms. Ape-like. And of the birthday boys they'd seen so far he appeared the least troubled by being summoned back to the police station.

He sat right back in the chair and gave them a bland smile.

Joanna eyed him for a moment. 'What did you think of Molly Carraway?' she asked.

Jones had not been expecting this approach. He considered for a moment. 'I didn't know her.'

'But you gained an impression?'

'Nice,' he said. 'She seemed a nice girl.' He smiled. 'A rotten flirt – very sexy. Very beautiful.'

Joanna nodded. 'And what do you think's happened to her?'

Jones shrugged. 'I think,' he said, 'someone's got her.'

'Kidnapped?'

Slowly he shook his head.

'Did you see Molly leave the club last Friday?'

He shook his head. 'No.'

Joanna let him go then, but with a feeling that she was missing something.

'Let's take another look at the CCTV of people leaving the club,' she said. 'She must have left the club at some point.'

'Well, she isn't still there,' Korpanski said. 'We've had a thorough search of the premises.'

'Quite.'

It had been a cold night, flakes of snow drifting in front of the camera like the snow on a Hollywood Christmas film. A few of the girls stood around, shivering, waiting for taxis or cars that picked them up. Even on poor quality CCTV film with no sound you could almost *feel* the cold. Some of the girls were wearing coats, but most weren't. A few were sliding around on the icy surface in high heels, clutching on to one another, giggling. One fell right on her bottom and struggled back to her feet, still laughing. A couple of snowballs were lobbed into the air.

Then a couple came out: the girl muffled in a coat, her hair over her face, the man supporting her. Joanna peered closer. He was almost carrying her. And as Mike and Joanna watched the coat slipped and revealed a sliver of red dress. 'That's her,' Joanna said. 'That's Molly.' It was no wonder they had missed it before. It would have been hard to pick her out.

She slowed down the picture and sat with her chin on her palm. 'He's taking her,' she mused.

Korpanski was watching too. 'She could be drunk,' he said, 'or she could be drugged.'

'She could even be practically dead.'

Both peered closer, looking for signs of life. But there were so many people milling around the club doors they couldn't be sure. They could quite understand how on that night no one had really noticed Molly. The clubbers had been distracted by the snow. And now they had lost the view as revellers crowded around.

It was a sobering thought that this had been the last sighting of the girl.

They sat and looked at one another until the door burst open and DC Alan King stood in front of them. 'Sorry,' he said, 'I thought you were out. I thought the room was empty. Sorry,' he said again.

The intrusion galvanised them into action.

'Kayleigh's still our key, Mike,' Joanna said slowly. 'If we can persuade her to tell us the absolute truth we might find out who our perpetrator is. And Molly.'

They found Kayleigh at home with both her mother and her father. Once the two detectives had squeezed into the small sitting room it seemed that the walls bulged with the effort. Even the Klimt seemed to have expanded to fill any space, dominating the room and leaving little room for air. The inhabitant's emotions were similarly intensified.

Peter Harrison was on the sofa, his daughter sitting very close to him. Kayleigh was wearing low-cut jeans, a T-shirt and furry lilac slippers and was snuggled in close to her father who seemed perfectly at ease. In contrast Christine, dressed smartly in a royal blue dress and flat black pumps, sat stiffly in the chair by the window, almost detached, outside the situation as though she sat behind a sheet of plate glass.

Joanna observed the trio and sat down. In her father's presence Kayleigh had blossomed. She shone with an inner happiness and new confidence. The three of them sat, waiting for Joanna to speak.

She spoke to Kayleigh first. 'We know some of what happened the night you *believed* you were raped,' she said, noting that neither of Kayleigh's parents contradicted the statement. 'We think the true story behind that night will help us find out what's happened to Molly. So why don't you tell me, again, exactly what you do remember.' She wanted to advise the girl not to embellish her story with anything she was not certain of but she resisted the temptation. She didn't want to influence Kayleigh's story at all.

As though they had already discussed this scenario Kayleigh glanced at her father, who gave her an encouraging nod. 'OK,' she said, then gave an impish grin, which altered her face even more. Joanna had never noticed before that the girl had dimples. Kayleigh leaned back comfortably against her father and began. 'I was chattin' to this bloke at the bar, right? He seemed really friendly.' She turned to give Peter Harrison a cheeky smile. 'Quite attractive, I thought. From down London way. A bit older than me but he'd bin around.' She lifted her eyebrows. 'You know? I asked his name and he told me, Peter. We chatted some more. I started tellin' him my dad was called Peter and he lived in London. He asked my name. I can't remember which one of us twigged first me or him but I was well pissed by then. He'd kept buying me drinks.' She looked vaguely proud of herself. 'I said I was eighteen and a half and he believed me. Then he asked me some more questions, like my birthday and where me mum lived – stuff like that. When he realized I was his actual daughter he changed. He told me to get on home.' She clutched his arm. 'Got all Dad-like, gave me some money, told me to get a taxi and left me. But I didn't go home. I went back into the club. I was sort of happy and a bit sad as well because he was my dad and I'd never remembered meeting him before though I must have done when I was a baby.' She sucked in a deep sigh. 'I thought how nice it would have been if we'd done things together, you know, gone walkin' or shoppin' or whatever blokes do with their daughters.' She gave a sentimental smile at Harrison who, far from looking uncomfortable, seemed to be taking this all in – with relish.

This was when Kayleigh stopped looking at her father and fixed her gaze instead on Mike Korpanski, her expression defiant and challenging. 'The money he gave me for a taxi home – well,' she said defensively. 'I was in a right funny mood, havin' just met my dad for the first time in livin' memory. I couldn't bear the thought that he'd just walk out of my life. I might never see him again and I thought he was nice. Really nice.'

Christine Bretby shifted uncomfortably in her seat.

It caught Kayleigh's attention so she turned her attention on her mother instead. 'I know you think I'm pathetic and useless,' she burst out. 'I know you wish I'd never been born.'

Joanna risked a look at Kayleigh's mother. Her face was taut. Frozen. She was taking refuge behind the fact that this was not real. It was not happening. It was a soap on the TV or a story in a magazine. It was not real. Joanna studied her face and realized that Christine Bretby was floating away from this situation into a romantic haze, towards the Klimt.

Perhaps Kayleigh realized this too. She stopped looking at her mother and carried on. 'I felt terrible. So I spent all the taxi money on a few shots.' She aimed her gaze now at the carpet, avoiding either parent's censure. 'I passed out in the car park.' She looked Joanna squarely in the face. 'You might not believe me,' she said, 'but I know I was raped. I felt it but I couldn't do anything. I couldn't seem to move.'

'Just a minute,' Joanna said. 'The description of your attacker? Are you saying you made it up?'

'Not exactly,' the girl said slowly. 'I remember bits of it: the weight of the guy, the smell of tobacco, the feel of him. The swimmy feeling. And more than anything else the cold. When I came round the next day I was terrified. The police officer was askin' me for a description.' Her eyes flickered across to her father. 'I didn't want to say I was pissed and couldn't remember, that I didn't even know who'd done it.'

'The man you described was your father.'

'It just came out. And once I'd said what he looked like I could hardly change it, could I? You kept askin' if I'd been raped. I knew I had but I didn't know what he looked like. So I had to make bits up, fill in the parts I couldn't remember. I didn't know who did it.' She gave a cheeky grin at her father. 'I knew they'd never pin it on you. I knew it wasn't you and you'd hardly go for your own daughter, would you?'

In Kayleigh's mind, Joanna reflected, making up the bits that were missing made sense. She stopped talking, sat very still and quiet, her thin shoulders bowed, waiting for the axe to fall.

And it did.

Christine's eyes were blazing. 'So you made the details up?'

'I went along with it,' Kayleigh defended.

'Just like you did with my Neil.'

The girl looked frightened now. 'There was only you, Mum,' she said. 'Me and you. It had always been like that. I didn't know what would happen to me without you. Once you'd got married you didn't want me around, did you?'

Christine fidgeted with a large, noisy bracelet, jangling an orchestra of sounds with the tiny ornaments, hearts, arrows, a tiny book.

Now it was Kayleigh who had the upper hand. 'You didn't want me, did you? Be honest with me. You didn't, did you?'

Her mother looked up. 'I wanted a family. We would have had more children.'

'That was why I did it – said what I did. I worked out a plan to get rid of him.' She looked defiantly at her mother. 'And it did work, didn't it? I'm not so stupid. I saw 'im off, didn't I?'

'You little –' Christine Bretby was on her feet; hatred in her eyes. 'You've ruined my life with your lies.'

Surprisingly it was Peter Harrison who brought the situation under control. 'There's no need for that, Chris,' he said mildly. 'The girl's had a tricky life.'

'And whose fault is that?'

'Mine,' he admitted. 'It's my fault. I see it now. I haven't been the dad I should have been. But I'm going to act different now. I'm going to take on my responsibilities.'

'Oh, yeah?' Her scorn was blistering.

The three of them glared each other out. Christine was hardly bothering to disguise the dislike she felt for her daughter.

Kayleigh Harrison drew in a deep breath and bounced the hostile stare right back. 'I don't want to be with you,' she said bluntly. 'I want my dad.'

The child had a perfect right. But it was unexpected. It threw Joanna; Mike gulped but that was nothing to the effect it had on Peter Harrison. He looked stunned. 'I –' he began. Holding his hands up defensively. 'I –' His ex-wife and daughter both turned their attention on to him, full beam. 'I live in a flat.'

Ex-wife and daughter continued to stare at him.

And Harrison finally caved in. 'A trial period?' he squeaked.

'Are you sure about this, Kayleigh?' Joanna asked gently. The girl focused her attention on her.

'Yes, I am,' she said simply. 'I want to be with someone who loves me and believes in me.'

Joanna gave Mike a quick, worried glance. Harrison might be Kayleigh's father but she wasn't sure his feelings towards his daughter were completely paternal. After all, they had met at a nightclub when he had been plying her with drinks and trying to pick her up. Hardly a great start for belated parenting skills. She eyed Kayleigh uneasily, wondering whether the girl was about to tip from the frying pan into the fire. But Kayleigh's stare back at her didn't invite comment. It challenged her to voice her feelings and Joanna realized that the girl was perhaps wiser and more mature than she had given her credit for. And the gaze Kayleigh beamed at her father was simply adoring.

'I just want to ask you one thing,' she said to her mother. 'What did I do that was so very wrong?'

Christine didn't even hesitate. 'You were born.'

They were shocking words but Christine hadn't finished. 'Then you cocked up my life,' she said. 'Now get out.'

Joanna caught Mike's eye. This had turned into a 'domestic'. Time for them to beat a hasty retreat and return to the briefing.

But at least this time they had gained some ground. They had separated Kayleigh's father from Kayleigh's rapist. Gone now the London accent and to some extent the description. They were back somewhere much nearer to home.

As Korpanski inched the squad car into a parking space she confided in him.

'I think the girls were drugged,' she said. 'I need to speak to Matthew.'

Korpanski protested. 'We're supposed to be having a briefing.'

'It'd be more use if I got some information out of Matthew,' she said. 'You take the briefing. You can explain the story about Kayleigh and her father. I'll see you later.'

'OK,' he said.

She rang Matthew. 'Hi,' she said when he picked up. 'Where are you?'

'At the Path lab. Why?'

'I want to ask you some questions.'

'Delighted. We can have a coffee together. OK?'

She found him in the lab, peering down a microscope. For a moment she simply watched him. He was absorbed, quite unconscious of her approach as he fiddled with the focus. His hair flopped over the lens. He was wearing a white coat. She would have watched him for longer but he straightened and saw her. For a moment he simply grinned at her. 'Hi, Jo,' he said.

She felt her face twist into a huge smile. 'Hello, you,' she answered.

'Let's go into my office. We can have a bit of peace.'

'Great.'

She followed him in and the first thing she saw was the photograph on his desk. It had been taken at a restaurant in Spain the night they had got engaged. She studied it and could already read the doubts and confusion in her face – feelings which were only now beginning to melt away. Matthew followed her gaze.

'It already seems a long time ago,' he commented, 'doesn't it?'

'Yeah.'

'So . . .' He sat in his armchair. 'What can I do for you?'

'Help me,' she said. 'The "date rape" drug?'

'Ah, Rohypnol. Actually I don't know why there was all that fuss about Midazolam – any of the benzodiazepines would have done. And they're more freely available and therefore cheaper.'

'English, please?'

'Well –' he drew in a deep breath – 'the desired effect is sedation with amnesia. So any of that class of drugs would work equally well.'

'Any of the class of drugs,' she repeated slowly.

Matthew nodded. 'Diazepam, Lorazepam, Temazepam, as well as the infamous Midazolam or Rohypnol. Understand?'

She nodded. 'And much more readily available.'

She thought for a while before asking. 'Did you test Danielle Brixton for benzodiazepines?'

'Yes and it was positive. But she also had a very high blood alcohol.'

'What about Kayleigh?'

'She wasn't tested. But I have to say if it was left to me I'd choose Lorazepam. Short half-life, wears off after four to six hours. And,' he added, 'it's much more easily available. And then there's ketamine,' he said slowly. 'Nasty, dangerous stuff. Now if it was that –' He looked at her. 'It would fit,' he said. 'Danielle – vomiting; Kayleigh – forgetting.'

'Were they tested for ketamine?'

He shook his head.

'And Molly,' she queried.

Matthew looked at her. 'Oh, shit, Jo,' he said.

TWENTY-ONE

Friday, 10 December. 8.30 a.m.

She decided to ring Andrew Downey in case he could add anything to the events they were slowly pulling together. She switched the telephone on to loudspeaker so Mike could listen in. As she'd expected Downey responded cheerfully to the telephone call.

'You know I'd do anything to help you find that girl,' he said.

'You think she's still alive, then?'

'Never say die,' Downey responded.

'When you were out clubbing with your friends I take it you didn't dance with any of the women?'

'Nope.'

'You probably sat and drank – and looked around?'

'What are you getting at, Inspector?' His voice was silky.

'Tell me what you saw.'

There was the briefest of pauses before Downey replied. 'Nothing. If I had seen anything I would have told you.'

'Did you speak to Molly?'

'Hardly.' By the inflection in his voice she could tell he was smiling. 'Do you have any idea of the noise levels in those places? It's no place for a conversation. You dance; you drink. You don't talk – except in the quiet room.'

Joanna decided to try a different tack. 'If you had to pick out one of your pals,' she said, 'and charge him with the crime, which one would you pick?'

'That's an awful question and unfair, I think.'

'Yeah.' Joanna brushed the objection aside. 'I can see what your objection is but have a go.'

'No,' he said.

'You're a good and loyal friend,' Joanna said. 'Now, then. If you knew something about one of your pals . . .?'

She let the sentence waft in the air.

'I wouldn't grass on a pal,' Downey said, 'unless he'd done something really bad.'

'Like murder?'

Downey wasn't to be drawn. 'Then I'd have no choice.' His words were honourable but Joanna wondered.

'Let's talk about your mates, then. Gary Pointer first. What do you think of him?'

'He's a nice guy. Personable.'

'You know what I'm asking you, Andrew.'

'I can't answer that,' he said. 'He's my mate.'

Joanna waited.

And Downey answered. 'I don't know,' he said. 'There's no reason he should and I can't believe he would.'

Joanna narrowed her eyes. In her book this was tantamount to a 'yes'. 'Thank you,' she said.

As soon as he'd put the phone down she turned to Korpanski. 'So what do you make of that, Mike?'

'Interesting. I'm still not quite sure where you're headed, Jo, but I'm a patient man.'

'We've a few more things to do yet; questions to ask.'

'Such as? Oh,' he complained, 'don't pull the old rabbit-out-of-a-hat one with me, Jo. We're supposed to be buddies. Mates. Colleagues.'

She couldn't resist playing with him. 'So what's *your* version of events, Mike?'

'Not sure yet.'

'And neither am I.'

'The search for Molly . . .' She nibbled her fingernail. 'We have done all the usual things, haven't we, Mike?'

'House-to-house, boards up, checked mobile phones, sightings. Oh, yes,' he said. 'We've done all the usual things.'

She sat back in her chair. 'Let's go through things more slowly then because we're missing something, Mike. Molly – or Molly's body – is somewhere.'

'Yes.'

'A man is involved – we believe this has a sexual motive.'

'Yes again.'

'Our American friends from Patches are, we think, off the hook.'

Korpanski nodded.

'And Andrew Crispin is not the man that Molly left with. Besides, he was at Patches until well after two.'

Again Korpanski nodded.

'She danced with lots of guys.'

'But you seem to be homing in on Hennessey and his buddies.'

'Well, they were at Lymeys the night Danielle died, at Patches when Kayleigh was raped and again at Patches on the night Molly went missing.'

'Now that we have a believed sighting of Molly leaving the club we have a vague description. We know her abductor was tall and slim. That lets quite a few potential suspects off the hook.'

'Yes.'

'What did you think of Clint Jones?'

'Clint Jones was not the guy who we're assuming abducted Molly Carraway.'

'How can you be so sure, Mike?'

'He doesn't look right. Doesn't walk right. Men who work out and become overweight develop a sort of rolling gait,' he said. 'I've seen it myself. I think it might be to do with some of the food supplements.'

She smiled. 'Do you think Clint's mother was a fan of Clint Eastwood?'

'That too.' Korpanski laughed.

It was Joanna who sobered up first. 'How can we laugh,' she asked, 'when that poor girl's body is somewhere?'

Korpanski put his hand on her shoulder. 'It's just a defence strategy, Jo,' he said. 'It doesn't mean we're psychos. It's just our way of coping.'

Gary Pointer arrived at midday.

She started off by thanking him for attending, which put him nicely at his ease, and studied him. Out of the pals he was by far the most attractive. Tall, slim, with a bright, sentimental look. There was something gentle about him; something that drew you in.

'My pleasure,' he responded politely with not a hint of sarcasm.

'You know we are investigating the disappearance of Molly Carraway?'

He nodded, wariness growing now, but no alarm or apprehension. His conscience appeared clear.

So why was her radar bleeping? Even as she asked her questions she was wondering this. What was alarming her? 'You know we are linking Molly's disappearance with two other assaults on young girls outside nightclubs.'

'Yes.' He was still being pleasant. 'So I understand.'

'On May the eleventh of this year a young woman died outside a nightclub in Newcastle-under-Lyme. Her name was Danielle Brixton.'

'Yes?' His face held puzzlement – only that.

'She had been sexually assaulted. The post mortem showed that she died because she inhaled her own vomit. She had been drinking heavily.' Joanna flipped the photograph of the fresh-faced schoolgirl on the desk. 'She was sixteen years old,' she finished quietly.

'How on earth do you think I can help you?' Pointer asked, his eyes just starting to worry.

Joanna ignored his query and continued. 'On the thirtieth of November another girl was sexually assaulted outside Patches nightclub in Leek.'

Pointer nodded. 'Kayleigh, I presume.' He was still playing the innocent. 'I still don't see what it's got to do with me.'

'Patience, Gary.' Korpanski was watching Pointer, hardly blinking. The stare from his black eyes was as much a blast as the beam of an interrogation light. Joanna noted that Pointer deliberately kept his gaze away from Sergeant Mike Korpanski.

'Danielle was found dead outside Lymeys back in May. She'd been drinking heavily and had inhaled her own vomit. She was sixteen years old.'

The only sign that Pointer had heard her words was a swift nod.

Joanna continued. 'Kayleigh, whom you've rightly identified, was abandoned outside Patches, in the snow. She was found by one of your friends, Steve, in the car park the following morning. She was suffering from hypothermia and nearly died. According to the doctors she would have died in less than an hour had your mate –' she used the word sarcastically – 'not discovered her.' She paused to let her next words take full effect. 'We are treating the assault on Kayleigh as attempted murder.'

'And then we get to Molly Carraway who has disappeared, also from Patches nightclub, just a few days later, some time on the night of Friday the third of December or early hours of December the fourth. We believe the three cases are connected.' She leaned forward on her elbows so there would be no mistake. 'Committed by the same man.'

Was it her imagination? Had Pointer paled? No. His eyes held polite curiosity.

'We haven't found Molly yet but the search is on. There is another factor in these three cases.'

Instead of carrying straight on, she waited.

Pointer simply regarded her with no sign of unease.

'We've studied CCTV footage of people leaving Patches between midnight on the Friday and one a.m. on the Saturday. We have picked out a woman we believe to be Molly. She is with a man who fits your description.'

Pointer's eyes flickered but he remained steady.

'This is where it gets interesting, Gary.'

'According to Molly's school friend she was having an affair with a married man.'

'Lets me off the hook then, doesn't it? I'm not married.'

'No.'

Pointer lifted himself from his chair, as though preparing to leave.

'Just a minute, please, Mr Pointer.'

He looked mildly surprised.

'I said that a *friend* had *reported* this, not that it was so.'

Pointer sat down again. 'Why would a man claim to be married if he wasn't?' He grinned comfortably. 'Most guys do the opposite: pretend they're single to persuade the girl to have a relationship with them.'

'Yes,' Joanna agreed mildly. 'This is true.'

Floating through the air she caught a memory from years ago. Matthew hadn't lied. He never had. And she had known from the first that he was married. He had never deceived her. She laid her hands on the table, looked at the black pearl engagement ring and wondered. 'There are, of course, other reasons why a man might pretend to be married when he is, in fact, single.'

Pointer blew out a sharp breath but apart from that made no comment.

'Perhaps to excuse the fact that the relationship had to be kept secret,' Joanna said. 'Molly is underage – just fifteen years old. Kayleigh is even younger. Fourteen.' Gary Pointer looked upset. 'This is nothing to do with me,' he said. 'I don't know these girls. I've had nothing to do with them.'

'Take me through that Tuesday night: the night Kayleigh was assaulted.'

He pulled his shoulders up. 'It was just a normal lad's night. Shaun's birthday. A lot of ragging and playing around. None of us was driving so we had a shedful and, well . . .' He left it to her imagination.

'Go on, Gary.'

'Well – we were dancin' and playin' around, foolin' around. I remember the girl in the silver skirt.'

'On Friday night Molly was wearing a short red dress with high-heeled silver shoes. She had a pair of reindeer antlers on, I believe.' Joanna knew exactly what she was doing – deliberately blurring the two nights in his mind.

'They were all dressed like that: little Santas.'

Joanna was watching him. Was he a rapist? Callous and careless?

Either he was an expert at deception or something here just wasn't right.

'Give me a minute,' she said to Pointer. 'Mike?' He looked up, read her dilemma correctly and followed her out of the room. 'It wasn't him,' she said.

Korpanski didn't agree. 'He's got *something* to do with it, Jo.'

'Do you see him as a murderer?'

Korpanski's eyes rested on the door as he shook his head, reluctantly.

They re-entered the interview room.

'Look, Gary,' Joanna said, almost kindly. 'We don't think you've abducted or murdered Molly but you were having an affair with her, weren't you?'

He didn't have to answer. His response was enough. He simply dropped his head in a shame-faced nod. 'Stella lost a baby,' he muttered, 'back in October. She seemed to – freeze up. She didn't want anything to do with me.' He was begging, beseeching her to believe him.

'I was terrified she'd find out.' He looked up. 'It was only once or twice.' His eyes were still cruising along the floor. 'I knew she was under sixteen. I'd have lost my job,' he said. 'It was just madness. But I wouldn't have killed Molly,' he said, 'and I'd have nowhere to take her if I'd abducted her.' He paused for a minute. 'I didn't love her,' he said, 'she was just available, just there – when I needed someone.'

Joanna made no moral judgement. 'Do you know where she is?'

He shook his head. 'No. I've tried to text her but her phone's off.'

'Did you speak on Friday night?'

'Yeah – but I was so worried my mates would find out. They know Stella and they wouldn't think much of me.' He looked up. 'Whatever you think of my friends they wouldn't take kindly to me playing around – especially after Stella lost the baby. I talked to Molly on the Friday night. She said she wanted to meet me so I went into the quiet room for a bit. She got a bit heavy; asked me when I was going to leave Stella.' He looked up help- lessly. 'I couldn't leave Stell, could I? I didn't want to. Molly had read it all wrong. She thought I wanted to break up my relationship and go off with her.' He looked repulsed by the idea. 'I couldn't have walked out on Stell,' he repeated. 'And her having lost our baby?'

Oh, no, Joanna thought. *You couldn't possibly leave your partner, could you? But you could cheat on her with a minor.* In the next moment she felt a hypocrite. Matthew had left his wife, hadn't he?

'You're free to go, Gary,' she said.

She should have been Christmas shopping, making last-minute wedding arrangements. Instead she was hunting a callous rapist. She had no time off over the weekend. It was spent checking statements, speaking to the Carraways and making absolutely no progress.

Saturday, 11 December. 3 p.m.

As the light was fading Joanna sent Mike home to do some family Christmas things and wandered up Derby Street towards Patches. The weather had turned dull, mild and wet; often the way when Christmas looms.

The shops were wild with festive spirit, Derby Street illu- minated with fat red Santas and fatter white snowmen, big red bells and baubles. Bright stars and angels. And who should she bump into but Christine Bretby with Neil, hand in hand, Christine transformed into the woman from the Klimt. Big red lips, a golden sheath of a dress, white fur jacket, thick hair, dark and tousled, eyes smudgy, mouth curving into a scarlet siren's smile. 'Well, hello.' Joanna could think of nothing to say.

'Kayleigh's livin' with her father now,' Christine said. 'London sounded more exciting to her than Leek so she's already gone. I raised no objection. It's about time Peter took her on as a father. I've had her for her first fourteen years. He can have her for the rest.' Her voice had lost none of its sharpness.

Neil Bretby gave Joanna an awkward smile. 'Best let bygones be bygones,' he said. 'I've missed her.' His arm stole around his ex-wife's shoulders protectively.

It was as Joanna walked on that in front of her eyes she began to see not the gaudy Christmas lights or the dull grey street, not the shoppers, muffled against the weather, but the star, sharp as crystal, white and bright as magnesium, leading her towards the truth. It was as though a floodlight had been switched on in front of her eyes. It blotted out everything else.

She returned to the station, sat, alone in the dark, in her office, picked up the phone and asked three questions.

TWENTY-TWO

Monday, 13 December. 5.30 a.m.

She couldn't sleep. She reached out and touched Matthew. Dead to the world. Her mind teased out the phrase. Dead – to – the – world. Like Molly? In her mind she went through the three cases bit by bit, statement by statement. And sat up. There was no point lying here, awake, listening to Matthew's breathing. She slipped out of bed and peeped through the curtains. Outside was black as the grave. Again the phrase resonated around her mind. She went into the shower room and peered at her face in the mirror. In two and a half weeks she would be married. No longer Joanna Piercy but Mrs Matthew Levin. She stared at herself, trying to get used to the idea. Then she cleaned her teeth, scrubbed her face and stood under the shower, still in something of a dream.

Matthew wasn't even stirring when she returned to the bedroom. Leaving the door ajar she dressed by the light on the landing then went downstairs. Quick make-up and breakfast. She left a note for Matthew and drove into work. Then sat at the computer, still in a half-conscious state; thinking, studying statements, trying to piece it all together. She realized now that Kayleigh's description of the man who had assaulted her had led them astray. But that wasn't all. In fact, as she peered into the screen and studied all the evidence, she realized it was all here. Easy. They'd had it from the beginning. She half laughed and then frowned. If they had not been misled by Kayleigh's story, Molly might not have . . . She sat forward. What had happened to Molly? The stamp was there in all three cases – never a deliberate murder – more an accidental one.

Mike arrived, yawning, almost three hours later. She sat him down and shared her thoughts with him. He was silent; his dark eyes fixed on her face as she gave him her reasoning. ' "Lots of girls were dressed like that". Harrison's statement. Of course. It was Christmas, Mike. There would have been lots of Santas in little red dresses. Even quite a few wearing reindeer antlers. Molly didn't ever leave the club. And who was there until it closed? Crispin.'

Korpanski said nothing so she pressed on with her argument. 'Go through the cases one by one. Danielle, Mike. He found her, probably half comatosed, outside Lymeys. He raped her, then went home. Maybe stopped off for a kebab.'

As she'd expected, Korpanski raised his objection. 'We don't know he ever worked at Lymeys.'

'He had a record of GBH, Mike, what other job would he be fit for but nightclub bouncer?'

'But—'

'I rang Westheisen yesterday evening. He said he'd worked for them since they'd opened. They haven't been open that long. We only have to check his work record.'

'So Kayleigh?'

'Practically a blueprint of Danielle's except that Kayleigh, being Kayleigh, and a complete stranger to the truth, gave a description of her dad – tall, slim, et cetera, et cetera. So we were misled, looking in the wrong direction for the wrong person. Harrison did not rape his own daughter and Kayleigh knows it which is why she blurted out his description. But that wasn't all, Mike.' She paused. 'If I'm right Kayleigh wasn't raped outside the club but inside. She doesn't really remember anything, does she? Why? Because she'd been drugged. She never left Patches.'

'But she said . . .' His voice faded away.

'Exactly. We thought she was raped near where she was found. Partly because her clothes were there and partly because she told us so. But Kayleigh doesn't always tell the truth, does she?'

Korpanski shook his head. 'So . . .?'

'If she was raped inside the club we need to look at someone who worked *inside* the club.'

'And Molly?'

'I have a suspicion,' she said, 'but I need to check it out first.' She watched his face, then spoke softly. 'I want to bring him in, Mike. I want to charge him. Today.'

He blew out his cheeks. 'Your evidence is a bit thin here, Jo; conjecture, circumstantial – nothing concrete.'

'I know,' she said. 'But he was there, he lets the young girls in deliberately.

'Molly's still missing,' she continued. 'We've lost enough time as it is. I want a warrant to search his flat, car and anywhere else he has access to. Remember him riding off on his motorbike?'

Korpanski blinked. 'What's that got to do with it?'

'You can't ride a motorbike through snow, Mike. He would have been in his car that night so he could move the body.'

Crispin looked surprised when he opened the door of his flat to them. 'Inspector,' he said politely. 'Sergeant?'

'Good morning.'

Crispin still looked bleary-eyed. Another late night at the club? 'What can I do for you?' He was still playing his polite self.

'We'd like you to come down to the station and answer a few more questions,' Joanna said briskly.

Crispin looked from one to the other.

'About Molly Carraway.'

'I'll get my coat.'

The duty solicitor proved to be Ruth Gaul, an intelligent young woman with large brown eyes, short curling hair and a very brisk manner. 'Might I ask what my client is being questioned about?'

'It's in connection with a series of serious sexual assaults against three young women,' Joanna said. 'And there's a possibility of a murder charge.'

Ruth Gaul blinked. 'I see,' she said. 'And you have evidence of my client's involvement?'

'Circumstantial so far,' Joanna said, 'but we have applied for warrants to search his home and other premises he is involved with.'

'I see,' Ruth Gaul said. Then: 'I need to speak to my client – alone.'

Mike and Joanna left her with Crispin and went in search of a coffee. They'd just sat down when the call came over on her mobile. Joanna listened carefully before she shared the information. 'In May Andrew Crispin was "helping out" at Lymeys,' she said. 'He wasn't on their employment list because he was only there because the usual bouncer was off sick which is why he didn't show up on their original investigations.'

Sergeant Barraclough was waving a piece of paper. 'We have the warrant,' he said triumphantly.

They looked at each other and downed their cups. 'So what are we waiting for?' Joanna said. She authorized the search of Crispin's property.

Half an hour later they were called back into the interview room. Ms Gaul spoke for Crispin. 'My client denies all knowledge of any of these crimes,' she said with a tight smile.

'So, he wants to do it the hard way?'

Ms Gaul waited, tension etching lines across her face. She wasn't enjoying this.

'OK,' Joanna said. She'd been expecting this response from Crispin. 'We'll question him now.'

She and Mike faced him across the table once he was seated. 'Let's go back to the night of May the eleventh this year,' she began. 'It was a Tuesday,' she reminded him, 'and you were working at Lymeys nightclub in Newcastle-under-Lyme.'

Crispin's face went chalk-white but he managed a 'No comment', through gritted teeth.

Joanna pressed him – gently for now. 'Were you there that night?'

'I can't possibly remember that far back,' he protested. 'It's ages ago.'

'OK,' Joanna said, still gentle, with a quick glance at Korpanski, 'let's put it another way. How many bouncers worked at Lymeys?'

'Two,' he said sullenly.

'And how many would be on the door on any one night?'

Crispin couldn't see where this was going. You could tell that from his face. 'There was usually just one on a night.' He grinned, as though forgetting where he was, why and what he was about to be charged with. 'Sometimes two on a Saturday or a particularly busy night.'

'And you helped out there sometimes.'

'Very occasionally.'

'You understand that we shall be reviewing the cases of Danielle and Kayleigh, in the light of Molly Carraway's disappearance,' Joanna said, knowing full well that they had nothing against Crispin on either of those two cases; neither were they likely to find any extra evidence which would secure a conviction. 'We're still looking for Molly.'

Crispin's face did not move a muscle. There was absolutely no sign that he had heard what she had said. She almost wondered whether maybe he hadn't heard and that she should repeat it. Then he licked his lips and spoke. 'I don't know –'

Joanna cleared her throat and caught Korpanski's eye.

Someone knocked at the door. Joanna knew they had something. They wouldn't interrupt this unless –

'Excuse me,' she said politely, getting to her feet and walking to the door. Danny Hesketh-Brown whispered in her ear.

Ruth Gaul looked woodenly ahead then muttered something to Crispin.

They had a swift exchange before she addressed them again. 'My client wishes to change his statement,' she said flatly, avoiding their eyes. Crispin was sitting at the table, arms folded, jaw set, staring ahead. Ruth Gaul continued but now Joanna could hear revulsion in her voice. 'He admits having been at Lymey's nightclub on May the eleventh and on the other two nights in Leek,' she began. Then: 'But he denies sexual assault.'

'And Molly?'

'He claims that he did see her.'

Crispin took over. 'She was very drunk,' he said. 'I was outside having a cigarette round the back of the club. We started chattin'. She was a nice kid.' He scratched his nose. 'I, umm . . .' Was he wondering just how much evidence they had; what had been said outside the door? 'She seemed a bit the worse for wear.' His eyes swivelled around the room. He knew he was chancing it. 'I, umm, tried to wake her up. I gave her a drink.'

That was when he began to look worried because Joanna was simply nodding, as though she already knew all this.

'When I came back out she was just lying there.' He spread his hands, appealing for them to believe him. 'I knew it'd look really bad for me. I didn't know what to do with her.'

'Where is she?'

'I put her in my car to try and warm her up,' he said. 'Then I realized she was dead.' He held his hands out. 'What could I do? What would it look like? Me – a decent man with a dead young girl in my car. I panicked, didn't I?' His face assumed the picture of innocence. Piggy little eyes wide open.

'Where is she?'

Ruth Gaul held up her hands.

TWENTY-THREE

At two o'clock Joanna and Mike drove out to Leekbrook to the place where Andrew Crispin serviced his motorbike, to join the SOCO team. Matthew, as the Home Office pathologist, would be on his way. The vans had already gathered and the scene had been sealed off from prying eyes or unwelcome guests.

Barra met her at the door. They entered between a narrow corridor of police Do Not Cross tape. It had once been a petrol garage plus service area but most people bought their petrol in a supermarket these days; either that or at one of the big chains. And small, servicing workshops had likewise suffered over the last ten years. Too much expensive equipment needed. So the premises had fallen empty and derelict. But it was still a workshop and like many people who have spent time in prison, Crispin was a tidy creature. There were shelves neatly stocked, oil marks on the floor and a lovely old motorbike in three sections. Korpanski eyed it reverently. 'Harley Davidson Hummer,' he said. 'About nineteen fifty. Lovely.'

'This isn't so lovely, Sergeant,' Barra said drily. 'Take a look at this.'

Like many garages this one had an inspection pit in its centre: six feet deep, concrete, straight sides like a grave. Barra had pulled aside the cloth which must have covered it. Joanna peered over. At the bottom lay a young girl long dark hair, a bright red dress the colour of fresh blood rucked up over slim thighs. As she watched a rat ran over her.

They'd found Molly. Adored daughter. No university tuition fees now. No more worrying where she was at night. It was all over.

Joanna stared.

'Hi.' Matthew was here, dressed in his forensic suit, bag at the ready. He caught up with her and saw what she saw.

Matthew Levin didn't waste time on sympathy. He simply patted her on the shoulder and jumped down into the inspection pit to begin his task. Joanna watched him. You could always tell a pathologist who had attended many murder scenes by their manner. They were quiet, efficient, knew exactly what to do, which made their movements economical and their comments spare.

'No marks on her,' he said only moments later. 'Looks like there's been some sexual activity. She's not wearing any knickers. Probably been here ever since she was abducted.'

He looked up. 'I'll speak to the coroner,' he said. 'We should get her moved. I'll complete the examination down at the mortuary.'

Dusk was dropping from the sky as Joanna went back outside with him. 'Thanks, Matt,' she said. 'Thanks for coming so quickly and, well, just getting on with it.'

He kissed her on the mouth, very gently. 'I just can't wait to take you away from all this,' he said.

She kissed him back. 'But only for two weeks.'

Matthew gave a short laugh. 'I'd take you away for ever, Jo. But I have the feeling you'd resist.'

'I'll see you later,' she said. 'And don't ask what time.'

She took PC Bridget Anderton with her and knew as they walked up the path towards the watching faces that Beth and Philip Carraway already knew what had happened to their daughter. Joanna hardly needed to explain. 'I'm so sorry,' she said. 'We've found Molly.'

The pair of them sat, frozen together like statues in an ice tableau. They seemed to have lost all power of movement or speech. Even the blinking of their eyes looked robotic and jerky.

Bridget Anderton glanced at Joanna then back at Molly's parents. 'Is there anyone you'd like me to ring?'

Philip Carraway managed a jerky shake of the head. Beth was in misery too deep to respond to even this simple kindness.

'I shall leave WPC Anderton here with you,' Joanna said.

Philip Carraway managed to give a slow nod and Joanna left. There was a police initiative to bring a victim's relatives and the perpetrator of the crime face to face. *Maybe*, Joanna thought, as she slipped the car into gear, *in some cases, with some people, it might help.* But not here. No way could she see that Beth and Philip Carraway could possibly benefit from ever meeting Andrew Crispin.

So now, back to the station and Crispin himself. Ruth Gaul was still with him, taking notes as he spoke. She eyed them cautiously as Joanna and Mike entered and sat down.

'We've found Molly,' she said. She did not address Crispin specifically but made her next question sound like rhetoric, addressed to the room in general. 'What goes wrong with these girls?'

Ruth Gaul frowned but made no comment.

Crispin looked slightly interested. 'What do you mean?' he asked, crossing his thick legs.

'You don't mean for them to die, but they do, don't they?'

Gaul's antennae were up but Joanna ignored them. At her side Korpanski was wearing his famous wooden expression.

Joanna continued. 'You just want to have a good time, don't you, Andrew? And they make out so do they.'

Crispin's eyes flickered over her.

'But then they get just too drunk. Danielle completely lost it, didn't she?'

Again Crispin's eyes flickered over her.

'Bloody well died on you.'

'She didn't—'

'Too late, Crispin. No, maybe she didn't die *on* you. You weren't even there when she expired, were you?'

Gaul gave him a quick, warning glance.

'And Kayleigh. Well, that was interesting. Kayleigh survived. But she'd been so drunk and it had been so dark she couldn't describe you. But you couldn't take that chance again, Andrew, could you?'

His eyes were watching her, mesmerized. 'You witch,' he managed.

'So you had to try something else.'

And then it burst out of Andrew Crispin like a lanced boil. 'Fucking ketamine,' he said. 'Fucking stuff. No good. She just clapped out.'

'May I have a word with my client?' Ruth Gaul sounded just about as pissed off as she could be.

'My client,' she said calmly, when they trooped back in twenty-five minutes later, 'is prepared to make a statement. He denies any knowledge of the death of Danielle Brixton or of the recent assault on Kayleigh Harrison. However, he is willing to assist you in the enquiry into the *accidental death* of Molly Carraway as a result of her *accidentally* ingesting a dose of ketamine.'

How did she do it? Joanna thought wearily. Defend a complete psycho like Crispin, find a loophole in the story that he can slither right through.

Answer? Like her. Someone has to. And now she understood why there had been no blood near the torn out earring. Molly had already been dead. And the dead don't bleed.

TWENTY-FOUR

She was home before midnight and Matthew was still up, waiting for her.

'Tell me about ketamine,' she said. 'What is it? What's it used for? Why is it so popular as a recreational drug? Will you be able to find traces of it in Molly's body? Why did he use it?'

'It's primarily used in anaesthetics,' he said, 'and for chronic pain – more in veterinary medicine than with humans. It produces something they call dissociative anaesthesia – the patient isn't exactly knocked out but they don't *remember* what has happened to them and that's why it can be used as a "date rape" drug. I suspect this is why your guy used it. If he expected Molly to survive then he would obviously not want her to remember clearly what had happened to her. And certainly not who had raped her. Unfortunately it has side effects: hypotension, depression of the respiratory centre, a high incidence of extraneous muscle move-ment, hallucinations, nightmares and other transient psychotic effects. It would be difficult to titrate the dose to induce a state of complete relaxation and amnesia without killing your patient. We don't use it much. As for your last question about finding traces in Molly's body: possibly. It has a half-life of two to three hours. If she died in that time frame we should not only be able to work out what was given but also what dose was administered.'

'Mmm.'

'And now,' he said with only a hint of reproach, 'how about we get on with the wedding?'

TWENTY-FIVE

They had chosen the wedding venue together, both loving the high moorlands venue, but even they could not have organized the snow-capped peaks and the bright sun which made her dress sparkle and shimmer as she left the car to walk the few steps through the studded oak door and stand, for a moment, in front of the mirror. Her wedding dress was Pacific blue, with a halter neck which left her shoulders bare. She had worn a white fur stole but now she took it off to allow the maximum benefit of the crystals randomly scattered over the skirt. As she walked in on her brother in law's arm she felt everyone turn around and stare. 'Scatter the crystals,' she had said to the dressmaker, 'at random.' And so she had, each crystal sewn on by hand.

The dress clung to her hips from the front but had a train at the back which rustled and spread as she walked. Her hair was loose and she had plaited some of the dress material with flowers to form a circlet which sat on her head, long ribbons down her back. Matthew was grinning at her and she grinned back, knowing that he had worried what she would wear.

Not black.

And so she walked slowly towards him, through the small collection of friends, relatives, acquaintances: Eloise, who had worn funeral-black trousers, and Matthew's tight-lipped parents, who stood next to their granddaughter in a show of solidarity. She walked past Sergeant Mike Korpanski, reading his radar, one eyebrow raised – either he never thought she'd go through with it or he was wondering how long it would last – feeling the hostile gaze of his wife scorch her back as she moved forward. She caught Chief Superintendant Arthur Colclough's warm, fatherly smile, mirrored by that of his wife who, although she had pretended otherwise, had always had a soft spot for Joanna; had watched her morph from hot-headed, newly appointed Inspector, to the woman who was still maturing in front of her. It was a relief to reach Caro's eyes and see her smile, even if her hands were wrapped round her swollen belly. Then Tom's broad grin, her sister Sarah, and Alan and Becky, Matthew's friends who had let him live on their top floor when he and Jane had first split up. They had looked after him until he and Joanna had finally bought Waterfall Cottage together.

And now she had reached him. She handed her small bunch of flowers to Lara, her niece, in dark red.

Another red dress.

'Thanks, Jo,' Matthew whispered. Then reassured her: 'It will be OK.'

Would it?